Chocolate
Magic

E.G. FISHER PUBLIC LIBRARY
1289 Ingleside Ave.
Athens, TN 37303

6/6/05

D1417468

Also by Karen Sandler
in Large Print:

Just My Imagination
Table for Two

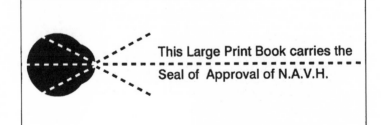

This Large Print Book carries the
Seal of Approval of N.A.V.H.

Chocolate Magic

Karen Sandler

E.G. FISHER PUBLIC LIBRARY
1289 Ingleside Ave.
Athens, TN 37303

WHEELER
PUBLISHING

Copyright © 2004 by Karen Sandler.

All rights reserved.

This novel is a work of fiction. Names, characters, places and incidents are either the product of the author's imagination, or, if real, used fictitiously.

Published in 2005 by arrangement with Karen Sandler.

Wheeler Large Print Softcover.

The text of this Large Print edition is unabridged.
Other aspects of the book may vary from the original edition.

Set in 16 pt. Plantin by Carleen Stearns.

Printed in the United States on permanent paper.

Library of Congress Cataloging-in-Publication Data

Sandler, Karen.
    Chocolate magic / by Karen Sandler.
        p. cm.
    ISBN 1-58724-978-2 (lg. Print : hc : alk. paper)
    1. Candy industry — Fiction.   2. Divorced people — Fiction.   3. Seattle (Wash.) — Fiction.   4. Business intelligence — Fiction.   5. Large type books.   I. Title.
PS3619.A54C47 2005
813'.6—dc22   2005003212

To all my chocolate-loving friends
— you know who you are.

National Association for Visually Handicapped
----------------------- *serving the partially seeing*

As the Founder/CEO of NAVH, the only national health agency solely devoted to those who, although not totally blind, have an eye disease which could lead to serious visual impairment, I am pleased to recognize Thorndike Press★ as one of the leading publishers in the large print field.

Founded in 1954 in San Francisco to prepare large print textbooks for partially seeing children, NAVH became the pioneer and standard setting agency in the preparation of large type.

Today, those publishers who meet our standards carry the prestigious "Seal of Approval" indicating high quality large print. We are delighted that Thorndike Press is one of the publishers whose titles meet these standards. We are also pleased to recognize the significant contribution Thorndike Press is making in this important and growing field.

Lorraine H. Marchi, L.H.D.
Founder/CEO
NAVH

★ Thorndike Press encompasses the following imprints: Thorndike, Wheeler, Walker and Large Print Press.

~ 1 ~

Katarina Roth froze in the act of pinching off another bite of her chocolate chip croissant as Mark Denham ambled into Starbucks, a petite blonde sashaying at his side. Tucked into the back corner of the coffee bar, Kat had no hope of slinking out without Mark spying her. She was trapped, with nothing to hide behind but an oversized cappuccino cup and a half-eaten croissant.

You'd think with a population of millions in the greater Seattle area, she and Mark would never cross paths. And she hadn't been down to Pike Place Market in months. The nerve of him choosing today to escort that knockout blonde for a lunchtime coffee and tête-à-tête.

Damn, there ought to be a law against ex-husbands parading blondes in front of their ex-wives in public. Mark ought to at least have the common courtesy to sprout a post-divorce potbelly or a few gray hairs so he wouldn't look so damned yummy.

Appetite gone, Kat stuffed what was left of her chocolate-filled croissant back into the white paper bag. As Mark and his companion turned away from the counter, lattes and pastries in hand, Kat ducked behind her cappuccino cup, gulping a mouthful of tepid coffee. Mark hadn't seen her yet and to her relief, he seated himself with his back to her. If she moved quietly enough and quickly, he might miss her entirely.

Crumpled bag in her hand, she left the cup behind and threaded her way through the tables and chairs of the crowded coffee bar. The bag slam-dunked into the trash, Kat thought she'd made good her escape when he called out her name. Praying he'd think he'd mistaken some other tall, skinny woman with a short mop of hair for his ex-wife, she dodged through traffic across Pike Place and slipped inside the first shop she came to.

Using a revolving display of cookbooks as camouflage, Kat peered out the store window at Starbucks across the street. Mark still stood there at the entrance, looking left and right, obviously searching for her. Why it seemed so important to him to track her down, Kat had no idea. Maybe he just wanted the chance to flaunt the blonde on his arm.

Finally, Mark turned and reentered Starbucks, no doubt returning to his companion. Reluctant to walk past the coffee bar and risk seeing Mark and his chippie together, Kat turned away from the window to wander along the narrow aisles of the store she'd entered. It was a kitchen wares shop, a pretty ironic refuge for a woman whose idea of cooking was nuking a frozen dinner in the microwave. Nevertheless, as her gaze leisurely scanned the cluttered shelves from top to bottom, she found the plethora of incomprehensible gadgets fascinating.

Unfortunately, not intriguing enough to keep her mind from her ex-husband. Just the thought of him elevated her heart rate. Despite her best intentions, she still reacted to his six-foot-plus body as strongly as she had during their short, tempestuous marriage. Her heart may have stopped loving him, but her libido had yet to get the message.

Even now, she could remember clearly his bare broad shoulders above her as they made love, the intensity in his face, the feel of his legs tangled with hers. The texture of his muscles under her hands, the way they flexed as he thrust into her, the moment of her release and the triumph reflected in his eyes.

A sudden flush of heat drove her to remove the jacket of her dove gray power suit and sling it over the crook of her arm. The matching heels pinched her feet so she slipped them off and stuffed them in her handbag. So much for dressing for success.

The little blonde had been wearing red, and the suit fit her petite body like a glove. Too impatient to wait for tailoring, Kat bought her suits off the rack. Unfortunately, clothing long enough to fit her tall frame was always baggy in the shoulders and hips.

Seeing Mark just added to the aggravation of the day. She had enough on her plate with the pressing problems that awaited her back at the office. She'd hoped for a respite spending her Friday lunch hour at Starbucks, then a little relaxation roaming through the Pike Place Market shops. Instead, a close encounter with her ex had unsettled what little peace she'd gained in half a cup of cappuccino.

Shaking off her irritation, Kat lifted her gaze to the kitchen store's back window and the distant view of Elliot Bay beyond. Seattle's April sky refused to surrender its gloom, although the drizzle had ceased by mid-morning. If the weather report could be believed, the upcoming weekend would be sunny. If only the same could be said for the financial picture at Roth Confectionery Company.

As she returned her focus to the exotic merchandise crowding the store shelves, the urgency to return to her office closed in on her. She longed to blow off the afternoon, to retreat to her Capitol Hill condo and watch sappy old movies on the Romance Channel with her cat, Rochester, draped across her lap. Her assistant took an afternoon off at least once a month, with Kat's blessing. Why couldn't she do the same?

Because she was Roth's CEO. And if she wasn't there to solve the problems, no one else would.

With a sigh, Kat continued down the aisle to the end, pausing at a display of coffeemakers. Amidst the Brauns and the Krupps, an arrangement of foil-wrapped chocolates overflowed a crystal bowl. Coffee Buddies, the accompanying sign read. Another fine product from the Denham Candy Company. Leaning against the display, a chubby-cheeked chocolate "Buddy" doll grinned rakishly at her.

If you asked her, Buddy looked too damn cheerful. Glaring at the cartoon character, Kat plucked up a chocolate, stared down at it in her palm. Envy tweaked at her as she studied the neatly wrapped cube. It wasn't the high quality of the product that galled her, the way they melted so evenly in coffee to flavor it. And she didn't resent that Coffee Buddies were a smash from the day they hit store shelves . . . not much, anyway.

What truly maddened her, what was nearly too much to bear, was that Roth had been a heartbeat away from releasing their own version of the treats when Denham beat them to market with Coffee Buddies. Roth's Coffee Pals, although delicious in their own right, were also-rans in popularity. In fact, if sales didn't pick up, they might have to discontinue the item since the fine European chocolate required to make them was so costly.

If it had been Hershey's or Mars or Ghiradelli who'd trounced them, she could have handled the defeat. But it was Denham. The company whose headquarters was a short drive up Fairview from Roth's. The company chosen the number-three best place to work in Washington state, right after Roth Confectionery. The company co-featured with Roth two months ago in *Fortune* magazine.

The company owned and operated by Mark Denham, her infuriating and drop-dead gorgeous ex-husband, creator of winning candy products, escorter of knockout blondes.

With a growl, Kat dropped the chocolate back in the bowl, then turned to head out of the store. Just as she reached the door, Mark emerged from Starbucks across the street, the blonde glued to his side. The petite woman gazed up at Mark as she spoke, gesturing animatedly with her paper sack from the coffee bar. Mark nodded occasionally, flashing his devastating smile in the bimbo's direction.

Damn, they were crossing the street. Kat retreated again into the cooking store, crouching in the back until she was sure Mark had passed.

As she straightened, she caught sight of the brimming bowl of Coffee Buddies, the perky cartoon Buddy grinning at her. She could almost see him prancing on the shelf, little squares of chocolate bouncing around him as they taunted her, "Neener, neener, neener, we like Denham better . . ." Buddy's imaginary voice bore a striking resemblance to Mark's high tenor when he was a ten-year-old and she a lowly six-year-old.

Feeling a little like that six-year-old now, Kat stuck her tongue out at Buddy and snatched up a handful of the candies. I'll get you, Buddy, and your little friends, too.

One eye out the front window, Kat approached the register and spilled the handful of chocolates on the counter. "I'll take these."

The grandmotherly clerk gave Kat a sunny smile as she rang up the sale. "Aren't those the most scrumptious treats?"

"I suppose." Kat fished a few dollars from her wallet, then scrounged in the bottom of her purse for the change. "But Coffee Pals are better."

"Coffee Pals?" The clerk blinked at her through thick glasses. "What are those?"

"Never mind," Kat sighed.

As she slipped from the store, she checked Pike Place, left and right. No sign of either ex-husband or sashaying blonde. A Coffee Buddy melting in her mouth, Kat returned to her car, reluctantly savoring the delicious smooth taste of the chocolate. They really were wonderful, and the marketing darned clever, with Buddy creeping into the hearts and minds of both children and adults. It still irked her that Denham's concept had been so similar to her own for

Coffee Pals. It had forced Roth to revamp their marketing strategy at the last minute.

As she drove up Pike Street, she nearly had her third Coffee Buddy to her lips before she caught herself. Darn things were just as difficult to resist as their maker. She dropped the unwrapped candy into the bag and tossed the bag on the seat beside her.

Pulling onto Interstate 5 for the short drive back to her office, she could almost hear the Coffee Buddies whispering, "Don't you want another?" Her arm snaked out of its own accord, nearly reaching the bag when someone cut in front of her as she was about to exit the freeway. That took all her concentration, distracting her from the enticing bag of candy.

By the time Kat reached Roth Confectionery's headquarters overlooking Lake Union, considerations of her afternoon's tasks dominated her thoughts. Entering her twelfth-floor corner office, a stack of pink message slips in her hand, she was irritated to discover she still clutched the stash of Coffee Buddies. Resolutely, she tossed the remaining treats in her wastebasket before she leafed through her messages.

Her jacket tossed over the back of her chair, Kat glanced out her floor-to-ceiling window. Lake Union spread out before her and on its opposite shore she could just make out the Space Needle. When she'd become CEO, her parents had given her the choice of corner offices — this one with its view of the Seattle Center or the larger northwest corner suite. It had been a no-brainer — the northwest office over-looked Denham Candy Company headquarters. Gazing out at Mark Denham's enclave as she sipped her morning French roast would have wreaked havoc on her blood pressure.

Kat returned her attention to the stack of messages. She dreaded the upcoming meeting with marketing. Maybe she could sneak off to visit Roth's research and development department instead? As she contemplated that possibility, her phone buzzed and she started like a guilty child.

She lifted the receiver. "Yes, Norma?"

"Someone to see you, Kat." Norma low-ered her voice to a stage whisper. "It's Fritz."

"Oh, Lord." That was all she needed today. Her walking disaster of a cousin. Cousin-in-law. Ex-cousin-in-law? "Tell him I'm busy."

"Fritz, she's . . . Fritz!" Norma called an instant before Kat's office door opened.

Fritz's grin would have rivaled Buddy's. "Cousin Kat! It's so great to see you." He strode toward her, five feet, six inches of trouble in a chocolate brown Armani suit.

As he rounded her desk, arms outstretched, his hip bumped against a Lenox porcelain candy dish, upsetting it. Kat dove for it, catching it just before it tipped off the desk.

"Sorry, Kat." He pulled her into his arms, gave her a Heimlich hug that popped the air from her lungs. "How ya doing, Cuz?"

"Great," she gasped. "And you?"

He stepped back, still smiling. "Good. Really good." He didn't quite meet her gaze.

His evasiveness set off warning bells inside Kat. She scrutinized him worriedly. Always a slight young man, he seemed a little thinner than he'd been two years ago when she'd seen him last. How old was he now? Twenty-three? No, twenty-four, eight years younger than she.

The heart-stopping Denham good looks had skipped Fritz's gene pool. Late-life son of Mark's stuffy Uncle Neddy, Fritz took after his frail, dainty mother. Cute as a puppy, and just as vexatious.

"So what brings you here?" Kat asked carefully.

Nonchalantly, he leaned one hand on her desk, jostling a framed picture of Kat's mom and stepdad. Kat rescued the photo, putting it out of reach.

Straightening, Fritz shoved his hands in his trouser pockets. He grinned wider. "Your dad didn't tell you?"

Unease tickled the pit of Kat's stomach. "Tell me what?"

A rap on her office door pulled her attention from Fritz. Her assistant, Norma Wilson, opened the door and stuck her head in. "Marketing is waiting for you in the big conference room. The Chocolate Magic strategy meeting — remember?"

The marketing meeting now seemed a welcome diversion from the chaos that was Fritz. "Gotta go," Kat said as Norma bowed out again. "Can we do this later, Fritz?"

"Hey, no problem." He waved his hands, striking the desk lamp which leapt to its death. Fritz retrieved it, righting it on the desk with an apologetic shrug. "I can replace that bulb for you if you want."

"No need." Kat grabbed up her jacket and held it before her like a shield. "Norma will take care of it. Why don't we

18

do lunch sometime?"

"Sure! Sounds great. After all, we'll be seeing a lot of each other."

She'd nearly reached the door when her belabored brain absorbed what he'd said. She stopped, turned to face him. "We will?"

His hands plunged back into his pockets. "Well, I don't start here officially until Monday, but we could have lunch any-time."

"Start." She blinked, once, twice. "Here?"

He rocked back on his heels. "Your dad really didn't tell you?"

She shook her head.

"He hired me today. To work at Roth." He flung out his arms to either side and the lamp bit the dust again. "I'm your new community relations advisor."

Kat shook her head. "He can't. Hire you, I mean. Not without telling . . ." Except it wouldn't be the first time her father had done an end run around her. Although still on the Roth board of directors, he'd retired as CEO only a year ago. Kat knew her father trusted her, but he still hadn't quite gotten used to letting her run the business.

But Fritz! What could her father have been thinking?

She walked back toward her cousin, intent on prying him from her office. "Look, I really have to go." She reached for his arm. "If you could just —"

"So, how's Mark?"

The unexpected question jolted Kat to a stuttering stop. "I have no idea." Gorgeous as ever. Dating knockout blondes. Ignoring the nasty little voice inside her head, Kat marched back toward the door. "Look, I've got a meeting."

"So you're still single? Got a boyfriend?" His gaze roved her desktop as if in search of love interest evidence. "Engaged maybe?"

"None of the above," Kat said, her hand on the doorknob. "Come on, Fritz. I have to go."

Without missing a beat, Fritz slid open the center desk drawer, glanced through it, shut it again. As he moved to open the upper left drawer, Kat hurried back across her office. "Hey! Leave my stuff alone!"

Fritz ignored her, pulling open the drawer. Kat grabbed his wrist, startled at how thin it seemed. Whatever else was happening in this boy's life, he wasn't eating enough. Shaking off her hold, Fritz fished inside the drawer all the way to the back. His grin grew sly as he retrieved the bit of folly Kat had hidden back there.

He held up the photo before him, tapping his chin as he examined the radiant bride, the devastatingly handsome groom. Kat didn't have to look; that picture from her wedding day was burned into her memory.

"How interesting," Fritz said. "You still have his picture."

"So what?" Kat plucked the framed photo from Fritz's hand, stuffed it back in the drawer. "It's just a good picture of me, so I kept it."

A crafty light brightened his blue eyes. "Uh-huh."

"Never mind." Kat shoved the drawer shut with her hip, then tugged on her jacket. "I have to go. We'll deal with your employment status later."

"Of course, of course. After all, I've got work to do." He giggled, then with a skip in his step he crossed to the door and opened it for Kat.

Suspicion blossomed inside her. "What work?"

He flicked his fingers in an airy wave. "You know, community affairs stuff." He laughed and unease did another two-step in Kat's stomach.

She narrowed her gaze on him. "Look,

21

Fritz, just hold off doing anything until we have a chance to talk."

He just smiled, stepping in behind her as she slipped through the door. "See you later, Cuz."

"Wait!" Kat tried to grab his sleeve, but he moved too quickly. "Fritz, did you hear me? Don't do anything!"

He winked as he passed Norma's desk, then disappeared around a corner into the hallway. Kat felt a sudden sympathy for Pandora when she opened the box.

Norma looked up at Kat with a wistful smile on her matronly face. "My, that boy has grown."

"Go after him," Kat told her. "See what he's up to. I've got to get to the marketing meeting."

"Sure thing, Kat," Norma said, quickly rising from her desk. "I'll take care of it."

As Norma hurried after Fritz, Kat worried her lower lip. What was she going to do about her cousin? She couldn't just fire him. That wouldn't be fair to Fritz, not to mention how it might hurt her father's feelings. It had been so hard for him to retire, Kat didn't want to discourage him from giving input into how Roth should be run. But to hire Hurricane Fritz without asking her first — that strayed far beyond the bit of fatherly advice he usually dispensed.

There must be some way to handle the situation without ruffling anyone's feathers. But as she headed down the hallway to the elevators, she couldn't seem to put two thoughts together. Between seeing her dratted ex-husband with a blonde and unearthing a wedding picture she should have tossed long ago, her mind was mush.

Her thoughts kept circling back to the photo of her wedding day, to the joy suffusing her face. Why the hell had she kept the picture? Because she hadn't had the heart to throw away the only reminder of such a happy day?

But it was exactly that day that was the beginning of the end for her and Mark. If anything, the picture was a harbinger of the bad times to come. It drove home the reality that happiness couldn't be trusted, that marriages were fragile, ephemeral things.

She really ought to toss the photo, to purge her life of all reminders of Mark Denham. She vowed to take care of it the moment she returned from the marketing meeting.

But as she stepped into the elevator, she knew in her heart of hearts she would keep the picture. If only she could figure out why.

Mark Denham leaned back in his office chair, scanning the March reports from his sales force. The southeastern division had recorded record sales, especially in Florida, and projected a truly phenomenal Mother's Day return. Marketing had outdone themselves with their latest advertising campaign and production was turning out a tremendous volume of Mother's Day Kits for Mom, specialty boxes of chocolates in beautiful floral shapes.

He should be ecstatic. He ought to be turning handsprings in his office in delight. The business picture for Denham Candy Company couldn't be rosier. Then why the hell did he feel so empty?

He could answer that in two words: Kat Denham. It had hit him hard today seeing her at Starbucks. At least he'd thought it was Kat. He'd only caught a glimpse, but what he saw had been achingly familiar — the slender neck exposed by the short cut of her hair, the set of her narrow shoulders in the ill-fitting gray suit, her trim calves. In the moment it took him to excuse himself from Lydia, the newest member of Denham's sales force, the woman in the gray suit had disappeared.

Leaving him with this roiling in his gut that still hadn't eased. He couldn't remember one word Lydia had said as he'd rushed her through their quick lunch. He'd turned the woman over to his VP of sales the moment he'd returned to Denham headquarters. Holed up in his office ever since, he'd fought a losing battle to banish Kat Denham from his mind.

Of course, her name wasn't Kat Denham anymore. She'd resumed using her maiden name the moment they'd separated. It had cut like a knife when he heard she'd taken back the Roth name so quickly, despite the brevity of their marriage. He really couldn't expect her to continue to call herself Denham, especially when Denham and Roth were such fierce competitors in the candy-making business. But that one act seemed to sever completely the link between them.

Tossing aside the sales report, he removed his wire-rimmed reading glasses and rubbed at his eyes. Damn, they should have just stayed friends. Why did he have to go and propose to her after fifteen years of perfectly good friendship? Had it been lust? He could still remember the day she'd returned to Seattle after five years away, with a brand-new MBA from Stanford. At twenty-six, she took his breath away, her willowy beauty like a punch to the gut. He managed to keep his hands off her for two years, keeping up the front of friendship when all he wanted to do was get her into bed.

But he'd loved her when he'd proposed, hadn't he? It sure as hell had seemed like love. But compared to the blissful peace his own parents had enjoyed for nearly forty years, his marriage to Kat had been more like a war zone. Obviously there was some crucial element to love he didn't understand.

So he'd lost a friend as well as a wife when their marriage failed. And even now, two years later, he couldn't seem to go a day without thinking of her.

He glanced at his Rolex — ten after five. All afternoon he'd had to squelch the urge to call her, just to see how she was, how things were going for her.

His phone buzzed and he picked it up, grateful for the distraction. "Yes?"

Rod, his gruff-voiced admin assistant, growled into the phone, "Someone's here to see you."

His heart galloped into overdrive as his mind leapt to a hasty conclusion. Kat! It had been her at Starbucks, and now she

26

was stopping by to say hello. Schooling his voice to neutrality, he asked, "Who is it?"

There was a pause, then Rod answered, his voice low. "Your cousin, Fritz."

Fritz! Even as Mark thrust aside his disappointment that it wasn't Kat, he was searching his office for an avenue of escape. "Does he need money?"

Retired military who'd been with Denham's for six years, Rod was a veteran of the Fritz wars. He spoke in a near whisper. "Don't think so. He's wearing some fancy designer suit."

Curiouser and curiouser. Last he'd heard, Fritz had been booted out of USC, his fourth ejection in as many years. Mark sighed and gave in to the inevitable. "Send him in."

When Fritz first walked into his office, Mark's polite smile faltered a moment. The suit was Armani, the young man's hair neatly styled, but something haunted the depths of his bright blue eyes. Then Fritz grinned and the darkness vanished.

"Hi, Mark." He stretched his arm across the desk to shake Mark's hand.

Fritz shook vigorously, in the process upsetting a foot-high model of Buddy next to Mark's in box. Buddy and in box threatened to tumble over the edge, requiring quick action from Mark to save them from disaster.

Mark scooped the endangered items closer to his side of the desk. "Hey, good to see you, Fritz." Sitting back down, he gestured to a visitor's chair. "What can I do for you?"

Fritz seated himself without incident and flashed Mark a toothy smile. "I'm here on behalf of Roth Confectionery. I'm their new community affairs advisor."

Mark's bonhomie faded. "Did Kat send you over here?"

"In a manner of speaking." Fritz tipped his chair onto its back legs, banging into the bookshelf behind him. "Roth is starting up a new fund-raising campaign for local charities. And they'd like Denham Candy to participate."

"Participate?" Mark's gaze narrowed on Fritz. "How?"

"By joining forces in the campaign." Fritz's patter would have made a politician proud. "We call it 'Kandy for Kids' since most of the earmarked charities benefit children. And if Seattle's two biggest candy rivals join hands in this campaign, we have a lock on significant media interest."

Fritz's earnest smile never waned under

Mark's scrutiny. "You say Kat sent you here?"

Fritz didn't even blink. "I'm sure you know Kat is a big booster for local causes."

He did indeed, having encountered her at a few of the charity events he'd attended. Chance meetings were difficult enough to handle; inevitably either she or he would leave early to avoid each other's extended presence. But to intentionally choose to be in the same place at the same time with Kat Roth . . . that would be lunacy.

Yet how could he say no? "Which charities had you planned to support?"

Fritz named several that Mark knew were Kat's favorite nonprofits. Coincidentally, more than a few were the same organizations Mark endorsed.

Legs crossed, Fritz bounced a foot and nearly clipped a corner of the in box. "So what do you say?"

Mark tried to think. It sounded like a worthy endeavor. But how could he become involved without Kat turning his life upside down again? His sense of self-preservation kicked in, offering him an out. He smiled at Fritz. "Denham will be glad to take part. My VP of human resources will be at your disposal."

"No, no." Fritz rose to his feet, and the chair fell backwards to the floor. A bonsai on the bookshelf behind Fritz shook ominously. "You have to do it yourself. Kat is taking time out of her busy schedule for the campaign. If Denham's CEO doesn't reciprocate . . ."

Fritz didn't have to finish. If Denham Candy didn't participate to the same extent as Roth Confectionery, Denham would come off looking like the bad guy. "You have a point," Mark agreed reluctantly. "Count me in, then. Just let me know where and when."

Nearly dancing in his apparent relief, Fritz outlined the plans Roth had already conceived for the Kandy for Kids campaign — a two-man scull race on Lake Union with Seattle-area businesses participating, a pre-game celebrity softball game at SAFECO Field, a family picnic for underprivileged kids. "Kat thought you two could meet for dinner tonight to hash out the details."

Meet Kat? For dinner? Just the two of them? "I don't know . . ."

"We'll be in touch." Fritz danced over to the door, suddenly in a hurry to leave. "Talk to you soon."

He ducked out of the office before Mark could say another word. A few moments later, there was a knock at the door. Was Fritz back? "Come in," Mark called.

Rod stepped inside, his beefy frame filling the doorway. "I'm about to leave. Mind telling me what that was all about?"

Bemused, Mark raked a hand through his hair. "Denham's will be participating in a new fund-raising campaign — Kandy for Kids."

"And?" Rod pressed.

"It's a joint effort." Mark shook his head, still wondering how he'd gotten himself hornswoggled. "With Roth Confectionery." He raised his gaze to Rod. "With Kat Roth."

Rod's brow rose speculatively, but he didn't say a word. He didn't mention the number of times Mark had told his assistant he would never get tangled up in anything related to his ex-wife. Rod also didn't expound upon his bizarre theory that Mark still loved Kat. The older man just flashed Mark a smirk and backed out of the office.

But Mark could hear Rod's booming laughter all the way down the hall as he left.

~ 2 ~

Sinking into her desk chair, Kat stared unbelieving at her administrative assistant. "You lent him your car?"

Amazingly, Norma blushed, the color taking a decade off her forty-some years. "He needed it to go down to Denham's. To talk to Mark. About the new fund-raising campaign."

Alice and her rabbit hole had nothing on Kat in that moment. She pressed her hands to her desktop, on either side of her shadow cast by the setting sun. She wished she could fly away from here, away from troublesome ex-husbands and pesky ex-cousins-in-law. If she could, she'd follow the sun's orange glow clear back to its source.

Dropping her hands into her lap, she looked up at Norma. "Let's assume I just spent the last four hours in a grueling meeting with marketing." Which she had, and had the scars to prove it. "Let's assume

I haven't the slightest notion what you're talking about. Then explain it all from the beginning."

Norma began to look a little unsure of herself as she stood opposite Kat's desk. "You asked me to keep tabs on Fritz."

"Yes. That much I remember."

"He told me you'd just hired him on as community affairs advisor."

Kat scowled. "I didn't hire him. My father did." She waved a hand at Norma. "Go on."

The older woman settled herself on the edge of a visitor chair. "Fritz told me about Kandy for Kids."

"Kandy for Kids?"

"The fund-raising campaign."

Kat was about to ask, "What fund-raising campaign?" then decided against it. It would only prolong the agony. "Continue."

The rest spilled out in a flurry of words. "Fritz said Kandy for Kids would be a joint effort between Roth and Denham and he needed to go down the street to talk to Mark. So I lent him my car."

The blush was back in Norma's cheeks and she sat ramrod-straight in her chair. Bad enough she gave Fritz the keys to her car. That she did so to provide him transportation to the enemy stronghold amounted to insurgency.

Norma's gaze dropped to her lap. "I thought you knew all this."

If it were anyone else, Kat would have torn strips off them for putting her in this position. But not Norma, a sweet, loving woman whose self-esteem had taken enough of a beating when her husband left her five years ago for some sweet young thing.

"Of course I knew, Norma," Kat lied, her tone even despite the turmoil inside her. "Just not the details. Is Fritz back yet?" Might as well lay blame on the shoulders that deserved it.

At the mention of Fritz, Norma smiled. "No. He's only been gone an hour."

With a sigh, Kat turned her chair slightly to look out the window. The fat ball of the sun, its red-gold face striated with wispy clouds, hung over the city beyond Lake Union. Below her, commuter traffic moved slowly along Fairview. One of those cars could be Mark's. He could be driving along right now, muttering under his breath about what Kat had roped him into this time.

She'd have to call him. Even though the thought of hearing his voice again set off a wrangling in the pit of her stomach, she'd call him, tell him the whole thing was a joke. A late April Fool's prank. He'd be irritated as hell. But Kat had long ago given up hope of getting along with Mark.

Norma intruded on her reverie. "Where did you want me to make reservations for dinner?"

She bumped along down the rabbit hole again, confusion whirling inside her. "Dinner?"

Before Norma could enlighten Kat, the phone rang, tweaking her nerves even further. She snatched up the receiver, barked out a hello.

The voice that answered was full of reproach. "Katarina, how can you talk to your mother like that?"

Kat rubbed at the tension between her eyes. "I didn't know it was you, Mom."

"So you talk to your clients that way?"

Ten, nine, eight, seven . . . deep long breath. "No, Mom. How are you?"

"Fine. Wonderful. Oh, Tony's been having a little back trouble, but —"

"Mom, I'm kind of in the middle of something — could I call you back later?"

"No need. We'll just talk to you tonight at dinner."

Why did everyone seem to know about

this except her? "Look, Mom, about dinner —"

Fritz chose that moment to return, barreling into Kat's office with a wide grin and wind-tossed hair. Norma lit up like a Christmas tree at the young man's appearance, setting off warning bells inside Kat.

Her mother reclaimed her attention. "You're right. We'll be too busy planning the Kandy for Kids campaign to chat."

Good God, the situation got more complex by the moment. "That's exactly what I need to tell you. This campaign —"

"We'll just have to set another time to have a little talk. See you tonight." Her mother hung up before Kat could utter another word.

She'd no more set down the phone than the door swung open again and her father strode in, his compact body bristling with energy. "Hi, love, sorry to interrupt," he called out before rounding her desk to give her a peck on the cheek. "Just wanted to let you know Patti and I can make it tonight."

A sudden, vivid image of a steamroller popped into Kat's mind, its bulk rumbling inexorably toward her. "Now, wait a minute, Dad —"

"I have to say, Katarina, I'm thrilled to

36

see you extending an olive branch to Mark this way. And for such a good cause." He turned and smiled at Fritz, stuck out his hand. "How are you doing, son?"

When the phone rang again, Kat eyed it with trepidation. The Seattle Mariners, maybe, calling to RSVP for dinner?

Her moment of whimsy did nothing to prepare her for Mark's deep voice on the other end of the line. "Hello? Kat?"

For a long moment, she couldn't speak. The chatter between Norma, Fritz and her father faded, her world narrowing and centering on the phone receiver in her hand. "Hello, Mark."

He paused, too, as if caught in the throes of the same memories. "Where are we meeting tonight? For dinner."

Now's the time, Kat thought. Tell him it's all a mistake. There is no Kandy for Kids campaign. No dinner planned for tonight.

But the words stuck in her throat. As much as she hated to admit it, she wanted — ached for — a chance to see him, to be with him. Even with her parents there avidly looking on, even knowing the impossibility of a relationship between them.

"Kat?" Mark's voice caressed her ear, setting off a heat inside her.

She glanced up at her father, although she knew she'd find no help there. He still chatted with Norma. But Fritz had fallen silent, his blue eyes on her. The intensity of his gaze surprised her. He must have sensed she was about to pull the brakes on the crazy train he'd set in motion.

She should. She had to. But maybe it would be easier to go ahead with dinner, have them all meet so she could tell them all at once.

"Papa Gianni's," Kat said finally, and saw Fritz relax. "Down on Pike Street?"

"I know the place," he said. And of course he would. He'd given her an engagement ring there.

She dropped her face in her hand, tried to think. There were hundreds of restaurants in Seattle. There had to be one that wouldn't generate a flood of memories. "Or maybe Rosie's Café. That might be —"

"Papa Gianni's." His tone brooked no argument. "Should I make the reservation?"

Kat sighed, acquiescing to the inevitable. "Thanks, no. Norma can do it. Eight o'clock?"

"Fine." He cleared his throat. "I hope you don't mind — I invited my parents."

The words were innocent enough, but

Kat caught the message behind them. His parents' presence would be a buffer between them. He didn't want to be alone with her. That made perfect sense, considering the volatility between them. But it hurt nonetheless.

She forced a laugh. "No problem. Your parents apparently invited mine. And I'd planned to bring Norma and Fritz along as well."

Take that, Mark Denham. I wouldn't want to be alone with you, either.

If her ineffectual jab wounded him, you couldn't tell it from his voice. "See you soon, then." She held the phone to her ear a moment after he hung up, then set down the receiver as she rose. "Norma, give Papa Gianni's a call. Reservations at eight o'clock for ten people."

Her father returned to her side to give her another kiss. As he straightened, Kat grabbed his arm. In a low voice, she said, "We have to talk." She looked significantly from her father to Fritz and back.

"Not now, honeybunch." He pulled away. "Patti's in the Benz down in the parking garage. We'll meet you at Papa Gianni's." Her father escaped.

Norma out at her desk phoning the restaurant, Kat fixed her gaze on her cousin.

"You've succeeded in turning my life upside down."

He smiled and shrugged. "I'm just trying to do my job, Kat."

Kat frowned. "I asked you not to do anything until we talked. And to force me to have dinner with my despicable ex-husband —"

"Despicable?" Speculation glittered in his blue eyes. "If he's so despicable, why is his picture still in your desk?"

Kat wasn't about to answer that one. "This Kandy for Kids campaign ends tonight. We'll tell everyone it was a joke, or a mistake, or a misunderstanding — whatever it takes to pull the reins in on this runaway horse. Then I'll find something for you to do around here that will keep you out of trouble."

His smile faded, and for the first time, his expression grew serious. "I'm sorry, Kat. I don't mean to be such a screwup."

Kat could have kicked herself for hurting his feelings. She opened her mouth to apologize, but Norma returned and the somber moment might never have been. Fritz was full of smiles for Kat's assistant, insisting he ride over to the restaurant with her, inveigling the car keys out of the older woman. Norma glowed; she probably would have given Fritz the whole car if he'd asked.

Kat's cousin escorted Norma out of the office, leaving Kat behind to gather up her purse and jacket and follow them in her own car. As she guided her Camry along Interstate 5 toward Pike Street, she contemplated her assistant's burgeoning adoration for Fritz.

Norma had been an extended member of the Roth family for years. Her philandering ex-husband had been a longtime employee of Roth before he danced off into the sunset with his sweet young thing. Because of the Roths' close association with the Denhams, Norma had literally watched Fritz grow up. In fact, if Kat weren't mistaken, Norma might have changed the infant Fritz's diaper a time or two.

So what could have possessed Norma to show such interest in Hurricane Fritz? Kat hoped she wasn't setting herself up for another heartache. She'd had enough hurt in her life without taking another blow from a man, even a young pup like Fritz.

As she pulled into Papa Gianni's crowded parking lot, she decided she had enough troubles without borrowing Norma's. Her assistant would just have to

41

watch out for her own heart. It was enough for Kat to keep hers out of peril.

It had been less than a ten-minute wait between Mark's arrival at the restaurant and Kat's appearance, but it seemed to extend into an eternity. First there was the interminable welcome from Gianni Giancarlo, ecstatic to see the Denhams and Roths together again in his establishment. Then the conga line through the restaurant to the back banquet room where Mr. Giancarlo had set up a private table. Finally the juggling at the table, as his parents and the Roths played musical chairs in an effort to seat him next to Kat.

The older folks' maneuvering shredded nerves already rattled by his anticipation of seeing Kat. When he couldn't take it anymore, Mark grabbed a chair at the head of the table and lowered himself into it, leaving the rest of them to figure out the seating.

So he had his back turned toward her when she finally entered, had only the warning of Phil Roth's smile when he spied his daughter. Mark forced himself to sit still, ready to rise to seat her next to him when she reached the table. But she walked right past him to the other end.

42

"I'm sorry," she said, her smile seeming to include everyone but him. "Would you all mind moving down?" She gestured to the side of the table with the empty seat. "I need to sit next to Norma."

He should object, should insist she sit next to him. But the sight of Kat's face rendered him speechless, the heart shape, her soft eyes the exact color of dark chocolate. Her body might be camouflaged by the baggy gray suit, but he knew its every line, every warm curve.

Before he could think to protest, they had all shifted around, his father moving to stretch his long legs out to Mark's right, his mother next to his dad, then his cousin and finally Norma. Kat settled herself opposite Mark, her parents and stepparents to her right.

She might have thought it safe to position herself so far away. But despite the length of the table, despite the dense foot-high centerpiece of dried flowers half-hiding her, he could feel the attraction between them, palpable and enticing.

When had he seen her last? Not counting earlier today, when he'd caught only a glimpse. Two months maybe, when they'd both turned up at the pre–Valentine's Day Chocolate Affair. She'd been manning

Roth Confectionery's booth, her attention focused on pouring coffee liqueur into tiny cups made of white chocolate. She'd spilled some of the dark liquid on her thumb and then sucked it off, sending a sudden erotic shock straight through him. He'd remembered all too clearly licking the sweet dark liqueur from her breasts in a night of particularly wild lovemaking. He'd had to back away, leave the event, making excuses to the organizers.

Now she sat six feet from him, her gaze locked with his. She couldn't possibly know what ran through his mind, how even in this crowded restaurant he ached for her. Her eyes widened, her lips parting slightly, and it was all he could do to suppress a groan.

Then she broke eye contact, grabbing up her menu and ducking behind it. He ought to feel relief, but instead tension zinged along his spine. Lord, why was nothing ever easy with Kat?

"So, what are the specials tonight?" she asked, her breathy voice sending fingers of sensation up Mark's spine.

Everyone around the table spoke at once, reeling off the list Mr. Giancarlo had recited. The noise flowed around him as he stared down the table at the back of Kat's menu, waiting for her to lower it. She must have sensed him; her hands trembled where they gripped the laminated cardboard. When the table talk drifted into a discussion of what each person planned to order, it was all Mark could do to keep from striding down the length of the table and plucking the menu from Kat's hands.

She closed it finally, laying it carefully on the table. Mark watched her speak alternately to Norma on her left and her father on her right. She managed to turn her head from side to side without her gaze ever passing over him.

Annoyance nibbled at Mark. Damned if he'd let her avoid him. "So, Kat," he called out down the table. Conversation immediately died on either side. For a moment Kat kept her head averted to her father, then she turned to Mark, her chin tipping up slightly. Mark cleared his throat. "Who have you lined up for the scull race?"

As if the strain of sharing the same room at the same time with Mark Denham wasn't enough, now he had to lob entirely nonsensical questions at her. "The scull race."

Mark kept his intense green gaze on her, a look of disapproval on his face. "The

45

business sponsors. And the participants. Who have you got lined up so far?"

No one, of course, because until that instant, she didn't know anything about a scull race. She glanced at Fritz; he just gave her a shrug and a sheepish grin. "Uh . . ." Tell him the truth. Before you're dug in any deeper. But now everyone at the table had their eyes on her — parents, stepparents, her former in-laws.

And Mark, who all by himself could empty her brain of intelligence. Somehow, under his steady regard, she couldn't quite squeeze the truth out of her mouth. She flicked a hand in a negligent gesture. "We haven't quite pinned everyone down."

"Haven't quite . . ." Mark seemed to bite off the words; his parents, her parents, Norma and Fritz all swiveled their heads back toward him. "The scull race is scheduled for Mother's Day — less than a month off. If you haven't managed even a modicum of organization for this fund-raising effort . . ."

As the Ping-Pong game returned to her end, Kat felt her hackles rise in automatic response to Mark's tone. "Kandy for Kids is organized. I just haven't nailed down all the details." What the hell was she doing? She was defending something that didn't even exist!

Mark leaned back in his chair. "Then it's a good thing you brought Denham in on this. Now you at least have a hope of pulling it off."

Reaching for the empty wineglass at her place, Kat curled her fingers around its stem. Ten, nine, eight, seven . . . "We included Denham Candy strictly for public relations purposes. If you can't be a team player —"

Kat's father gripped her wrist. "Honey, Mr. Giancarlo needs to take our order. You two kids can talk about this during dinner."

Finger by finger, Kat unwrapped her hand from the wineglass. Papa Gianni stood beside Mark, order pad at the ready. She'd so narrowed her focus on her ex-husband, she hadn't even seen the restaurant owner enter the room.

As the jabbering resumed around the table, everyone seeming to give their order at once, Kat strove to gather her wits around her again. She shot a glance at Fritz, who returned a guileless look, his lips curving into a smile. He seemed completely unrepentant at the havoc he had wreaked in Kat's life.

When Mr. Giancarlo stopped at her seat

to take her order, Kat picked an item almost randomly off the menu. She'd wait until the restaurant owner had finished, then she'd get everyone's attention to make her announcement. Maybe instead of declaring Kandy for Kids a figment of Fritz's imagination, she'd tell them, regretfully, that the program seemed unfeasible, considering how difficult it would be for Roth and Denham to work together. She'd keep it congenial and impersonal, express her respect for the Denhams, thank them all for coming, but it just ain't gonna work, baby.

No need to mention the hunka-hunka burning lust she still felt for her ex-husband.

But once the orders were finished, a waiter immediately appeared with bottles of the house red — compliments of Papa Gianni's. Then the fussing over corkscrews and tasting and serving the wine. Once every glass had been filled with the crimson Chianti, Kat had to endure toast after toast to the Denhams and Roths and Kandy for Kids.

As she sipped her wine, Mark watched her from the other end of the table. Where earlier she had done her best to ignore him, now she felt she had something to prove. If he intended to keep his eyes on her throughout dinner, she'd damn well return the favor. Never mind the tumult of emotions mixing with the wine inside her, never mind the powerful erotic memories evoked by his presence.

After the wine came the salads, then the soup, then the entrée. Eating her meal gave her the excuse to look somewhere other than at Mark, giving her a breathing spell from the unwanted connection between her and her ex-husband. She conversed with those at her end of the table, Norma and Fritz, her father and stepmother Patti. She dimly heard Mark's end of the table brainstorming the Kandy for Kids campaign, throwing out ideas at a breakneck pace.

Although she refused to look at him, Kat's awareness of Mark never ceased. She knew each time he looked her way, could feel the weight of his gaze as real as a touch.

When the *zuppa inglese* arrived, Kat thought she would scream from the tension. That or take Fritz by the scruff of his scrawny neck and shake him to relieve her anxiety. Instead she cut a corner off the rich rum-soaked sponge cake with her fork and slipped the bite into her mouth. A bit of custard filling slipped and she had to lick it from her lips. Then she made the huge mistake of glancing up at Mark.

She froze, the tip of her tongue still out. She read his face as clearly as the pages of a steamy romance novel, saw every sensual image that danced through his mind. Damnably, the images burst inside her as well — the exact sensation of his tongue skimming across her lips, dipping inside, tangling with her own. His breathing growing hoarser as his arousal increased, his eyes dilating with passion as they stared into hers.

Good God, what was she doing? She jerked back as if to break the link between them. Her fork went flying and as she grabbed for it, her hand struck the wine bottle at her end of the table. As it wobbled in place, Fritz lunged across the centerpiece to right the bottle, but he only made matters worse. It took Kat's last-minute nab to keep Norma's lap from being doused with wine.

Fritz blushed deep red as he lowered himself again. As everyone around the table congratulated her on saving the wine bottle, Kat puzzled over Fritz's reaction. Usually he was oblivious to his klutz attacks.

Kat picked up her spoon to finish her dessert, but her appetite had fled. Pushing the luscious cake back from her, she sagged back in her chair. It wasn't until the check arrived and everyone at the table started bickering over who had the honor of paying it that Kat roused herself.

This was her last opportunity to call an end to this folly. As her father and Ian Denham played tug-of-war with the bill across the table, Kat rose and called out, "Excuse me."

They ignored her. Clearing her throat, she yelled more loudly, "Excuse me!"

Still no response. Mary Denham had started arguing her husband's case, her soft voice lost in the din. Tamping down her frustration, Kat put two fingers to her mouth and with all the lung power she possessed, gave out a shrill warning whistle. It cut through the cacophony, quieting the room.

"This has really gone far enough," she said, her gaze passing from one face to the next. She forced herself to look at Mark exactly as long as she did each of the others. "I can't let this go on a moment longer."

Nine expectant faces turned toward her. Their emotions seemed transparent — her parents' love, Ian and Mary Denham's caring, Norma's kindness. Mark's barely veiled heat. And Fritz . . . Fritz seemed to plead with her, to beg her for . . . what?

She returned her gaze to Mark. She could see the challenge in his eyes, like a schoolboy goading her — I dare you, Katarina. I double-dare you.

That alone decided her. Not Fritz's plea, or her parents' and in-laws' enthusiasm for the project. Not even the potential for good that Kandy for Kids could bring.

Mark tipped the scales with his silent taunt. Double-dare you back, Mark Denham, she answered him in her mind. Quadruple-dare you.

"This has gone far enough," she said again. She leaned over the table and plucked the check from Ian's and her father's hands. "This is Roth's party. And Roth is paying for it." Reaching down for her purse, she pulled out her corporate credit card, dropped it and the check on the plastic tray. A few moments later, Mr. Giancarlo appeared to take it to the register.

They all shuffled toward the door, Norma and Fritz with their heads together, thick as thieves, the older folks in animated conversation. Kat felt a hand on her shoulder and knew immediately it was Mark's. She lurched to a stop, sudden tension singing through her.

She looked back over her shoulder and wondered why all the oxygen had vacated the room. He stared at her, the silence charged by his touch. If he didn't let go soon and disengage his compelling blue gaze, she just might reach melting point and puddle to the floor like tempered chocolate.

She shifted, turning toward him, and Mark finally dropped his hand. Her shoulders sagged with relief. "Yes?"

If he didn't stop looking at her mouth, she'd have to smack him. Or put him in a lip lock. He blinked, as if remembering how to speak. "It's a great idea. Kandy for Kids, that is."

She wriggled her shoulders a bit, but couldn't quite shake off Mark's touch. "It was Fritz's idea actually."

"Right." He rocked back on his heels. "I just . . ."

His gaze had drifted back down to her mouth. She had to resist the urge to fan herself with her baggy jacket to siphon off the heat. "You just?" she prompted.

"It's really good to see you, Kat. You look great."

For about three seconds she let the compliment wash over her, then logic took over. Terminal bed head hair, wrinkled suit suffering a power outage, and her face . . . Maybe that explained his fascination with her mouth. With the last of her Sweet Cinnamon lipstick faded, her mouth had vanished in her face and he was searching for it . . .

His gaze drifted down again, no doubt riveted by that empty space between her nose and chin. The least she could do was say something to give him a point of reference.

"Thanks," she said brightly. "You look good, too."

With the inanity of her comment ringing in her ears, she inched toward the door. "We should go."

"Wait."

He put his hand on her again, just above her elbow. Who would have thought the crook of her arm would be such an erogenous zone? Even through the baggy sleeve of her jacket, she felt the heat of his palm, the imprint of each finger. She remembered with crystal clarity just what his touch could do to her.

Why couldn't it have been as easy as this? Why couldn't they put their animosity aside and just enjoy great sex? There wouldn't have been much depth to their marriage, but at least they'd have had a rollicking good time. That should have been enough.

It would have never been enough. Her heart a stone in her chest, she prodded him to finish. "What?"

His gaze searched her face and the stone threatened to crumble. "I just wish . . ."

She didn't want to hear the rest. She couldn't. Kat tugged away, turning her back on him and hurrying out the door. The first slap of chill Seattle evening air cleared her mind and cooled her body. When she heard the restaurant door open then close behind her, she spared Mark only the briefest glance before heading for her car.

The rest of the crowd was still chatting in the parking lot and it took a full five minutes to say good-byes and climb into cars for the trip home. Fritz dragged a large, battered Louis Vuitton suitcase from Norma's trunk and a second, smaller one from the front seat before bidding her farewell.

Kat unlocked her car, then leaned against it to speak to Fritz. "Where are you staying?"

"I, ah . . . forgot . . ." He didn't quite meet her gaze. "To make a reservation. At a hotel. Where I would be staying. If I'd remembered, that is."

She tried to follow his circular logic and failed. "Why not stay with your dad?"

He shrugged. "Gone somewhere."

"Surely he wouldn't mind if you stayed at his —"

"I don't have a key."

Fritz's flat statement took Kat aback. She had keys to both of her parents' and stepparents' houses. Just in case, as her mother liked to say.

How could Fritz not? Kat opened her car door and hit the unlock button. "Get in. If you promise to behave yourself, you can stay in my spare room."

"Thanks, Kat." Grinning, he tossed the large suitcase in the trunk of her Camry. The smaller Louis Vuitton he settled carefully between his feet in the front seat.

As she took surface streets to her condo on Melrose, she wondered if Fritz even had the money for a hotel room. Then she dismissed that thought. He was wearing an Armani suit — two or three seasons out of style and a bit big for his slender frame — but an Armani nonetheless. He must be doing fine.

They pulled up to the condo and into the parking garage below. Easing her Camry into her space, she killed the engine then reached in the back for her purse. She caught Fritz staring at her. "What?"

"Just wondering . . ."

"What?"

"Why don't you trust Mark?"

The simple question plunked inside her like a pebble in a well. And like water moving in reaction to that pebble, emotions rippled through her — irritation, defensiveness, despair. It was the same damn question her shrink had asked those first few tumultuous months after the divorce.

She gave Fritz the same answer she'd given the shrink. "It has nothing to do with trust. We are simply incompatible." She ducked her head down as if finding her purse required an extensive search. "Not that it's any of your business."

Purse in one hand, she reached for the small Vuitton suitcase at his feet. "The trunk's popped. You take the big one and I'll get that one."

He pulled the bag out of reach. "Thanks, no."

"I'm not hauling that monster in the trunk."

"I'll get them both."

Who was hiding something now? "Whatever."

Luggage retrieved and car alarm activated, they headed for the elevator. Up in her condo, Kat occupied the next half-hour getting Fritz settled in the extra room, providing him with bedding and pillows and pointing out the bathroom.

When she crawled into bed at last, Rochester curled on the pillow beside her, she could finally let go of the craziness of the day. Her muscles relaxed as she stretched out on the cool sheets, and her mind quieted.

If only she could push Mark from her thoughts. Again and again his face intruded, the wisp of sadness in his eyes, the tone of regret in his voice. Then Fritz's question . . . Why don't you trust him? Before now, the answer had always seemed so clear — because he's a man, and men can't be trusted. But now that justification seemed petty and childish.

Troubled, Kat tossed and turned for hours, finally falling into a fitful sleep near morning.

~ 3 ~

Kat woke to find a reproachful feline face looming over her, four paws digging into her chest and belly. Rochester glared, yellow eyes fixed on her in a feline mind meld. "Feed me" radiated from that baleful gaze.

As she nudged Rochester off and climbed out from under the jumbled covers, she knew a moment of sheer peace. Saturday stretched out before her, a quiet day of rest. Light slanted through her bedroom window, the rare sunny morning filling her with well-being.

She was about to stride from her room in her hip-length babydoll when a clatter in the kitchen brought all of yesterday back to her. An infuriating, but all-too-appealing ex-husband. An impossible fund-raising campaign. And Fritz, a one-man disaster area, who had single-handedly thrown her life into disarray.

And who was elephanting around in her kitchen, making enough noise to raise the dead. Rochester, thumping his twenty-plus pounds to the floor, crept to the bedroom door, then looked back over his shoulder. Disgust clear in his face, he shouldered open the door and stalked from the room. A moment later, Rochester's spitting hiss marched in counterpoint to another crash and Fritz's yelp of alarm.

Kat threw on jeans and T-shirt in record time, raced through her morning bathroom routine, then headed for the kitchen. Calamity awaited her — dirty dishes covering every counter in her compact kitchen, something that might have been pancake batter baked on to the coils of her electric stove and Fritz backed up against the refrigerator with a hissing, growling Rochester holding him at bay.

"Rochester, knock it off." Kat scooped up the black and gray mass of fur, staggering a bit under his bulk as she headed for the laundry room. A bowl of cat crunchies placated Rochester for the moment.

In the kitchen, Fritz still held his ground, leaning against the refrigerator, a spatula in his hand. A goopy white smear marred the front of his navy polo shirt. "Do you need a special permit for a cat that size?"

"Rochester is harmless." Kat reached over and turned off the stove as the pancake batter smoked. "You want to tell me what you're doing in here?"

Fritz swiveled his head from the laundry room door to her, staring for a long ten seconds before he answered. "Making breakfast." He blinked, tried on a smile. "As a thank-you for letting me stay."

Surveying the mess, she wished he'd been a little less grateful. A plate holding three charred circles caught her eye. She lifted a blackened disk. "Ever made pancakes before?"

"No, but it looked easy enough. The box said just add water."

Kat ran a spoon through the watery mixture in a bowl by the stove, feeling much more cheerful about her stunted cooking skills. She could at least make pancakes from a mix.

She picked up the box and dumped in another two cups. "Tell you what. If you clean up a bit, I'll finish these."

Fritz handed her the spatula, then headed for the sink. Over the sound of running water, he asked, "Did you sleep well?"

She poured a portion of pancake batter onto the griddle. "Like a baby," she lied.

"Why do you ask?"

Fritz dumped a handful of utensils into the soapy water. "Thought I heard you outside my door a couple times during the night."

"The condo's haunted." She'd been pacing up and down the hallway, trying to tire herself out. "Restless spirits. I hope they didn't keep you up." She looked back over her shoulder at him.

He looked pensive as he swished through the water with his fingers. When he noticed her watching him, he reached into the water for a dish and scrubbed it vigorously. "I slept fine."

"So . . ." With a twist of the wrist, Kat turned the pancakes. "How's your dad doing?"

He didn't answer for so long, Kat wondered if he'd heard her. "He's great," Fritz said finally with patently false cheer. "Doing really well."

Her cousin had no idea about his dad, Kat realized. The idea stunned her. So accustomed to the sometimes overwhelming familial closeness of the Roths and Denhams, Kat couldn't imagine a father so isolated from his son as Neddy was from Fritz.

She would have pressed him further,

but Rochester reappeared, licking his chops as he savored his breakfast. Fritz danced aside as the cat passed him, but the Maine coon had apparently finished expressing his opinion of the interloper. He leaped onto one of the chairs in the breakfast nook and proceeded with his morning wash, his disinterest in Fritz blatant.

"You don't like cats?" Kat asked.

"They don't like me." Keeping one eye on Rochester, Fritz gave the dish in his hands a perfunctory rub with the sponge. "They can smell my fear."

Kat laughed. "Unless your fear smells like tuna fish, Rochester couldn't care less."

"I'll keep my distance, just the same. No point in taking chances." He set the dish, still soapy, into the drainer.

"You have to rinse that." She waited until he retrieved the dish and held it under the running water before rescuing the pancakes from the griddle. "So when did you see your dad last?"

As the silence stretched, she set aside the plate of pancakes. "Fritz?" She caught a bleak look on his face before he turned away.

Her telephone bleated, the ringing pattern signaling she had a visitor downstairs. She grabbed up the receiver. "Hello?"

"Kat?" Mark's low voice dragged her heart to a stop, then slapped it into high gear. "I'm here."

"Mark?" A tremor stretched his name into two syllables.

"For breakfast. Remember?" He laughed. "It's only been an hour since Fritz called. You can't have changed your mind since then."

Kat whirled to spear Fritz with her gaze. He smiled at her, unrepentant. To Mark, she said, "Come on up." She tapped out a code on the phone to release the door.

Turning off the stove, Kat advanced on Fritz, giving him the evil eye. "How could you invite Mark for breakfast without asking me first?"

Fritz's eyes widened in innocence. "You were asleep. I didn't want to wake you."

She growled at him, nearly toe-to-toe now. "You have gone beyond annoying. You have trespassed into downright irritating and exasperating."

Fritz laughed. "You like men who irritate you."

"The hell I do!" A loud rapping at the door spun her around, sent her stomping into the living room.

Fritz followed along at her heels. "You like men who rile you."

"I do not!" Giving Fritz a dark look, she reached for the door.

"Wait." Fritz put out a hand to stop her. "I'd rather Mark not know I'm here."

"I want him to know you're here. I want him to know breakfast was all your idea."

"Wait. Please." He peeled her fingers from the doorknob. "When I called him I implied I was staying at the Hilton." Shifting his bare feet, he looked away a moment, then back at her. "I just don't want anyone else to know I didn't have a place to stay."

Mark knocked again. Kat shouted through the door, "Just a minute, the dead bolt's stuck." Then she turned to Fritz. "You just forgot to make a hotel reservation. Otherwise you would have had a place to stay."

"Yes. That's right, I did forget. But no one else needs to know that."

Kat studied Fritz's face, his guileless blue eyes, and wondered what he was keeping from her. "Get back in the spare room." She waved him down the hall. "Go on, shoo."

As he ducked into the bedroom, Kat unlocked the dead bolt, tugged at the door. Mark stood just outside, six-foot-one of tantalizing male.

"Hello, Kat." His low voice trilled up her spine, scattering her thoughts.

As she gazed up at him, she had to struggle a moment against the knee-jerk ache in her chest. Damn, why did he always have to look so yummy? "You're right on time."

As he stepped inside, his familiar scent drifted toward her, drenching her with memories. The pattern and rhythm of his touch, the flavor of his skin. She squeezed her eyes shut to banish the images.

"Taken to wearing men's shoes?"

Her eyes flew open. "What?"

He pointed to a pair of Hermès loafers under the entryway table. Kat remembered Fritz slipping them off last night when he'd first come in.

Mark nudged the shoes with his sneaker-clad foot. "Not really your style."

She shut the door, then faced him, chin tipped up. "How do you know they're not my lover's?"

Something flickered in his face, an emotion she couldn't quite pinpoint. "Are they?"

She didn't have to answer. They were divorced, both free agents — witness his cozy luncheon yesterday with the blonde. She could have a hundred lovers; it wouldn't be his concern.

"No." Bending, she picked up the shoes. "Excuse me a moment."

She took the well-worn loafers down to the guest room and cracked the door open wide enough to toss them inside. When she returned, she found Mark in the kitchen, leaning one shoulder against the refrigerator, chewing on what had to be a stone-cold pancake. She couldn't seem to take her eyes from the line of his jaw as it worked, the white teeth nipping another bite from the rolled-up cake.

He finished the flapjack and crossed his well-muscled arms over his chest. The black T-shirt he wore clung faithfully to the lean lines of his body. His faded denim jeans seemed to have a love affair with his legs.

"Who were you talking to earlier? Before you opened the door?"

She'd forgotten the subtleties of his smile, how it could be sweet one moment, hot and seductive the next. Right now it seemed a cross of both and it pulled at her heart even as it teased her more basic instincts.

She shook her head to dispel her treacherous reactions. "No one. The cat."

His gaze strayed to where Rochester

slept peacefully on a kitchen chair. Kat backpedaled. "I mean I would have been talking to the cat if he'd been in there. So really I was talking to myself, I suppose."

She expected him to press the issue, to fall into the familiar pattern of parry and thrust that always escalated into a fight. Instead he shrugged, reaching for another pancake.

Kat snatched up the plate. "You don't need to eat them cold. I'll make some more." Switching on the stove again, she poured a generous dollop of batter onto the griddle.

She could feel Mark watching her as she fussed over the giant pancake. When he spoke, his voice caressed her ears. "I confess I was surprised at the invitation this morning."

"I was, too," Kat muttered. She threw a glance at him over her shoulder. "That you agreed to come, that is."

"Why wouldn't I?"

Kat tried a laugh; it came out sounding sickly. "I'm a lousy cook for starters." She shoved the spatula under the pancake, flipped it. It folded in half and she had to rearrange it on the griddle to restore a passably round shape.

"Your cooking doesn't scare me," he said.

Something in his tone turned her toward him. There was a cryptic message in his eyes, a mystery she couldn't decipher.

Wouldn't decipher. "I figured you'd had enough of me last night." She hefted the pancake from the griddle, slapped it on a plate.

"I've never had enough, Kat."

That struck straight to the core. Her hand trembled as she handed him the pancake. He set it aside on the breakfast nook table where Rochester eyed it with speculative interest.

She waved at him. "Go ahead and sit down. I'll get the syrup."

The plastic bottle of pancake syrup sat so far back in the cupboard she had to drag out the stepladder to reach it. Then she turned too fast with the bottle, and nearly toppled off the ladder.

She'd never seen him move so fast, grabbing hold of her as she swayed. "Are you okay?" he asked, his hands spread at her waist, steadying her.

Wonderful, she thought. Better than I've been in a long time. "Fine, thanks." She edged away from him and descended the ladder, thrusting the syrup at him. "Here you go."

As she busied herself with putting away

the stepladder, then with pouring pancakes for herself, she sensed his gaze on her. She was grateful they'd never lived in the condominium together, that memories weren't clinging to every surface as they did in the guest house on his parents' estate. She could barely stand to be in the same room with him without the past intruding.

She flipped her pancakes, focused on the golden brown circles as if her life depended on it. "Seeing anyone new?" She would have swallowed her own tongue if it could have pulled the question back down her throat. Her skin prickled and burned as she waited for his reply.

Silence beat out the seconds . . . one, two, three . . . "Are you?"

"I thought I already answered that."

"You said the shoes weren't your lover's. You never said there wasn't one in your life."

She took a sidelong glance at him, tried to parse what might be going on behind his intent gaze. "No. No, I'm not. You?"

He seemed to want to dance around the issue. "Why do you ask?"

Because I saw you with a blonde bimbo yesterday. Because I can't stand the thought of you with anyone else. She scooped up her pancakes. "Just curious."

Avoiding his gaze, she took her plate and sat opposite him at the table.

But he didn't seem ready to let it go. When she reached for the syrup, his hand closed over hers. "What if I was?"

She tugged, but he didn't release her hand. "What do you mean?"

"If I was seeing someone else, would that matter to you?"

"Why should it?" She kept her tone neutral. "We're divorced. We've broken our ties."

His eyes darkened to emerald. "Have we?"

She sat transfixed by his gaze, by its intensity. "Yes," she whispered. "We have." This time when she pulled away from him, he released her.

His head bent to his plate as he methodically cut a bite of pancake. She realized with a start that he still hadn't answered. She resisted the urge to rise from the table, to take hold of him and shake the information out of him. Are — you — seeing — anyone?

Then she saw the considering look on his face and terror washed away the impulse to know. She could just see him gathering his thoughts, working out a way to tell her. Yes, Kat, I am. There's this

71

bleached blonde . . .

He squeezed a puddle of syrup on his plate as the pregnant pause went into overtime. "Talked to Eric Matthews this morning."

Kat blinked. Eric Matthews? What did Mark's longtime friend, his best man at their wedding, have to do with the blonde bimbo?

As she struggled to understand his context, Mark continued, "Had to call in a favor or two, but Microsoft's on board for the scull race."

Who the hell cared about the scull race? What about the bimbo? Irritation reared its ugly head inside Kat, at her irksome cousin for bringing her ex-husband back into her life, at the unanswered question dangling between them.

She stabbed a square of pancake so viciously syrup slopped over the side of the plate. Grabbing up a napkin, she scrubbed at the sticky mess and nearly swept her plate to the floor. Flustered, she glanced over at Mark.

A line cut between his brows. His fork rapped against the edge of his plate, tap-tap-tap, tap-tap-tap. "You don't want Microsoft involved?"

How could she not? It was an incredible

coup. But why did he have to be so damned competent?

"I just wish you'd asked me first." Whine, whine, whine. She sounded like a petulant little girl. "You just muscled in and took control."

Mark's tapping increased in tempo. "Eric and I jog Saturday mornings. I had to call to cancel after your invitation to breakfast."

Any moment, she'd be wrapping that tapping fork around his neck. "A little heads up would have been appreciated."

He shrugged and the tapping ceased. "The subject came up. I took the initiative."

Took the initiative. Stepped in and solved the problem. Something twisted in Kat's chest, an emotion she couldn't quite pin down. What was it about his easy competence, his willingness to take on responsibility that tore at her? She had her own skill in working out the bugs, in leading a project. It wasn't envy she felt; she had too much confidence in her own abilities. Yet there was something . . .

She didn't like the tug inside her, the way it unsettled her. She pasted a pleasant look on her face. "Thank you for taking care of Microsoft. Your connection there is better than mine."

He smiled and her IQ plummeted. "Is Sarah still over at Starbucks?"

He has such a damned fine smile. She kicked her brain cells back in line. "She is. I'll call her Monday."

"Peg and Jim still with the *Post-Intelligencer* and the *Business Journal*?"

Kat nodded, a little dazed by the crinkling around his blue eyes. "I'll e-mail them later today."

They stared at each other and Kat could almost hear her thoughts grinding to a halt. She needed to redirect her focus or she'd be a goner, throwing Mark on the living room sofa and having her way with him, never mind Fritz in the other room.

"Let's get to work, shall we?" The Mouseketeers had nothing on her for chipper cheerfulness.

Moving briskly around the kitchen, Kat cleared the plates, waving off Mark's offer to help. Once she'd swiped the table clean of sticky spots, she dumped a stack of Post-it pads, colored pens and highlighters in the center. Seated opposite him with the supplies as a symbolic barrier, she grabbed a hot pink pad and purple gel pen, ready for action.

Like a combatant choosing his weapon,

Mark slipped a neon blue pad from the pile and selected a black pen. As he uncapped his pen and centered the pad in front of him, the opening measure of "Dueling Banjos" twanged in Kat's imagination.

"About the costume ball," Mark said, his gaze on her, pen poised. "How about a black-and-white ball instead?"

Kat had to redirect her mind from its erotic fandango before Mark's suggestion could register. "Maybe," she said slowly. Then her enthusiasm for the idea sparked. "Yes. But masked. No one knows who's who until midnight."

Nodding, Mark started scribbling madly on his pad. "Donors could contribute anonymously to the Kandy for Kids fund."

"They could compete for the honor of the highest donation." Kat snatched up her own pad and made her own notes. "We'd keep tabs on the current winner, announce it throughout the evening."

"Yeah. Give them the opportunity to up the bid."

"How about a silent auction?" Kat asked.

"That's good." Mark peeled a square of blue paper from his pad and slapped it on the table. "Solicit goods and services

75

from the community."

"Right. Give the smaller businesses a chance to take part."

They spent the next hour mapping out strategies, squares of hot pink and neon blue paper filling the table. Aside from the occasional tantalizing thrill when his fingers brushed hers, the thread of tension between them eased. They'd always collaborated well on a business level. World War III they reserved for personal issues.

But there were no issues between them anymore. They'd left those childish impulses behind when they divorced. Now they were fellow businesspeople, icons of industry, masters or mistresses of their respective domains . . .

As she was giving herself a pat on the back for her admirable maturity, Mark's drop-dead gorgeous blonde companion popped up in Kat's mind, as intrusive as a snotty, pesky little kid that just won't leave you alone. Determined to be a grown-up about it, Kat shook off the unwelcome reminder of Mark's no-doubt active love life. She told herself it didn't matter. She really, truly didn't care. She was really fine with whatever Mark chose to do. It really didn't concern her if he was out there schtupping every sweet thing that came along.

"You're drilling a hole in the table."

She jumped at the sound of Mark's voice. "What? I'm not —" But she was. In a frenzy of denial, she'd dug the pen deeper and deeper into the Post-it sheet until she'd ripped clean through it and carved a purple-tinged cavity in her formerly impeccable washed pine table.

"Kat." Mark's hand covered hers. Her lungs, always troupers when she dragged them onto the treadmill at the gym, chose that moment to cease functioning. He could always sabotage her with a touch, no matter how many harsh words between them, no matter how vicious the fight.

She hauled in a ragged breath, let it out on a wispy, "Yes?"

"No," he said, and although the question had never left her mind, for a moment his answer confused her. "No, I'm not seeing anyone," he clarified.

Her heart did cartwheels in her chest, bouncing around like a cartoon image inside her. "Oh," she managed, afraid if she kept talking she'd reveal the joy welling up.

He opened his mouth, his gaze meeting hers and she knew he had something more to say. She could see it spilling across his face, could see it in the faint smile curving his lips, but it was in a language she

77

couldn't translate.

He took his hand back, began plucking up Post-its from the tabletop. "I'd better get going."

"I can have Norma transcribe these." She gestured at the yellow squares. "E-mail them over to you."

His hands full of bits of paper, he paused. "If it's not too much trouble."

"Of course not." She took the stack from him carefully, not wanting to risk another touch. "I'll give them to her Monday."

He nodded, then turned to head for the door. One hand on the knob, he looked back at her. "There's still the silent auction to plan."

"Right." Why wasn't he leaving?

"And the benefit concert." He let go of the door and leaned against it. "We'll have to make a decision on that soon. The Seattle Symphony is booked solid for the year."

Kat started to wonder if Mark was permanently cemented to her floor. "I'll have Norma give the Arts and Cultural Affairs office a call." She gave his arm a little nudge.

The gentle hint flew right past him. "If you want to get together this week, have Norma contact Rod."

He stared down at her, sinful as a Chocolate Decadence Truffle and twice as luscious. Maybe a quickie on the living room sofa wasn't such a great idea, but in her room with the door shut, if they were quiet, Fritz might never . . . No, no, no! Bad, Kat! Bad!

A slightly hysterical giggle bubbled from her lips. "I'll check my calendar." She repositioned herself into a farewell-to-guest stance, complete with emphatic wave. "Bye."

Still he stood there, immobile and tantalizing. Then his gaze dropped to her mouth, a sequel to last night's obsession. She could still feel a trace of the Wicked Watermelon gloss she'd applied this morning and knew she couldn't blame his fixation on a disappearing mouth. Then he took a breath and the memory of his tongue against hers cut in sharp as a blade.

She grabbed the doorknob and nearly shoved him off his feet opening the door. "Sorry," she gasped out.

He took the hint and finally stepped out into the hallway. For an instant, she thought he might lean in and kiss her, but she shut the door before he could so much as move.

Pressed against the door, she listened,

waiting for the sound of his footsteps. She sensed him standing there on the other side, could picture him raising his hand to knock. That image faded as she heard him head down the hall toward the elevator.

She wasn't sure how long she stood there before she realized Fritz stood beside her. Her returning awareness of the room came in snatches — Fritz's worried face, the edges of the Post-its digging into her hands, Rochester on the kitchen counter munching leftover pancakes.

Fritz laid a hand on her arm, his expression oddly colored by guilt. "Are you okay?"

"Fine. Excuse me," she said as she plunked the stack of paper squares on the table, then plucked Rochester from his booty.

As she went through the motions of washing dishes and gathering a load of laundry, she ignored Fritz's worried look. How could she explain her muddle of feelings to her ex-cousin-in-law? She barely understood them herself.

~ 4 ~

E.G. FISHER PUBLIC LIBRARY
1289 Ingleside Ave.
Athens, TN 37303

Eleven o'clock Monday morning, Mark pulled his silver BMW roadster into Roth Confectionery's underground parking structure. A baby-faced attendant leapt to open his door, eagerly taking the keys Mark handed over with some trepidation. Retrieving his computer bag from the front seat, he tried not to wince as the valet peeled out, sending out a fervent prayer for the protection of the roadster's impeccable exterior. The wistful look on the other attendant's face didn't augur well for the safety of his car. Hopefully they wouldn't be joyriding around the parking garage the moment his back was turned.

Instant karma, most likely, to punish him for not calling Kat before driving over. A twinge of guilt bubbled up as he stepped up to the elevator and stabbed the button. He should have phoned to warn her. She probably would have found a way to evade him, given the opportunity. He really just wanted the chance to go over the list of potential donors for the silent auction he and Rod had compiled.

Right. And chocolate came from fairy dust instead of cocoa beans.

He stepped into the elevator and leaned against the mirrored wall as it climbed to the thirtieth floor of Roth Tower. There was simply no way he could not see Kat today. He'd been preoccupied with her all weekend, from the second he left her condo Saturday until this morning when he'd made the decision to drop in unannounced. Every hidden fantasy he'd harbored about Kat in the two years since their divorce had clamored for its moment in the sun and by eight a.m. Monday he'd felt wrung out by his body's edgy anticipation. He didn't know if seeing Kat would make things better or worse, but by God, it was the only thing he could think of to do.

With a muted ding, the elevator arrived at the top floor and the doors slid open to reveal Norma at her desk, Fritz standing over her. Her matronly face lit by whatever nonsense his ill-fated cousin was sharing with her, Norma didn't even notice Mark until he was opposite the wide cherrywood desk.

Norma sat up abruptly as Fritz cleared a

penholder off her desk with a startled jerk of his arm. As Fritz busied himself with picking up the scattered pens and pencils, Norma lunged for her phone. Mark put his hand over Norma's to forestall her giving Kat the heads up.

Mark smiled as he plucked Norma's hand from the phone. "Why don't I just go on in."

Norma's eyes widened. "She's out of the office."

"No, she isn't, Norma." He gave her hand a squeeze. "You tell her I'm here and she'll be doing a Spider-man down the side of the building to escape."

"I'm sorry, Mark." Her chin tipped up, but he could hear from her tone she was wavering. "I have orders."

He broadened his smile. "I just need a minute. I'm sure Kat won't mind."

With a sigh, Norma gestured toward Kat's office. When Mark reached the door, he heard a faint thunk from the other side. He turned the knob, pushed . . . and dropped to the floor just as a dart came screaming toward his head.

Kat shrieked. On hands and knees, Mark cautiously peered around the door. Kat stood behind her desk with another dart in her hand and Mark froze as he waited to see if he was its target.

Kat bristled, as prickly as the needle-sharp weapon in her hand. "What are you doing here?"

Sitting carefully on his heels, he raised his computer bag as a shield. "Could you put that down?"

She looked down at the dart in her hand and flung it to her desk. Unfolding himself from the floor, Mark stepped inside Kat's office. When he shut the door behind him, he discovered a movie poster–size image of cheerful Buddy of Coffee Buddies fame tacked to the inside. Darts and puncture holes pierced Buddy from topknot to shiny black toes.

He pulled darts from the heavy oak door. "There's always been something a bit maniacal about Buddy." Crossing the room to Kat's desk, he set down his computer bag and took aim. "A psychotic gleam in those big blue eyes." He tossed a dart and it flew straight and true toward Buddy's face. "I tried to tell marketing, but they just wouldn't listen."

As he drew back to throw another, Kat stopped his hand. "How did you get past Norma?"

She was leaning across her desk and her cream-colored V neck, baggy as usual,

84

gapped in front. A gentleman would never take a peek, but then, it wasn't much fun being a gentleman.

She caught him staring down her sweater and quickly straightened, patting her ID badge as if to add a layer of protection. "I have work to do."

He set aside the darts and grabbed his computer bag. "Yes, we do." As his laptop booted, he made himself comfortable on the edge of her desk. "The donor list isn't quite complete, but I think you'll be happy with what I've got so far."

He turned the computer display toward her, but she ignored it, narrowing her gaze on him. "Print the list and give it to Norma."

"As soon as I have your approval."

His imagination wandered along the slender line of her throat, the intriguing angles of her shoulders. Did she realize how delectable she looked in that pale, creamy sweater? She might have thought she was hiding her curves with the oversized sweater and loose-fitting mocha slacks, but he remembered every soft inch.

Her voice buzzed in his ears, reining in his wayfaring fantasy. ". . . have to go. They'll be here any minute."

"Who?"

She huffed with impatience. "The Business Understanding Youth group. They're touring Roth's testing kitchens."

"I'll come with you." He shut down his laptop and stuffed it back in his bag. "Give them the Denham perspective."

"I don't need the Denham —"

The phone buzzed and Kat snatched up the receiver as she glared at him. She listened briefly then hung up the phone again. "They're here. Good-bye." She turned and marched to her door.

Lord, why wouldn't he leave her alone? Bad enough her thoughts of him had developed into an obsession, that he haunted her dreams when she finally managed to fall asleep. He had the audacity to turn up at her place of employment, to flash that "kiss me" smile, ripple those "touch me" muscles, turning her insides from perfectly good nougat to a gooey soft center.

The group of BUY boys and girls waited at Norma's desk, visitors' badges clipped to the girls' prim sweaters and the boys' conservative blazers. As Kat approached, she ignored her six-foot-one shadow in the vain hope he would simply disappear. No such luck. When she introduced herself, ingrained courtesy forced her to introduce

Mark as well to the adult leader, Jennifer, and the twenty bright-eyed twelve- and thirteen-year-old business-mavens-to-be. When she gestured the mob toward the elevator, Mark moved right along with them.

With his easy smile and his eye-candy body in a gray polo shirt and charcoal slacks, he drew the admiration of every female in the group. As the young girls clustered around him, Kat entertained a brief homicidal fantasy of tipping him down an empty elevator shaft. It'd be a damn mess to clean up, and the OSHA paperwork would be sheer hell, but maybe . . . She put a damper on the macabre notion when she realized just how far astray her exhaustion was taking her thoughts.

Mark positioned himself right next to her in the packed elevator, his hand suspiciously close to her rear end. When she felt his fingertips brush against the soft wool of her slacks, she thought it had to have been inadvertent. Then he stroked her again, more firmly, and her traitorous eyelids drifted shut.

She snapped her eyes open again. "Stop that," she whispered.

"Stop what?" His hand spread to encompass more of her behind. If it didn't feel so damn good, she would have elbowed him for his impertinence.

Suppressing a moan, she muttered out of the corner of her mouth, "Move your hand."

He did, scribing slow, sensuous circles over her derriere. When she ought to be screaming in protest, instead she was nearly moaning in pleasure. By the time the elevator glided to a stop, she was leaning into him, ready to melt into his arms for a kiss. If it wasn't for the enthusiastic young girl behind them who pushed them apart as she exited the elevator, she'd be molded against Mark and making a complete fool of herself.

Gathering her dignity around herself as best she could, she marched from the elevator. He caught up, but if he thought she'd let him manhandle her again, she let a quick evil glare apprize him otherwise. One of the young boys, a towhead in a navy Brooks Brothers blazer, caught the look and shrank back in sympathetic male fear.

As she herded the bright-eyed BUY boys and girls toward the test kitchens, she kept the flighty crowd between her and Mark. The worst part of having him goose her in the elevator was that she'd enjoyed it so much. It had been a sharp reminder of the way his skilled hands could so quickly get her hot and bothered.

The flock of future B-school students preceded her into the kitchens. "As part of Roth's marketing plan, we offer free or nominally priced cookbooks on the back wrappers of our baking chocolates and Choco-Chunks bags. We test the recipes here."

Mark managed to do an end run around the gaggle of students and now hovered just behind her. It would only take one step back and she'd be pressed against him, his heat melting into her. The BUYers were staring raptly at a stainless steel double boiler, enjoying the fragrance of the Choco-Chunks melting over simmering water. They'd never notice if she rubbed herself against her ex-husband.

Good Lord, what was she thinking? She wormed her way into the circle of students, putting a human shield between her and Mark. When she glanced back to scowl at him, he gave her a cocky smile, as if he read every dirty little thought in her mind.

She refocused her attention on the BUYers, delivering a familiar patter about the method of tempering chocolate, the crucial temperatures required to ready chocolate for coating or molding and to avoid bloom on the finished product. Therese, the test kitchen's head chef, sprinkled more Choco-Chunks into the melted chocolate to cool it, then offered bits to the group. As the boys and girls reached out for their share, Kat sought out Mark.

He'd disengaged from the group and had drifted off toward another kitchen station. Kat's focus drifted along with him. What was he up to, prowling around her test kitchens? Was he trying to glean Roth's candy-making secrets? Truth be told, there really wasn't anything to glean in the kitchens or anywhere else on this floor. The Chocolate Magic team was safely tucked away in R&D, out of view of the parade of BUY kids and ex-husbands.

But, darn him, what if he planned to pin down her Aunt Sophie's chocolate rugelach recipe? Ian Denham had tried to wheedle the precise ingredients out of Aunt Sophie three years ago at Thanksgiving. The old lady wasn't quite in possession of all her marbles, but she had enough sense to keep the recipe to herself. Maybe that was Mark's goal all along, to invade her test kitchens and snitch Aunt Sophie's rugelach.

Mark caught her watching him and he winked before ducking behind a refrigerator. Kat called out to Therese, "Take over for me, would you?" then quickly extricated herself from the group. Briefly blockaded by the towhead in Brooks Brothers, she growled in frustration as she side-stepped the young man. He skittered out of her way, whimpering at her scowl, and she felt a brief twinge of guilt.

Rounding the refrigerator, she had Mark in her sights. He'd escaped to the far end of the test kitchens and had one hand on the door to the next room. He gave her a cocky salute before pushing through the door. Determined to put an end to whatever skullduggery he was up to, Kat followed.

She caught glimpses of Mark as he threaded through the adjoining file room, then lost him again when he exited out into the hallway. It was a short walk from there back to the elevators. He'd have access to any floor he liked, and although only employees with the appropriate pass code could access the Chocolate Magic research lab, she wouldn't put it past Mark to sweet-talk his way into the room.

She caught up to him outside the elevator and grabbed his arm before he could so much as press a button. "Where are you going?"

He grinned, the light in his blue eyes absolutely mesmerizing. "Can't stand to have me out of your sight?"

"I can't have you roaming the halls."

He gave her a look of pure innocence. "I was looking for a soda machine."

"You couldn't have asked?"

"You were busy." He smiled more broadly. "I hated to interrupt."

"And yet you managed to, anyway."

He shrugged, unrepentant. "You can go back inside. I'll find it on my own."

"Fat chance." She waved him down the hall toward the employee break room. Once they'd stepped inside the small kitchenette with its vending machines, Kat crossed to the soda machine and fished a dollar from the back of her ID badge holder. Feeding it into the machine, she punched the button for a Dr Pepper. She handed the icy can over to him.

"You remembered. I'm touched."

"How could I forget? You hogged half the refrigerator with DP the entire time we were married."

He popped the lid, carefully pressing the tab back. "Is that what did us in? Too much Dr Pepper?" He was still smiling, but there wasn't much humor in it.

An ache started up inside her. "Do you

really want to talk about that?"

"I guess not." He took a sip of the soda. "So how have you been, Kat?"

Kat folded her arms over her middle again. "I think we covered that Saturday. I'm fine. You're fine. We're all doing great."

"Yeah. Right." He stared down at the soda can, his smile gone. Somehow, that hurt most of all.

"Mark." He wouldn't look up. "Mark . . ." Another beat, then he lifted his gaze. "Why are you here?"

He stared at her, swirling the soda can. "Kandy for Kids. The donor list."

"You could have e-mailed it to me. Or faxed it to Norma. I would have looked it over, added my own data and sent it back. You didn't have to come down here."

"I just thought —"

"No, I don't think you did."

"Kat . . ." He reached for her.

She knew she ought to step back, evade him. She was a sucker for his touch, had endured the last few difficult months of their marriage because she was so damned addicted to the feel of his hands, his mouth. She'd feel his heat on her, and her brain would take a vacation.

She let him stroke her shoulder, draw his

fingers up along her throat. She refused to look into his eyes, refused to allow that connection. When his palm moved to rest on her cheek, she backed away, smacking her elbow on the soda machine before she could sidle out of his grasp.

"You lured me here."

"Katarina." He'd used her full name. Caution lights flashed. "I don't know what you mean."

"You walked out of the test kitchens just so I'd follow you."

"You have a very suspicious mind." He set aside the soda can and moved closer.

She retreated before he could touch her again. "You wanted to get me alone."

He gave a little huff of impatience. "You have nine thousand employees in this building. How alone could we be?"

As if to emphasize his point, Greg Marubayashi from marketing entered and headed for the coffeepot. "Hey, Kat. Hey, Mark."

Greg filled his mug and busied himself with creamer and sugar. Mark picked up his Dr Pepper and drank down the last of it, head tipped back, strong throat working as he swallowed. The Diet Coke guy had nothing on Mark.

Greg gave a cheerful wave good-bye as

he exited. Kat wanted to walk out with him.

The crunch of metal claimed her attention and she stood there, helplessly ogling the flex of Mark's biceps as he crushed the soda can. He tossed it into the recycle bin in a smooth slam-dunk, his gaze locked with hers. She knew that gleam in his eye.

It had been a game the first year of their marriage — he'd pursue, she'd pretend to evade. It had been heady and exhilarating knowing how much he wanted her.

She put the table between them. "I'm not playing, Mark."

He prowled around the table, the sound of her name as tantalizing as foreplay. "Katarina."

Her blood heated, turning her protest into a breathy invitation. "You should go." She shoved a chair in his path. "You're intruding."

He sidestepped the chair. "Call security."

Defenseless, she watched him move closer. "Please, Mark."

He cupped her shoulders, tugged her toward him. Erotic images flickered in her mind in a hyperactive movie trailer and suddenly one little kiss didn't seem like such a bad idea.

His mouth a micrometer from hers, she stopped him just in time. "No." She wriggled free, backed away. "Get out."

The heat in his beautiful blue eyes nearly dragged her back in his arms. "Kat —"

"Get out, get out, get out." Frustration turned her voice shrill and her words nasty. "I don't want you here!"

He stared at her for a long moment, pain chasing away the passion. "I'm sorry," he said softly, then turned and headed for the door.

Which was exactly what she'd wanted. She should be dancing for joy, doing back flips with exuberance. Instead she felt rotten, wanted to hide in a closet and gorge on a box of Roth's dark chocolate chews.

"God, I'm an idiot." She hurried out of the break room and caught up with him at the elevator. "Mark, I didn't mean to —"

"I left my briefcase in your office." He wouldn't look at her. "Okay if I go get it?"

"Sure, but Mark —"

The elevator arrived and he stepped inside. "Have Norma get back to me with any changes to the donor list."

"Mark —"

He must have hit the close door button because the elevator slid shut and it started up before she could think to slap the call button. The other car took its own sweet time arriving, then when she'd gone up a couple floors, she remembered she'd left the BUY kids to their own devices in the test kitchens. She stopped at the next floor and thundered back down the stairs. She'd have to call Norma from the kitchen, have her head off Mark.

In the test kitchens, Therese had the group suited up in white lab coats and paper hair coverings. Half the BUY kids were tempering their own pots of chocolate, the other half were rolling rum raisin fondant in the silky brown coating. Jennifer was holed up in the corner clutching a box of peanut butter fudge. Her glassy eyes told the sordid tale — she was a sugar addict in a fudge-induced state of sucrose nirvana.

Kat grabbed a wall phone and dialed Norma's number. "Is Mark still there?"

There was a long pause before Norma answered. "Already gone. He said he'd e-mail me the donor list."

Maybe she could still catch him in the garage. Call the parking attendants, have them withhold his keys. Blockade his car.

Jennifer sank her teeth into another square of fudge, her eyes closing in bliss. If the youth leader didn't get an intervention fast, she'd need a one-way ticket to a sugarholics halfway house to dry out.

Kat returned her attention to her assistant. "Norma, contact his office. Have him call when he gets in."

"Sure, Kat."

Kat hung up the phone and eyed Jennifer still wolfing down candy. First snatch the fudge, Kat decided, then administer coffee. With any luck, the woman wouldn't get nasty. It wouldn't do to have her make a scene in front of all those kids.

Pasting a soothing smile on her face, Kat set aside the problem of Mark and started cautiously toward Jennifer.

Despair filled Fritz as Norma set down the phone. Mark stood opposite her, briefcase in hand, his look so grim Fritz would have thought Denham Candy had been booted off the New York Stock Exchange. Mark's black funk drove one more nail in Fritz's self-made coffin.

Head bowed, Mark strode toward the elevator, then gave a halfhearted wave before stepping into the waiting car. The doors closed and the elevator swept him away, along with any prayer of Fritz successfully completing his objective.

Sinking to the edge of Norma's desk, Fritz tapped his foot in a rapid staccato. "Why didn't you tell her?"

Norma smiled up at him, and for the first time Fritz noticed the dimples creasing her cheeks. "I'd rather tell her face-to-face."

The friendly look in Norma's hazel eyes should have coaxed a smile from him in response. But he was so damn agitated he could barely think straight. His grand plans were going to hell in a handbasket, like everything always did in his life.

Norma's smile faded. "It's all my fault. I should have found a way to keep him here."

"No way, Norma. This one's on me." He tapped her gently on the arm. "Besides, we're in this together. *Compadres.* Partners in crime."

She gazed up at him a moment more, then she looked away, her cheeks coloring a bit. She stacked the already neat files on her desk, tidying up her impeccable work space.

"So what's our next step?" she asked briskly.

Doom weighed heavily on Fritz's shoulders. "What next step? They hate each other."

"They don't. I'm sure of it. We just have

to find a way to put them together and keep them there, then let nature take its course."

Now she was smiling up at him again, her hazel eyes shining. For an older lady, she really was pretty. He liked the way she styled her soft blond hair around her face, the way it dipped in just under her chin. And she always dressed so classy, in colors that set off her curvy figure just right. Her ex, Ronald, was a real jerk for leaving such a fine woman.

Embarrassment hit, knocking some sense into him. This was Norma he was entertaining such goofy thoughts about, the woman who had held him as an infant, who had even baby-sat him a time or two. He'd always liked her, always respected her, but that was as far as their relationship went.

If she'd just stop smiling at him, stop looking at him as if he really mattered, as if he was really worthwhile instead of a terminal screwup. A woman like Norma had a way of making a guy feel as if he actually counted for something.

He pushed away from her desk and started pacing in front of it. Man, he needed therapy. He needed a shrink. A lobotomy, maybe. A weekend at the funny farm . . .

"That's it." He stopped in his tracks, turned to Norma. She really was a good influence on him, giving him such stellar ideas. "A weekend getaway."

She looked surprised, and for an instant he wondered if she thought he was suggesting a getaway for them, for him and Norma. The idea shouldn't excite him, but it did. He pushed aside the crazy notion and forged on with his idea. "Does Roth still own that cabin up at Mt. Rainier?"

"The executive cabin? Sure. They just restocked it last week for the spring and summer."

"Great, great." His mind raced now, sinking its teeth into his newest plan. "This is what we're going to do . . ."

~ 5 ~

The Mark Situation proved to be a portent for the rest of the week, because it hurtled downhill from there. Problems with Chocolate Magic, dismal sales figures and a recalcitrant cat had turned the last five days into a nightmare.

And now, when she'd rather be nursing a TGIF margarita at Phil's Tacqueria, she was trapped in her Camry on Highway 706 two miles east of Elbe. Her shoulders ached from the three-hour-plus drive from Seattle that started with an agonizing crawl through Friday rush-hour traffic and segued into a sudden spring thunderstorm on Highway 7 that swamped her windshield and reduced her forward velocity to five miles an hour.

Barring the unexpected landing of space aliens on the highway, it was only five more minutes to the town of Ashford, nestled in the shadow of Mt. Rainier. Maybe ten miles more and she'd arrive at her destination — the Roth executive cabin.

She was hungry and cranky, and longed for a quick microwave meal and an extended session in the cabin's hot tub. She could put Mark out of her mind, get some perspective on the hellish week, somehow restore her equanimity.

Instead, she'd be lucky to get the microwave meal. Somehow, her father had roped her into conducting a management retreat, a weekend "team-building" exercise. Yuck. Touchy-feely "can't we all get along" activities gave her hives. She'd suffered through them at USC, had put up with them at Roth in her first few years there. When she took over as CEO, she swore she'd never do another.

When Norma had passed along her dad's request, Kat was vulnerable. Word of the latest Chocolate Magic debacle had just been dumped on her. Poor Norma knew Kat was at a low point and almost refused to give her the memo from her father. But Kat had insisted, her eyes glazing over as she read her dad's purple prose, rattling on about the latest fad in personnel connectivity and interleaved matrix structures. Half brain dead, Kat said yes before she'd had time to think. By the time Kat came to her senses, Norma had already forwarded Kat's agreement to her father.

She pulled into Ashford in the rapidly gathering gloom, past the Pizza Hut, the cafes and B&Bs. As she continued beyond Ashford, Mt. Rainier towered above her in the dusk light, an eerie glimmer limning the volcano's glacial snow. Seven more miles down Highway 706, then three miles along a private gravel road and she'd reach the cabin. Norma would likely be there already, and maybe one or two other staff if they'd left early enough to avoid the Friday crush of traffic.

The cabin. Where she and Mark made love the first time. Where they'd spent two days of their honeymoon before a crisis back at Denham cut it short. They'd packed more passion in those forty-eight hours than should have been humanly possible. Those erotic memories still visited her some nights, deep in her dreams.

For those two days everything seemed right between them. Now nothing was.

Okay, she'd been an ass on Monday. She could still see the pain in Mark's eyes, hear the hurt behind his carefully neutral tone. Her propensity for foot-in-mouth disease had got her into trouble again. The wrong words had a tendency to leap from her lips without benefit of forethought. Mark exacerbated it, especially when he touched her . . . or smiled at her . . . or stood in the same room as she did. In a way, it really was all his fault, but she was too much of a lady to blame it on him.

So engrossed with Mark, she sailed right past the turn for the cabin, then had to drive another mile in search of a turnout on the narrow, winding road. Once she reversed direction, she resolutely shoved aside the image of Mark's sad, puppy dog face.

Better to focus on the other disasters du jour of the past few days. Tuesday, the Chocolate Magic stabilizing ingredient, always the most problematical component of the formula, turned the day's test batch a nasty shade of green. On Wednesday, she was still digesting that disappointment when the Mother's Day sales figures dropped on her desk. She'd expected bad, but those numbers were just plain ugly. Then as a last straw, Rochester had made a mad dash to freedom yesterday morning, skittering past her when she'd opened the door for the morning paper. By the time she found him, he'd breakfasted on something, which he puked on the living room carpet the moment she brought him back inside.

She finally spied the marker for the private drive and slowed the Camry to make the turn. Norma had warned her the road hadn't been graded yet this year, but that still didn't prepare her for the six-foot-deep pothole that swallowed the Camry just after the turn. She bit her tongue and smacked her elbow on the side window, but no damage to the car. Foot ready on the brake, she squinted in the headlights' dim glare as she puttered on down the road.

Truly the last several days hadn't been much worse than the week before. The Chocolate Magic team already had another avenue to explore. Marketing put their heads together and had derived an excellent strategy to increase sales. Rochester might be in a snit over his minuscule weekend accommodations at the kitty B&B, but at least lizard or *whatever* he'd eaten would be off the menu.

To be honest, it had been the start of the week that had made the rest of it so difficult to bear. The Mark Situation.

He wouldn't answer her calls, didn't acknowledge her E-mails, ignored her faxes. He was always tied up in meetings or had just stepped out or hadn't arrived yet or had already left for the day. No matter what time of day she tried, she never reached him.

She suspected Norma knew more than she was telling. Whenever Kat asked if Mark had called, her assistant shook her head, blushed and turned away.

Fritz inexplicably had taken a powder, too, which made Kat even edgier. By definition, Fritz out of view meant he was up to no good. If she couldn't oust him from Roth entirely, she'd prefer to have him in plain sight, not skulking about, surreptitiously wreaking havoc with Kat's life.

A soft glow filtering through the thick trees caught her eye and she hit the brakes. Was that another car? She thought she glimpsed the glint of metal but as she peered through the windshield, straining for a better look, the light extinguished. Space aliens, no doubt, landing in the woods. She eased her car forward again.

Kat finally bumped down the last curve to the cabin. The headlights strafed the creek, the wide sloping lawn with its barbecue pit, the cabin and finally the carport. Where were the other cars? Norma's little Geo Metro should be in one of the two spaces in the carport; the others' vehicles should be lining the drive along the back side of the cabin. She'd asked Norma to notify the attendees they could leave work early to avoid the traffic. Surely someone would be here by now.

Visions of ax murderers dancing in her head, Kat rose from her car and looked around her. The cabin's one exterior light created shadows that striped the creek-side lawn. The firs and pines, dark silhouettes against a purple sky, writhed gently in the breeze.

Faint unease prickling across her skin, Kat leaned in to grab the fat legal-sized packet her father had sent over. What had Norma said when she'd left at noon? She had to tie up a last few loose ends. Make sure all the supplies and materials were ready for the weekend. Come to think of it, Norma had been a bit vague as to her own arrival time. It was Kat who had leapt to the conclusion her assistant would be here when she arrived.

Kat tapped the bulging lavender envelope against the top of the car door. So where was everyone else hiding? The team-building activities didn't start until tomorrow. Maybe the rest of the management team had checked into their rooms back in Ashford. Norma had the details of who was where so Kat would have to wait for her assistant to arrive before she could check on the weekend's guinea pigs.

Tipping the lavender packet toward the Camry's dome light she studied the logo on the sealed packet. Ornate with curlicues and flourishes, the letters CLR were inscribed across the front. CLR, which stood for . . . what? Calluses Look Raunchy? Cheap Losers Rejoice? According to Norma, Kat's father swore by this company and he'd thoroughly vetted them. More likely, he stumbled across them while surfing the Web and liked the color scheme of their home page. They were all doomed.

Resolute, she tucked the packet under her arm and slung her waist pack over her shoulder, then went to the trunk for her suitcase. As she trudged across the lawn toward the front door, a memory sprang from out of nowhere and hit her squarely in the chest. Her and Mark, playing the "chase me, catch me" game across a blanket of snow. He'd tumbled her down into the icy white fluff, then had carried her off to the downstairs bedroom. They didn't come up for air for three hours.

The envelope slipped from her hands and thumped onto her left foot. Whatever CLR had packed in there just about crushed her baby toe. At least she could focus on the physical pain instead of the ache in her middle.

She nearly dropped the packet again as she dug in the waist pack for the keys, then wearily opened the front door. Despite her exhaustion, she dragged herself up the stairs to the bedroom on the second level. No way would she sleep downstairs. There was so much baggage in that room, there wouldn't be room for her suitcase. Norma could sleep in the larger, downstairs room.

At the end of the landing, she nudged open the door and flipped on the light with her shoulder. The room was tiny but welcoming with its four-poster bed topped with a worn antique quilt, a window seat overlooking the creek, and a rag rug on the polished wood floor. It was cozy and charming and completely memory-free.

Setting her suitcase in the closet and the waist pack on the dresser, she considered opening the lavender envelope. The brief instruction sheet that had accompanied the packet had advised it be opened when all parties were present. She was tempted to take a peek anyway, but the bed looked so soft and comfy. She dropped the packet to the floor and sprawled across the top of the quilt. It would just be for a few moments. A little bit of rest, then she'd check her cell for messages. She really ought to go get it from the car, and if she wasn't so sleepy she would have.

Why wouldn't Mark call her back? The question drifted into her mind, adding to the ache inside.

She'd nearly drifted off asleep, when she thought she heard the sound of a car engine. She roused herself to listen. Had Norma finally arrived? But no, this engine was moving away from the cabin, not approaching. Probably someone driving on another of the small private roads crisscrossing the area. Sound traveled peculiarly in the woods.

She relaxed again and quickly fell asleep.

Mark's shoulders sagged in relief as his roadster rolled up the drive of the Roth executive cabin and eased into the carport. It was nearly midnight, the two-hour trip from Seattle mind-numbing. He'd had so many loose ends to tie up from a grueling week, it was ten before he could pack and head up here to the cabin.

Now he had a weekend sales seminar to face, filled no doubt with those "I love you, man" kind of exercises that always embarrassed the hell out of him. That had been one of the few points of agreement between him and Kat — an absolute loathing for pop psychology weekend bonding.

But there was no turning back now. The note his mother had dropped in his in box yesterday morning had been packed with accolades for CLR's cutting-edge productivity improvement program. After signing Denham up for the seminar, his mom had connected with Patti Roth and set up two-and-a-half days at the executive cabin. The only upside was he hadn't had to go over the material before he left Seattle or he wouldn't have made it up here until Saturday morning.

As he grabbed the fat lavender packet and extricated himself from the car, he realized the place was deserted. He would have thought one or two of the sales team might be here, drinking Roth's fine, aged whiskey and soaking in the hot tub before they returned to Ashford for the night. His mother's note hadn't included a list of who would be participating in this boondoggle. When Mark asked Rod, he discovered his assistant had been left out of the loop entirely. Mark supposed he'd find out soon enough in the morning when everyone arrived for the nine o'clock start time.

Retrieving his suitcase from the trunk, he wended his way along the gravel pathway to the broad front porch. Painful as it was being back here at the cabin, he was grateful it was spring instead of winter. The sight of snow on that sloping lawn, icicles dripping along the eaves, would have pushed him over the limit, especially after Monday's disaster. He didn't need any more reminders of lost chances and broken hearts.

He dropped his suitcase in the living room, then fished out his toiletries bag. Once he'd finished his evening routine in the downstairs bathroom, he grabbed his suitcase and headed for the bedroom. Flipping on the overhead light, he stopped short in the doorway, incapable of taking another step.

The wide king bed with its rich navy quilt seemed to sneer at him. The bed's fat white pillows exposed by the turned-down quilt flooded his mind with memories. There were a couple new pictures on the walls and the Roths had replaced the bedside lamp Kat had swept from the nightstand during a particularly acrobatic session in the bed. Even so, the room seemed frozen in time, a harsh reminder of the past.

He recalled with crystal clarity the night Kat broke the lamp. Her laughter as she climaxed under him, the room plunged into darkness, the lamp shattered on the floor.

Twenty-four months later, their marriage was shattered and Kat wasn't laughing anymore. At least not with him.

Lord, he was getting morose in his old age. Must have something to do with tipping past the midpoint of his thirties. He killed the overhead, then turned away from the bedroom and its memories. Switching off lights as he went, he headed upstairs.

A small nightlight glowing in the small second-story bedroom gave him enough illumination to avoid tripping over the furniture, so he left the overhead off. The upstairs bed hadn't been turned down, but whoever had last made it up had done a pretty poor job of it. The covers were rumpled, the pillows askew. He would have thought one of the sales staff had taken a nap in the bed, but there was no other sign of anyone.

A fanciful notion popped into his head — maybe it was Goldilocks who mussed the quilt. Jeez, he was more exhausted than he thought.

He dropped the lavender packet on the nightstand then stripped down to his skivvies. With a sigh, he pulled back the quilt on the bed and crawled between the sheets. He'd expected the linens to be cool; instead, the smooth fabric felt warm against his bare skin. Had the Roths installed some kind of bed warmer?

With a sigh he snuggled into the soft mattress, grateful to be finally prone. He ought to set an alarm to be sure he woke on time, but he just didn't have the energy.

In the distance, he heard a car engine start up and he wondered who would be driving off somewhere this time of night. Whatever. It had nothing to do with him.

He wouldn't have thought memories of Kat would have chased him into the upstairs bedroom. They'd never made love up here. But somehow, a trace of her scent tantalized him, tugged at his heart. Damning his overactive imagination, he closed his mind to his heart's trickery and tried to ease himself into sleep.

After nearly falling asleep on the toilet, Kat dragged herself from the bathroom and back into the bedroom. Stripped down to her panties, she'd left her clothes and shoes piled on the bathroom rug. No way was she searching in her suitcase for her sleep T. She'd slept in the nude often enough before; it wouldn't kill her to do it tonight. The fact that she slept in her birthday suit on a regular basis while married to Mark she wouldn't even consider.

Once she had the bed more or less in her sights, she shut her eyes, too tired to keep them open. When her thighs bumped the bed, she felt for the edge of the quilt and pulled it back. One knee up on the mattress, she planted a hand on the sheet and settled herself down. Rolling on her side, she scrunched down into the middle of the bed . . .

. . . until she pressed her back into something warm and firm and she leapt from the bed with a shriek.

The opening credits had just rolled on Mark's X-rated dream starring himself and Kat when a scream yanked him from slumber. The glare of the bedside lamp hit his pupils with the force of a klieg light and he had to cover his eyes to give them a chance to adjust. When he could finally make out Kat standing there in pale pink panties, arms crossed over her naked breasts, he thought he might still be dreaming.

But the Kat in his wet-dream-to-be hadn't been screeching. Nor had the dream-Kat been staring at him in horror, as if he had no right to be sleeping in the

Roths' bed, as if he were some kind of interloper.

"What the hell are you doing here?" she shouted.

In her outrage, one arm slipped, providing him an enticing glimpse of her left breast. She must have caught him looking, because she ran back into the bathroom, and when she reappeared she was wearing a rumpled shirt the exact shade of a cherry cream center. He couldn't seem to resist contemplating the color of her nipple — it had been closer to the cherry itself, and just as tempting.

Pushing himself up in bed, he scrubbed at his face as Kat stood over him, hands on hips. It wouldn't do to think about the trim waist set off by those slender hands, let alone the peek show he'd gotten when her arm had slipped. If the past week hadn't run him through the gauntlet the way it had, he would have copped a plea, apologized for disturbing her and gone to sleep in the car.

But he was tired and grumpy and horny as hell imagining Kat's body under that shirt. Damned if he would go down without a fight.

Arms folded over his chest, he leaned against the knotty pine headboard. "I'm here for Denham's sales team feel-a-thon."

She stared at him as if he'd just beamed down from an alien space ship. "You can't be."

The chill in the room had an interesting physiological effect on Kat's breasts. The tips pressed against the thin pink fabric of her shirt, drawing his eyes to her breasts again.

With an effort, he dragged them away. "You should have checked with your father before driving all this way. The cabin's booked."

Her brow furrowed. "My father . . ."

He felt pretty smug now that he was about to prove himself in the right. He didn't win many battles with Kat. "I'm sure your stepmother would have told him. My mother arranged with Patti for the use of the cabin this weekend."

Just seeing Kat here lifted the pall that had hung over his week. He should still be angry with her over Monday's nastiness, but somehow having her here washed it all away.

"But my father . . ." She shook her head and her hair, appealingly rumpled, brushed her brow. He wanted to hook those silky strands behind her ears, then follow the path of his fingers with his lips.

Then her hands came up to cover her face and her elbows concealed that nifty view of the front of her shirt. "Oh, my God," she murmured.

If he got up, he could pull her hands down, expose the front of her shirt again. He could tuck back her hair, kiss the shell of her ear, fulfill all those fantasies at once.

Then she dropped her hands of her own accord and sank down on the edge of the bed. This was even better. Now she was within easy reach. She was like a Christmas gift under the tree, and he couldn't decide which ribbon to untie first.

Number one on his top ten was to run a finger along the length of her bare leg from her knee to the hem of the shirt, then work his hand underneath . . .

She cut short his fantasy when she bent to grab something from the floor. When she straightened again, she held out what looked like the CLR packet he'd brought with him.

"How'd that end up over there? I set it . . ." His own fat lavender envelope still sat on the nightstand. He picked it up, compared the identical fussy CLR scrawled across the front. "Where did you . . ."

"My father. He sent me up here to conduct a management retreat."

He dropped his envelope on the bed. "I'm supposed to be running a sales productivity workshop."

She just stared at him, her Belgian chocolate eyes kicking up the fantasies again. "This is diabolical."

"It could be an honest mistake."

"Are you nuts?"

"Okay, not a mistake," he conceded. "They set us up, but it's not such a terrible idea. We both get a quiet weekend." Together, he added silently, alone. As his heart did a joyful two-step, he inched his hand toward her.

Turning to dump her envelope on top of his, she shifted, edging her hip just a shade closer. "I don't have time for this."

He walked his fingers along just beyond her periphery, intent on ambush. "Neither do I. But maybe that's the point. The family knows how busy we are, how much we need a break. They figured this was the only way we'd take some time for ourselves." His fingertips were millimeters from paradise.

"But why together? Why would they —" She grabbed his wrist, halting his incursion. "No."

He turned his hand to wrap his fingers

loosely around her arm. "No, what?" he asked, playing ignorant.

"No touching."

"Who says I was going to touch you?"

"You're touching me now." She tugged; he held on. "Let go."

"But you touched first."

"Mark, for crying out —" Her fingers grew lax, her eyes widened. "Was this your scheme?"

He pulled his hand back. "What?"

"Did you set this up?" She jumped from the bed. "Dragging me all the way up here to —"

"No!" He scrambled to his feet. "I told you, my mother —"

"I can't believe this!" She pivoted away, pacing the short length of the tiny bedroom before striding back toward him. "Using my father to get me up here alone!"

"I had nothing to do with it!" He felt like an idiot standing there in his underwear, so he grabbed his slacks and yanked them on. "I'm just as much a victim here as you."

She stomped back into the bathroom. "I don't care whose harebrained scheme this was. I'm going home."

He retrieved his mint green polo shirt from beside the nightstand. "I'm right behind you."

She emerged from the bathroom fully dressed in rumpled shirt and slacks, juggling toiletries. Tossing the stray odds and ends into her suitcase, she cast an evil look his way once or twice.

His patience as fragile as spun sugar, Mark returned her ire glare for glare. Snatching up his suitcase and his shoes, he hustled from the room in search of the shaver and toothbrush he'd left in the downstairs bathroom. If she thought he'd carry her suitcase down for her, she was sadly mistaken.

All his belongings stuffed back into his bag, he set the suitcase by the door and went poking around the kitchen for a flashlight. She'd have to tote her own barge and lift her own bale, but he was too much of a gentleman to leave her to poke around in the pitch-black night for her car.

She stopped halfway down the stairs when she saw him waiting for her. "I thought you'd already be gone."

"Sorry to disappoint you." He brandished the flashlight. "I thought you'd need help finding your car out back."

"You didn't need to bother. The front porch light is enough to see my way to the carport."

"Which would be fine if your car were

parked there. But since it's in the back —"

"What are you talking about?" She started down the stairs. "My car's in the carport."

Was she trying to piss him off? Mark counted to ten. "I know you're tired, Kat, and I can understand how you might forget where you left your car —"

"I remember exactly." She tossed her head as she closed the distance between them. "It's in the carport."

"The carport was empty when I arrived."

"You're out of your mind! My car is there."

Her hand fisted and she looked ready to slug him. He would have welcomed the contact, would have enjoyed a wrestling match if only to let go of the anger between them and channel it into something physical.

Then her suitcase slipped from her hand to clunk on the floor. "Oh, my God . . ."

She raced for the front door, fumbling with the knob a moment before she could turn it. Leaving his suitcase behind, Mark took off after her. As they trotted to the periphery of the porch light's illumination, he switched on the flashlight.

She stopped short and he bumped into

her. He would have apologized if his brain hadn't gone into a numbing shock.

The carport was empty.

~ 6 ~

From the front passenger seat of her Geo Metro, Norma watched Fritz guide Mark's BMW roadster down the secluded dirt road where they'd already hidden Kat's Camry. She hadn't had this much fun since Ronald, the stinker, left her for the bimbo. Just being with Fritz, participating in his harebrained schemes, made her feel like a teenager.

She supposed, technically, she and Fritz were committing grand theft auto, or whatever they called it on those cop shows that had kept Ronald glued to the TV. To her way of thinking, helping along the path of love took precedence over the niceties of car theft. She was sure there wasn't a judge in the nation who would convict her.

Besides, they weren't stealing the roadster and the Camry — they were merely relocating them. She and Fritz would relocate them right back where they belonged at the end of the weekend. They just wanted to force a little one-on-one between Mark and Kat, help them remember what they'd been missing in the two years since their divorce. By Sunday evening, Norma was sure they'd come to their senses and reconcile.

Fritz shut off the engine on the BMW, then climbed out and stood beside the car. Realizing he couldn't see her in the darkness of the thick woods, she switched on the Geo's headlights, then quickly shut them off again. They couldn't risk being seen.

In a jiffy, Fritz was climbing inside behind the wheel of the car, his rakish grin warming her heart. He was such a sweet boy, and such a gas to be around. Her two daughters, Lisa and Sarah, only in their twenties, weren't nearly as carefree and happy with life as Fritz. She supposed they took after their morose father, who never seemed to find much to enjoy about life — at least until he met the bimbo.

Fritz put his hand up for a high five. "We did it!"

As she slapped palms with him, Norma could just make out the bright white of Fritz's grin. "I thought my heart would stop when Kat almost caught us."

They'd only just turned on the dome light to retrieve a Diet Coke from the cooler, not realizing Kat was about to pass them. When they saw Kat's car slow, Norma had quickly snapped off the switch.

Fritz took her hand and gave it a squeeze. "But you saved the day."

What moonlight there was threaded wanly through the trees and Norma wished she could see Fritz's expression better. It felt so good to hold a man's hand again, even though the man in question was barely past puberty.

When he didn't let go right away, Norma would have thought she'd feel awkward linking fingers with such a young sprout as Fritz. But the connection warmed her, set off a little spark of joy inside.

Human contact, that's all it was. She'd had precious little of it in the last few years. Any woman likes being touched, even if the toucher was half her age.

Fritz finally pulled away and wrapped his fingers around the steering wheel instead of around her hand. "Well, now what?"

Norma sighed, already missing those long, slender fingers. "You don't know?"

"I guess I hadn't thought that far ahead."

"Do we go home?" Norma crossed her fingers. She most definitely didn't want to go home to her lonely little house.

"Uncle Phil expected I'd stay, just in case. He gave me a company credit card."

"So we go back into Ashford and find a room until Sunday."

He brushed her shoulder. "You wouldn't mind?"

A fluttery feeling started up in her stomach. "Why would I mind?" The words came out all breathy. She cleared her throat. "A trip away from home is a luxury for me."

A peculiar thought burst into her head and she almost laughed out loud at the ridiculousness of it. Her and Fritz sharing a room. Being out in these dark woods must have affected her brain.

Thank goodness he couldn't see her blushing in the dark. "Let's get going. I'm sure we can find a couple rooms somewhere in Ashford."

As he drove slowly back down the dirt road, Norma clutched her hands in her lap. An odd little feeling seemed to be brewing inside her, an entirely crazy and inappropriate emotion. She put it down to the nutty adventure she'd embarked on with Fritz, but deep down, she was afraid the strangeness growing inside her was a horse of an entirely different color.

128

★ ★ ★

Kat stared at the empty carport, thinking maybe if she looked long enough, she'd see her Camry there hidden within the shadows. But the vacant spot just stayed vacant and her stomach sank past her toes as she realized her car was well and truly gone.

She was dimly aware of Mark directly behind her, his heat soaking into her back in the frigid night air. "Who would steal a car out here in the middle of nowhere?"

"I don't know." The way he'd gasped out his response, you'd think it was his car that had been stolen.

She took a deep breath, and ordered her brain cells back into some semblance of normalcy. "Okay, this isn't a total disaster. We'll use your cell phone to report the theft, then take your car back to Seattle."

"My cell phone." She heard him swallow. "My car."

Why was he parroting her? Was he trying to annoy her? She turned to face him and his shell-shocked expression sent alarm through her. "Mark, what is it?"

"My cell phone was in the roadster," he said, his voice too high. "And the roadster . . ."

She grabbed his arm. "What about it?"

He pointed at the empty carport, at the spot she'd left her Camry. "I left it here."

She was exhausted, shaken, frappéd and fricasseed. That was why Mark wasn't making sense, why he looked so freaked. Her own mind, her own perceptions couldn't be trusted.

Keeping her grip on Mark — at least the warmth of his skin was real — she gave his arm a little shake. "You can't have, Mark. If you had, it would still be —"

The memory hit with the impact of a ton of cashew brittle dropped on her head. The glimmer of a car in the thick of the woods. Then the sound of an engine starting just as she drifted off to sleep. And again later, when she was dozing on the toilet.

"Them!" she gasped.

Mark's synapses were right behind hers. "They took the cars."

"Our parents?" She shook her head, unable to grasp the magnitude of her family's perfidy. "Drove all the way up here to steal our cars?" Sagging against the cool metal of the carport's aluminum support, she covered her face in her hands. "This is a nightmare."

"It has to be a prank." Mark raked his hair, rumpling it. Her fingers itched to touch it, just once. "Your dad's idea of a joke."

"What about your mom? What if she never talked to Patti? What if she made that up?"

Now he looked ready to tear out a handful of hair. "Why would my mother make up something so nutty?"

"How would I know?" She pushed away from the post, flinging her arms out. "Maybe she heard about the management retreat and had some screwy notion that if she sent you up here, then you and I would . . . that we'd . . . well, I don't know, something about putting us together."

He closed in on her, towering over her. "So your dad's innocent in all this."

She tipped her chin up primly. "Of course."

"And your management team is . . . where?"

That was one little glitch she hadn't worked out. She fluttered her fingers in the general direction of Ashford. "Somewhere in town."

"How do you know your father didn't set this up? Convinced my mother to run the sales seminar at the cabin, and all the while —"

"My father wouldn't do that!"

131

"So it's just my mother who's completely whacked."

Guilt twinged at her. She liked Mark's mother. "Not whacked, just . . . creative."

Like a brooding statue, he stared down at her. When he spoke, his voice was so quiet, she had to strain to hear the words. "I'm here for a sales seminar. I have the packet upstairs to prove . . ."

Sudden speculation lit Mark's expression. Those same wheels started turning in Kat's mind. The words slipped from both their lips simultaneously. "The packets."

"I left mine —" Kat said.

"Me, too." Mark did an about-face.

They hotfooted it back to the cabin, Mark just a step ahead of Kat. She had her key out first, he opened the door once she'd unlocked it, let her go ahead of him. Side by side, they nearly ran up the stairs.

The packets sat stacked on the still-mussed bed. Kat dithered. "Which is which?"

Mark grabbed the top packet. "Who the hell cares?" Pulling his reading glasses from his shirt pocket, he ripped the envelope open.

Kat snatched up the remaining packet and just about shredded the foo-foo lavender paper in her impatience to inspect the contents. The cover letter accompanying the two thick folders inside sailed to the floor. As she leaned over to retrieve it, Mark muttered a string of epithets that would earn him two rosaries his next trip to the confessional. When she scanned the letterhead herself, she let loose a few choice words Rabbi Satenberg would never approve of.

Kat met Mark's gaze over the incriminating letterhead emblazoned with Creating Loving Relationships in an overwrought font. All the nasty convoluted pieces thunked into place. "They were in this together," Kat said.

Mark nodded, his expression grim. "We've been had."

Okay, there's an upside to this, Mark told himself. A weekend with Kat. That ought to cheer him up. Sure, he was still pretty tweaked to discover CLR had more to do with sex than sales. And he had an overwhelming urge to call his mother and give her a sizeable piece of his mind. No matter how enjoyable the outcome, she'd had no right to orchestrate him the way she did.

That is, he'd call her if he had a phone. Which he didn't, since his cell was in his car and the cabin didn't have a phone.

But the sour look on Kat's face just before she'd collapsed on the bed certainly sapped the pleasure from the prospect of spending two days with her. At least he assumed it would only be two days.

"You don't suppose they'd leave us here past the weekend," Mark ventured.

Hunched over, head in hands, she turned long enough to glare at him before sinking into despair again. The scattered papers from the CLR folders lay in disarray around her. She'd dug through the mess of introspective crap for nearly fifteen minutes in a fruitless effort to unearth something related to management connectivity or matrix interactivity or whatever the hell she was searching for. She'd come up empty.

Her voice was muffled as she spoke through her fingers. "I've got to get out of here."

Kat, rumpled and at the end of her rope, still looked so hot it was all he could do to keep from joining her in that bed. "It's nearly two a.m. There's no sense in doing anything tonight. We'll go get our suitcases, I'll get you comfy downstairs and we'll work this out in the morning."

She dropped her hands. "Downstairs?

I'm sleeping up here."

No way was he using that other bed. "Not unless you're sleeping with me, babe. I've got dibs on this room."

She scrambled from the bed, knocking half the CLR paperwork to the floor. "I got here first. How can you have dibs?"

"Because . . ." Because I can't sleep downstairs without remembering how you felt in my arms. "Because I'm taller, and I need a . . . uh . . . longer bed."

"This bed isn't longer. It's a queen. The one downstairs is a king."

"The circulation's better." He waved a hand at the window. "You know I need good circulation."

She stared at him, no doubt wondering if he should be committed. She might have called the men in white coats if she'd had a phone.

She edged between him and the bed, and she spoke in the careful, reasoned tone one used on the unhinged. "I'm sleeping here, Mark. You'll have to go downstairs."

Leaping toward her, he feinted left, then right, trying to get around her. She saw through his subterfuge and jumped on the bed before he could get to it, splaying herself across it. He climbed on board, squeezing into the space her lean body didn't occupy. But she wouldn't give any ground and before he knew it, he was sprawled on top of her, both of them spread-eagled.

Now this was interesting. Kat panted and gasped for breath, her hair mussed, a lock of it trailing in her mouth. He'd ended up between her legs and Mr. BVD stood at full attention. If she raised her knees just a little, he'd be right where she wanted him.

Except of course she didn't want him there, and when she raised her knee, it wasn't to make friends with Mr. BVD. He rolled off her an instant before she made contact.

"Sorry," he gasped out, breathless at the near miss. "I didn't mean to —" Except he had, if he was being perfectly honest.

She looked a little stunned as she sat up, her breasts still saying hello from under her shirt. She gave him a sidelong glance as she admitted, "I don't want to sleep downstairs."

He pulled himself up and leaned against the headboard. "Yeah." That was sufficiently ambiguous that she wouldn't be able to tell if he was wimp enough to feel the same way or was just being empathetic. "So what do we . . ."

"We flip for it." She shifted to dig in her

slacks pocket and he wanted to dive in there with her. Producing a slightly warped gold foil–wrapped chocolate coin, she held it out in her flattened palm. "Call it."

The chocolate coin flew up, launched with a flick of her thumb. "Heads," he called as gravity pulled the quarter back down.

She grabbed it and slapped it on the back of her hand. When she revealed the coin, he saw Roth Confectionery embossed on the side.

"That's tails," she said, snatching the coin away and making to shove it in her pocket.

"Wait a minute." He grabbed her wrist. "Let me see the other side."

They tussled for a few intriguing moments before she gave up the goods. Huffing, she crossed her arms and lifted her chin in a lofty tilt.

He flipped the coin over. "It's the same on both sides. You cheated."

"Not exactly."

"We're flipping again," he told her as he reached in his own pocket. "With a real quarter."

But before he could fish out a coin, she turned to him, a pleading look in her chocolate brown eyes. "I don't want to sleep downstairs, Mark."

Oh, Lord, when she gave him that whipped puppy look, he had no choice but to be noble. And he hated being noble, especially when it meant he had to do something he really didn't want to do.

He got up from the bed. "You stay here. I'll go get your suitcase."

Her smile of gratitude filled his heart with so much warmth he couldn't help himself. One knee on the bed, he leaned over her and brushed a kiss across her forehead. It felt so damn perfect, so right, he wanted desperately to keep on kissing her, on her cheek, her nose, her mouth, her throat. He prayed she'd lay out the welcome mat, give him permission to keep going, even the slightest touch, the softest whisper would be enough. But she didn't move a muscle, didn't make a sound except for the sigh of her breathing.

He slid from the bed again, regret heavy in the pit of his stomach. As he headed for the door, he tossed, "Be right back," over his shoulder without looking at her. He didn't want to see her face, see the closed-off look in her eyes he was certain would be there. That would just be too damn much for his poor belabored heart.

Mark's kiss lingered on her forehead as

powerfully as did the witch's kiss Dorothy received in Oz. She wondered if she looked in the mirror, she'd see a silver mark there like the one on Dorothy's head. With her palm to her forehead, she was surprised she didn't feel the heat of it burn her skin.

When she heard the front door slam, she eased from the bed, then wrestled over whether to undress and climb into bed or to wait for her suitcase and her sleep T. It would be more comfy to sleep in the soft, baggy T-shirt, and she could use the extra warmth in the chilly room, but if she waited, she'd have to see Mark again. She didn't have an ounce of energy left to resist him. She might well end up in that bed with him, which would be a mistake of monumental proportions.

She switched off the overhead and in the glow of the nightlight plugged in by the dresser, she quickly stripped down to her panties again. Shoving the last of the CLR detritus from the bed, she climbed between the now-frigid sheets and tugged the covers up to her chin. The slam of the front door signaling Mark's return, Kat turned on her side and squeezed her eyes shut. She lay stiff and tense under the thin antique quilt, Mark's footsteps across the living room, then up the stairs loud as thunder to her sensitized ears.

Opening her eyes enough to catch a glimpse, she saw him hesitate in the doorway. An image burst in her mind with the brilliance of fireworks over Lake Union — Mark crossing the room, pulling back the covers, slipping into bed with her, pressing his body against hers. His touch, his scent, his ragged breathing as his excitement grew — they were as familiar to her as her own heartbeat. He was as addictive as chocolate and like any addict, Kat ached for just one taste.

He stood there with the suitcase, silhouetted by the light from the stairs, his broad shoulders a come-and-get-me invitation. The temptation to sit up, crook a finger, beckon him to join her was as irresistible as a double dark chocolate truffle. Just for tonight, she could relive the only good part of their marriage — the hot juicy sex.

She scrunched her eyes shut again. Bad Kat! Bad! She gave herself a mental slap on the wrist. Lack of sleep was making her loony. She needed to knock it off and purge all those steamy, delectable thoughts from her head. Just like double dark chocolate truffles, there would be no eating just one piece with Mark. It was the entire two-pound box or none at all.

Before her mental analogies descended even further into chocolate madness, Mark finally stepped inside the room. She expected him to set the suitcase by the bed, then turn and leave. But once he set aside her bag, he hesitated again, this time over the bed. Visions of Mark-flavored sugarplums danced in her head as she squinted another sidelong look at him. He leaned over the bed, closer, closer . . .

And picked up the CLR envelope he'd left at the foot. Before she could so much as entertain a second thought about scooting over so he could hop into bed beside her, he'd left the room and tromped down the stairs. He left her there with unfulfilled fantasies rampaging through her overactive imagination. Geez, couldn't he have at least made an effort to ravish her?

Bad Kat, bad! she scolded herself again. Nothing but G-rated dreams for you tonight.

To emphasize her determination, she punched her pillow into submission, then settled down again and forced her eyes shut. Fat lot of good it did her, because she was wide-awake, her sex drive lapping her better sense in the Mark Denham 100. If her libido didn't make a pit stop soon, she'd be trotting down the stairs and cuddling in bed with her ex.

With a huff of exasperation, she sat up and reached for the bedside lamp. About to snap it on, she reconsidered, rising to quietly shut the door first. No need to alert Mark that she was still awake.

Crawling back under the covers, she sat with her chin in her hand, wondering what to do next. She hadn't brought a book to read, figuring she'd be too busy with the management seminar for that luxury. She hadn't even brought any other work with her. She supposed she could pull her Palm from her purse and reorganize her address book, but that was just too pitiful.

She spied the rumpled CLR papers littering the floor. Maybe she'd just take a little peek at them. She was so desperate for distraction she'd take even the limited entertainment value of the interpersonal woo-woo BS that CLR had churned out.

Plucking a pale pink sheet from the messy pile, she read the prompt at the top. "List ten qualities you could change in yourself that could improve your relationship with your partner." Hah! She'd have to change everything about herself to make Mark happy. Everything except the sex.

She started to crumple the sheet, intent on tossing it aside when something stopped her. Qualities you could change. What could she change? If there was the slightest prayer fences could be mended, torched bridges could be rebuilt — were there things about her she could alter, to somehow make their marriage work?

Not that she wanted Mark back. She was happy as a vanilla cream–filled chocolate clam on her own. But just for yuks, maybe she'd work out a list. No way she could come up with ten. But maybe one or two. It sure beat lying here, wide-awake and restless.

Fishing the CLR-imprinted ballpoint from the scatter of papers, Kat clicked it open and started to write.

Mark made another vain attempt to conform his six-foot, one-inch frame to a sofa built for midgets before kicking the blanket aside in a fit of irritation induced by severe sexual deprivation. Here he lay, his feet jammed against the unyielding arm of the sofa, his body pretzeled and aching, when right upstairs lay the antidote for his troubles.

But he could no more climb those stairs than he could lie on that bed in the downstairs bedroom. Squeezed tight between his present and his past, he was a long,

long way from falling asleep.

Too agitated to lie prone, he sat up and switched on the floor lamp beside the sofa. As he blinked his bleary eyes against the bright light, his gaze fell on the CLR envelope he'd dumped on the side table. Creating Loving Relationships. Yeah, right. As if love could be manipulated. As if he and Kat could follow the instructions in those folders and love each other again.

Just the notion twisted something in his gut. It had all seemed so perfect four years ago. The Denhams and the Roths, best friends and friendly rivals for years, joined through their two children. The match had everything going for it, had no reason to fail — except he and Kat didn't seem to love each other enough. If they had, it would have been smooth sailing instead of the violent storm that erupted from day one of their marriage.

Picking up the envelope, he emptied it into his lap and put on his reading glasses. He hadn't read any further than the cover letter with its pop psychology buzzword mumbo jumbo. Since he couldn't sleep anyway, maybe he'd give himself a laugh by scanning the contents.

He plucked the top sheet from the first folder. "List ten qualities* that first attracted you to your partner." Her mouth, her breasts, the dark curls between her — He took another look at the prompt and saw the asterisk. Scrutinizing the fine print in the footnote, he read, "Nonsexual qualities." Trick question.

Outside of what she could do to him between the sheets, he couldn't think of a thing. Well, other than her quirky sense of humor. And the way she never fussed over herself, but still managed to look gorgeous. Did that qualify as sexual? He didn't think so.

The lavender pen that had been packed in the packet lay right beside him on the sofa. He picked it up, clicked it open and started to write.

~ 7 ~

The scent of fresh-brewed French roast drifted into Mark's nose and dragged him back to consciousness. He peeled one eye open and zeroed his gaze on Kat leaning against the kitchen counter, in a sloppy gray sweat suit. What was it about Kat and baggy clothes that made him want to strip her naked?

With a groan, Mark pushed himself up, every muscle aching from a restless night's sleep. Kat glanced up from her perusal of a cereal box, then raised the box to cover her face. If she wanted to hide from him, she should have concealed her feet as well since her dainty toes tempted him sorely. He had a fond memory of a chocolate pedicure followed by a wild night of lovemaking.

As if she'd read his mind, she curled her toes and tucked one foot behind the other. Mark shook off the pesky fantasies and shoved aside the blanket tangled around his legs. His BVDs did a lousy job of masking his interest in Kat, so he did the gentlemanly thing and turned his back on her as he pulled a pair of sweats and a T-shirt from his suitcase and drew them on. When he turned her way again, he caught her gaze avidly fixed on his butt, cereal box forgotten.

She blushed and executed a quick juggling act with the box before she got it under control again. She bustled around the kitchen then, grabbing a bowl from the cupboard, spoon from a drawer and milk from the refrigerator. She dumped way too much sugary cereal into the bowl, splashed on so much milk a trickle overflowed, then sat down and scooped up an oversized mouthful.

As she chewed, she mumbled, "There's bagels 'n' muffins in the freezer."

Scrubbing his fingers over his head, he could tell he had a bad case of bed hair. He abandoned his coiffure and padded into the kitchen and over to the fridge. "You'll be flying high if you eat that much sugar," he told Kat as mist from the freezer roiled around his face.

She swallowed and waved her spoon at him. "I can handle it."

"Yeah, that's what they all say." He poured himself a cup of French roast, then plucked a plastic-wrapped chocolate chip muffin from the freezer. "So what's the plan for today?"

You would have thought from her wary look he'd asked what time she planned to hop into bed with him. "I'm not planning anything with you."

"Did I ask you to?" He ripped the plastic from the muffin and crushed it in a tight ball. "I'm just curious. If you're going to be hanging around the cabin, maybe I'll grab a fishing pole from the shed and toss a line in the creek." He stomped so hard on the pedal for the trash can, the lid jammed. Slam-dunking the plastic wrap, he crammed the lid back into place.

She was mulling over her cereal again, picking at it now. "I thought I'd walk into town. Find a phone."

"That's nearly ten miles." He plopped his muffin in the microwave. Buttons punched, he took a belt of French roast, wincing as it seared his esophagus. "I hope you've got sensible shoes."

"I left my hiking boots at home." The coffee she sipped was pale as milk and likely contained half the sugar bowl. "I thought I'd be bonding with management this weekend, not traipsing through the trees."

All he could think about was bonding with her. He slammed back another mouthful of coffee and nearly choked when the microwave screeched. "You could just wait for them to bring the cars back. They're bound to eventually."

Clunking her spoon back in the bowl, she pushed to her feet. "I can't. I can't just sit here with you. I'll go mad."

Bundling the hot muffin in the paper towel, he walked past her. "I'll get out of your hair, then. You can freak out in private."

He kept going, out the front door and onto the porch. He slapped the muffin he'd lost the appetite for on the railing, then crossed the lawn to the chattering creek. The damp grass chilled his feet, getting squishier when he reached the edge of the water. Grabbing up a flat rock, he made a lame attempt to skip it across the surface, but in his unskilled hands, it sank immediately.

Why did she still get to him? Here he was, a manly man who ought to be able to laugh off Kat's sniping. But every time, like a four-year-old, he got his feelings hurt.

With a growl, he grabbed up a bigger rock and hurled it into the water. It made a satisfying splash and probably terrorized any fish he might have hoped to catch for dinner. The hell with the fish, throwing rocks was much more fun.

Just as he was contemplating the knee-high boulder at the edge of the lawn, mentally calculating how much water it would likely displace, he heard the front door open. Deciding the rock made a better seat than a projectile, he lowered himself to the chunk of granite and made a show of engaging in some deep thinking.

That required he ignore Kat's approach; deep thinkers weren't distracted by sexy, hot-tempered women. Most likely deep thinkers' deep thoughts weren't X-rated the way his were, so he had to be content with looking like a deep thinker rather than being one. He did manage to keep his lofty gaze fixed on the burbling creek rather than his willowy ex, only peeking sidelong at her once or twice.

"Look, Mark," she said when she stood beside him. "I didn't mean to be so rude."

"Sure you did." He was pretty proud at how manly he'd made that sound. The mud between his toes detracted a bit from the image, but that wouldn't stop him from taking the high ground.

"I'm not angry at you. It's the situation. Stranded here. Without my cell phone, without my computer."

He gestured at Mt. Rainier towering over them. "So go commune with nature. Hug a tree. Feed a squirrel."

"You know I'm no good with that." She paced away from him, her trademark edgy energy like an aura around her. "I have to be doing something productive. I'm lousy at recreation."

He could remind her of her expertise at bedroom recreation, but that would probably earn him Kat's right cross. "So read a book."

Scraping her hair back from her face, she paced back toward him. "I didn't bring one. I thought I'd be too busy."

I could keep you busy. Just as well he kept that one to himself. "Read through the CLR packet. There might be something interesting."

Her gaze wide, she froze, standing motionless one moment, two. Then she stalked away again. "It was garbage. I tossed it all."

He realized the list he'd scrawled last night was still stuffed under the sofa. He'd better deep-six it before she discovered it.

A fish rose in a still patch of water, setting off concentric circles as it scarfed a mosquito. "There are a couple old *Na-*

tional Geographic back issues in the living room."

She just grimaced, looking ready to pull that silky black hair right from her head. And that would be a damn shame.

Then a thunderbolt of an idea hit him. "I have a deck of cards in my bag. I know you're a lousy poker player, but —"

"Me, lousy?" She took the bait, stepping up to his challenge. "I'd have you on your knees, begging for mercy."

Now that was a pretty picture. Him, on his knees, at Kat's feet. His face pressed between her naked legs. But it wouldn't be him begging for mercy.

Thank God sweatpants hid a multitude of sinful thoughts. The rock under his butt wasn't the only thing hard.

"Just a few hands of poker, Kat." He crossed his legs. "Are you game?"

"Yes" nearly escaped from her lips before her radar went up. A few hands of poker. A little entertainment to help while away the interminable hours before she could go home. Why not?

Because it wouldn't be that simple, not when Mark was involved. But try as she might, she couldn't see anything in his intriguing blue eyes but a bland friendliness.

He smiled. "I'd almost think you trust me, Kat."

"Of course I do," she squeaked out, the lie rushing past her lips. "Sure. Poker. Why not?"

She didn't like that savvy look that flitted across his face. Mark had never been a devious kind of guy, but how well did she know him now? And here she was, trapped with him, miles from nowhere, at his mercy.

Now why did that send a little thrill coursing through her instead of a more sensible fear? Because the feel of him pressed against her last night still burned on her skin in a palpable memory. Because to be completely honest, she'd just as soon straddle his lap on that mini-boulder and see where that took them. If she wasn't mistaken, they'd christened more than one nearby boulder on their honeymoon.

He rose and she got an eyeful of what was going on inside his sweatpants. The ridge of his erection brushed against the soft knit, begging her to step a little closer. He knew where she was looking, and she knew he knew, but she just didn't give a damn. She wanted to look her fill. She wanted to experience the excitement again, the power of knowing she turned him on.

What if she hooked her fingers into the waistband of those sweats, then slid them slowly down his hips? She could put her hands on him, her mouth, her tongue. Her eyes drifted shut, her breathing caught, and her knees felt weak as water. She wasn't about to get any closer to him, but she damn well wasn't stepping away.

"Kat . . ." She heard the purr in his voice. "Why don't we make it strip poker?"

Her better sense, always apt to appear at the most inopportune moments, suddenly returned. She almost tripped over her own feet backpedaling and did stumble over a thatch of crabgrass as she trotted across the lawn in her aerobic shoes. "Maybe I will take that walk," she tossed over her shoulder as she made a beeline for the trees.

She thought he'd laugh, had her shoulders all tensed to ward off that mortifying blow. But she heard only the chuckle of the stream and the soft breeze sighing through the trees.

As Kat stepped into the same clearing with its termite-infested log for the fifth time, she realized there was a reason she'd never become a Girl Scout, aside from her aversion to wearing green. In her view, there was something extremely unnatural about nature, what with all the thorny bushes, nasty bugs and verminous chipmunks. If woman was meant to go tromping through the woods without a Palm Pilot and a cell phone, God would have never invented the integrated circuit. Not that God had invented it exactly, but surely such a miracle of the modern world came to be through His guidance.

The real issue here was that she was hopelessly lost. While in a car driving down the highways and byways, she had an unerring sense of direction. But on foot in the wilds of Mt. Rainier National Park, she was disoriented the instant she stepped off the cabin's landscaped front lawn.

She'd digested the two bites of Sugar Crunch cereal she'd downed at breakfast and her stomach rumbled its displeasure. How long before hunger turned to desperation and she started gnawing on tree bark for sustenance? The beady-eyed squirrel chittering at her from a branch overhead had better watch out. He'd be on a spit roasting over a crackling fire before he could say his squirrelly prayers.

That's if she had a clue how to make a spit or start a fire or even catch Mr. Fluffy-Tail. The smirk on the gray rodent's face told the tale — that squirrel knew it was perfectly safe around someone as wilderness-challenged as she was.

She groped in the pocket of her sweats for the hundredth time. There must be another chocolate mint in there somewhere. Still the same crumpled tissue and the cellophane wrapper from her last foray. The tissue she wouldn't part with in the event she had to use the brush as an alfresco Porta Potti. The wrapper might come in handy to catch rainwater. If it rained. If she didn't die first of hunger or squirrel bite.

Energy sapped, she sagged onto the rotted log, hoping the termites wouldn't mistake her rear end for lunch. How long had she been out here? She squinted up at the sun, completely at a loss as to how to interpret the hour based on its angle in the sky. Who learned how to tell time by the sun in this day and age? Clocks were everywhere and everyone had a watch. Of course, hers was on the nightstand in the cabin's upstairs bedroom, but if she'd remembered to strap it on, she wouldn't be peering up at the sun now.

She dropped her glare-spotted gaze back to the log, then whined in faint protest as a muscular foot-long lizard swaggered toward her. This was a lizard's lizard, a chocolate brown behemoth. Kat would no more face down that wide-bodied reptile than she would a rottweiler.

She jumped to her feet. "Hey, bud. The log's yours."

The lizard yelped in response, with the cry of an affronted toy poodle. Kat retreated a couple more steps. "I didn't mean to intrude. You want dibs on the termites? You won't hear any complaints from me."

Another high-pitched bark from the lizard, then it scurried out of sight under the log. She'd prefer to keep something that big and scaly within eyesight, but she wasn't about to go search it out. She'd just walk on in the other direction.

She'd no more than turned on her heel than the crunch of heavy footsteps sent a jolt of terror through her. That wasn't another lizard tromping through the underbrush. A creature making that much noise had to be massive. Was it a bear? Mountain lion? Sasquatch?

She'd be toast in a confrontation with a bear or mountain lion, but she might have an even chance against Sasquatch. Using the same keen powers of observation that enabled her to discriminate between the raspberry creams and the nut chews in a box of assorted chocolates, she scanned the surrounding area for a weapon. A crumbling tree limb leaning against the rotted log seemed her best option. She grabbed it up and held it at the ready.

With a shriek, she tossed it aside when a weevily-looking insect crawled from the branch to her pinky. Unarmed, she struck what she hoped would pass as a karate pose, at least in the animal kingdom. Sucking in a breath, she faced her potential attacker.

She swung her fist an instant before Mark pushed through the screen of trees into her clearing. Fueled by adrenaline, her fist kept going and would have left a wicked bruise on his cheek if his reflexes hadn't been hair-trigger. He snatched her wrist with her knuckles a millimeter from that fine masculine face. He held on tight, no doubt due to an entirely understandable sense of self-preservation.

The moment he loosened his grip, she threw her arms around him. "Thank God you're here."

Mark stood there in the sunlit woods, his arms full of Kat, her body slender under the roomy sweat suit, her scent faintly chocolate. If he'd known his reception would have been this enthusiastic, he would have come after her sooner.

Nuzzling her hair, he let his lips brush lightly against her ear. "Are you okay?"

She shivered and Mark was pretty damn sure it wasn't just from fear. "I'm fine," she gasped out. "Just a little scary to be lost for so long."

For so long? "I'm sure it was. Ready to go?"

She leaned back a little, but she didn't pull away. "You know the way to the cabin?"

Lord, he wanted to lie. Just wander the woods with Kat, find a deserted glade, do a little au natural frolicking amongst the trees . . .

But payback would be a bitch when she found out the truth. "I guess you got a little turned around."

He took her hand and tugged her the direction he'd come. He held back a tree branch as she ducked under it. "Did it take you long to find me? It feels like forever . . ."

Her words trailed off as he led her a few steps right, then left, then back onto the verdant green lawn surrounding the cabin. "This can't be."

He battled the urge to laugh. "All those

trees do tend to look alike."

"But I've been gone for hours." She clutched his arm, turning his wrist so she could see his watch. "Forty-five minutes. I've been gone forty-five minutes?"

"You were frightened." A chortle worked its way up his throat and it took an iron will to squelch it. "I'm sure it seemed longer."

She dropped his arm and confronted him. "Are you laughing at me?"

He coughed to cover a burgeoning guffaw. "Why would I laugh at you?"

She planted her hands on her hips and looked ready to belly-butt him. "Because you think I'm an idiot. You think I'm so damn lame I can't set one foot in the woods without losing my way."

His laugh-o-meter gauge was close to topping out at crisis levels. If he didn't divert the humor impulse, he'd be rolling in the grass and Kat would be so pissed at him, she'd hide in her room and refuse to show her face the entire weekend. Catastrophe loomed and he could only think of one way to avert it.

He kissed her.

Kat had about half a second to duck before Mark made contact, then maybe another second or two before things got serious. She sailed past both deadlines without so much as putting up a token resistance. She'd learned four years ago just how lethal Mark's kisses were. She knew the risks, the cost/benefit analysis, the price-to-earnings ratio. If pecks on the cheek from her elderly Aunt Bessie were junk bonds, Mark's kisses were blue-chip.

Chocolate chip. Thick, sweet fudge. Dark bittersweet with a hint of mocha. The smoothest, most delectable Bordeaux cream center.

She held him in a death grip, her heart hammering in her ears. His mouth moved over hers restlessly, his heat melting into her, the moist taste of him jacking up her senses until she thought she'd explode. He hadn't tried so much as an exploratory tongue battle, teasing her instead with just his lips. Here she was ready to wrap her legs around his hips and he was being shy.

She tried to make the first move, extending the tip of her tongue, running it along his lower lip. He just sucked at her, one hand against the back of her head, the other making a slow exploration of the hem of her sweatshirt. When she attempted to plunge deeper inside his mouth, he edged away, tracing an agonizingly slow trail along her cheek, her jaw, to her ear. He was being damn annoying, withholding a full-on tongue war, and she would have objected if her legs hadn't turned to vapor the instant she felt his wet kisses in her ear. Maybe she'd complain in a moment, once the oxygen that had vacated the general vicinity returned.

He'd worked his hand under her shirt and started up the groove of her spine. He had to know she hadn't bothered with a bra this morning; she was pretty much mashed against his chest. When his fingers grazed the middle of her back then hesitated, she could almost see the images in his mind — his hand over her breast, his palm stroking the tips until they were tight and sensitive, his other hand between her legs . . .

He shifted his focus to her mouth again and his tongue plunged inside. She couldn't moan, couldn't so much as gasp for air. Her skin burned, her nerve endings did the screaming for her. She was about to come just from a kiss.

He felt it in her, had always been so wickedly attuned to her physical response he could arouse her with the touch of a fingertip. Now he reached down and grabbed one leg, hooked it up over his hip, then widened his stance and wrapped her other leg around him. His hard length molded against her, pressed into her. She didn't have a chance.

He swallowed her first cry with his mouth. He drank up every shudder, each ecstatic convulsion as she rocked against him. She exploded like Mt. Rainier, molten rock flying into the heavens.

Bit by bit, her brain returned from its forced vacation and became aware of the awkwardness of her position. Her heel was jammed into his butt, his T-shirt was balled up in her hands and his face was pushed into her neck. Her body was still alert as a puppy and eager for part deux, but the cold chill of hindsight had its own agenda.

"Lordy," she muttered to the crystal blue sky. "Oh, Lordy."

Shell-shocked and idiot-brained, she let go of his T-shirt and pushed against him. He let her go readily enough, gently lowering her to the ground. He kept his gaze fixed on the grass at his feet as she straightened her sweatpants and jerked her shirt back around her hips.

"Well," he said, the single word a low, enticing rumble.

Damned if she didn't want to jump him

again. Just the thought of what they could accomplish horizontally in a bed had her heart racing. "Well . . ."

He lifted his gaze. "Should I apologize?"

"Ah . . . well . . ." A prickling heat rose in her cheeks, no doubt an allergic reaction. To Mark. She managed a marionette-style shake of the head. "N-no. Not at all."

His blue eyes were so intense, she thought she'd shatter just from the visual contact. "Should we go inside?"

Yes! Yes, yes, yes, yes — She shook her head so hard, she thought it might fly off her neck. "No. No. At least not to . . ."

"I thought not." He jammed his hands in the pockets of his sweats, the move drawing her gaze there. He obviously hadn't benefitted from their lawn interlude the way she had. "I'm going to take a walk."

He headed off into the woods, broad shoulders stiff as . . . well, stiff. A twinge of guilt tickled Kat, but it wasn't quite enough for her to shout at him, "Hey, let's do the deed!"

She stood there long after he'd disappeared among the trees, mortified, abashed, but oh, so mellow in the aftermath. Lord, that man could kiss.

★ ★ ★

It just wasn't natural, Mark decided, for a man to be driven so crazy-horny by a woman in a baggy gray sweatshirt. Maybe there was something just a little bit twisted about him that made thick shapeless fleece a turn-on.

He pushed on down the skinny ribbon of a trail, dodging red cedar branches and Douglas fir deadfall, wild blackberry brambles scrawling angry red scratches on his arms. A foxtail was poking his bare ankle and his already laboring lungs wheezed from the quick pace.

How the hell had one little kiss gone so far so quickly? Kat had outdone herself with her lightning response. She'd never been a woman who needed much foreplay unless they were on their third go-round. But her stellar performance this time had been mind-boggling.

He'd nearly bitten his tongue in two to keep himself from following in her footsteps. He hadn't come that close to coming in his pants since he was a randy fifteen-year-old. Even now, when his leg muscles were pleading for oxygen and he was sweating buckets, it was a struggle to divert his attention from Mr. BVD's full alert.

Out of deference for his heart, which was

threatening to go out on strike, he staggered to a stop in a thicket of willows. Hunched over, hands on his knees, he huffed and puffed and prayed he wouldn't keel over and become compost on the forest floor. He supposed there was an outside chance Kat would come looking for him, but he didn't place too much confidence in her ability to find him.

Besides, he couldn't die here and never have the opportunity to kiss Kat again. Of course, even if he made his way safely out of the forest, odds were he'd expire as an old man before she allowed his mouth anywhere near hers again. But dead men kiss no lips, so it behooved him to maintain the minuscule probability that the opportunity might arise by staying alive.

Regaining his second wind, Mark turned back the way he'd come. As he trudged along, his mind drifted back to dangerous territory — Kat and what she might be doing. What if she'd had a change of heart after he'd left? What if, even now, she'd stripped down to her birthday suit and waited for him in the downstairs bedroom? He could picture that all too clearly — Kat wriggling under the sheets, a come-hither smile on her face, one finger crooked and beckoning . . .

Without realizing it, his pace had quickened again, his heart rate galloped and his chest heaved like a bellows. Who needed Big Macs with Kat around to put such a strain on his cardiovascular system? The woman and her soft, slender body, silky black hair, crooked smile, was a cholesterol-free menace to good health.

And God, he couldn't wait to see her again.

~ 8 ~

Kat wandered back inside, still in a daze, without two thoughts to rub together. The cabin fairies hadn't cleared the bowl of Sugar Crunch from the kitchen table and the sucrose-laden flakes drooped limply in a sea of milk. In deference to her dentist and all his hard work keeping Kat's teeth cavity-free, she poured the soggy mess down the sink. Then, when she realized the sink had no garbage disposal, she slopped handfuls of the gunk back into the bowl so she could dump it in the trash.

How the hell had it happened? One moment she was feeling like a complete fool and working up a good, old-fashioned pique in self-defense, the next she was in lip-lock with her ex-husband. Only microseconds later, she was coming apart in his arms, from just a kiss and a well-timed hip thrust.

Egad, was she really that hard up? She hadn't even noticed the lack of sex the last two years, with all the grief she'd gone through with sinking sales figures and Chocolate Magic failures. She enjoyed the bedroom bop as much as the next girl, but just the thought of reentering the dating scene gave her heartburn. It was so much simpler just to stay home with a good book and a well-charged bedroom appliance.

It wasn't supposed to work this way. She should have been outraged, should have shoved him on his tokhes and slugged him. Kissing him back should not have been part of the program, let alone an orgasm. Geez, she might as well have a big red "come" button where Mark was concerned.

Rinsing sticky cereal from her hands, she considered her next move. There were two basic choices — stay put and wait for her father to return her Camry or hike into Ashford and try to rustle up some kind of car service. Since the roads were well-marked between here and town, she felt pretty confident she would find the way. But slogging ten miles just to avoid facing Mark again seemed pretty extreme. Not to mention the wimp's way out.

Okay, she'd stay. So how would she handle it when Mark returned? She started for the stairs, ticking off the possibilities.

Option one — ignore him. If she could pretend cabin fairies existed, she could imagine her hunky six-foot-one ex didn't. If he spoke to her, she'd pretend it was the cabin shifting on its foundation. If he touched her again, that was just a breeze against her skin. If he kissed her again, or rubbed himself against her, if he put a hand on her breast —

As she stepped inside the bedroom, she scratched option one off her list as completely infeasible. No one had that much imagination.

Option two — acknowledge what happened, but declare it was a Big Mistake. Yes, she came. Yes, it was on her top ten list of incredible experiences and Ms. V nestled between her legs still tingled with the aftershocks, but truly, they never shoulda. Surely Mark would agree . . .

Or would he? Kat flopped down on the bed and scrunched the pillow under her head. What if Mark got all boo-boo–faced about it? What if he regarded a mistaken orgasm as a blow to his fragile male ego? Then he'd be moping around the cabin making her feel guilty because she hurt his feelings and she hated feeling guilty.

Thumbs down on option two. She'd had quite enough of Mark's sad, puppy dog eyes. Women, the more emotional gender — what a crock.

Option three — acknowledge what happened, admit it was glorious, but, she would declare with a touch of ennui, she'd been there, done that. There was no need to revisit old territory, return to the old stomping grounds, begin again the beguine. Alas, as lovely an interlude as it had been, she'd simply had enough.

He'd be rolling on the floor with that one. Especially if he found that button again and pushed.

Ixnay on option three. She was a lousy liar anyway.

Option four — acknowledge what happened, admit it was glorious, but tell him the unvarnished, absolutely honest truth — her response had scared her spitless. It had tipped her world off its axis and confused the hell out of her. She didn't love Mark, at times she didn't even like him — how did he so easily get under her skin?

Even more than feeling guilty, she hated feeling vulnerable. If you were vulnerable, you were on your way to getting hurt. And when you got hurt, your life just flew out of control, opening the door to even more pain and heartache. She'd learned that lesson well from her parents' divorce and the raw agony her vulnerable six-year-old self had endured afterward.

Option four completely sucked. No way would she bare her soul that way to Mark, surrender that much power. He had enough power over her already, much as she might want to deny it.

Just one little kiss and he'd brought her to her knees. Figuratively, anyway, since her knees had been locked around his hips when the explosion hit. It was so damned unfair.

Flipping on her belly, she buried her face in the other pillow, just wanting to hide. But the pillow still smelled of him, his scent giving Ms. V another jolt of excitement. She'd have to strip the bed and wash the sheets to banish him completely. That would be too damn much work and besides, there was a certain comfort hugging a pillow that smelled of Mark.

Lord, she was such a loser.

Fritz serpentined through the tables of the Mountain Diner, making his way toward where Norma waited for him in a booth. He'd just gotten a royal chewing out by Kat's father, who'd been less than pleased with his machinations that had isolated Kat and Mark in the Roth cabin. He ought to feel crappy that he'd screwed up again, but then Norma's face lit up when she spotted him, and he just couldn't care very much that Phil Roth was pissed at him.

Fritz set his cell phone on the table and scooted in next to Norma. "He read me the riot act. He doesn't like them isolated up there. If there was an emergency, they'd have no way to get to a doctor."

Norma chewed her lower lip and Fritz reflected again on what a babe she was for an older woman. He liked the way her honey-colored sweater matched her eyes and the sun pouring through the window turned her blonde hair golden.

A jolt went up his arm when she touched him lightly on the back of the hand. "What do you think?" she asked. "Should we take the cars back?"

How would she react if he laced his fingers in hers? Just turned his hand over and caught hers, maybe even lifted it to his mouth to kiss it like in the old movies . . .

He pulled his hand into his lap, a little worried at how goofy he was getting. Maybe all this clean mountain air was infecting his city boy brain.

Norma locked her hands together on the table and color rose in her cheeks. Had he embarrassed her? Had she somehow figured out the crazy thoughts running through his head? God, he was such a loser, even his thoughts messed things up.

He nudged her on the shoulder. "Is that what you want to do?"

"What if something did happen?"

She looked so worried, Fritz couldn't resist patting her hand to comfort her. "If Kat were hurt, Mark would carry her the ten miles to Ashford."

Norma nodded. "And if Mark needed help, Kat would burn the cabin down to send up a smoke signal."

He stopped patting, but left his hand where it was. "I think we can give it another few hours. We'll sneak the cars back up there just after dark."

She sighed, turning to stare out the window. "I wonder if it's done any good, all these plans."

His gaze drifted down to her small hand under his. Her fingernails were so neat, glossy pale pink ovals neatly trimmed. His own were chewed down to the quick.

She turned toward him again, her sweet hazel eyes fixing on his. "You can't make two people love each other if they don't want to."

The sadness in her face hit his stomach

harder than any of the bullies had all those times in school. He wasn't sure how, but it had to be his fault. It usually was.

"We'll just do the best we can," he told her. When she still seemed troubled, he tossed caution to the four winds and lifted her hand to his mouth.

She looked so startled by the quick kiss, he thought for a moment she might slap him. Instead her surprise gave way to another smile and pink rose in her cheeks.

Fritz thought he'd never seen anything so pretty.

It was nearly noon by the time Mark made it back to the cabin. The chocolate chip muffin had tumbled from the porch rail and a hopeful squirrel was struggling to carry it off to the nearest tree. As runty as the fluffy-tailed rodent was, it had only dragged its booty as far as the tulip bed fronting the porch. It sat there, no doubt mulling over the engineering effort required to heft the loot up the nearest fir tree, when it spotted Mark. It took off, chittering and complaining.

Mark tossed the muffin in the direction of the squirrel's retreat, found the discarded paper towel, then headed up the porch steps. Somewhere between the tree root that tripped him and launched him into a patch of wild blackberry, and the fallen log that gave way when he stepped up on it, dumping him on his butt, he'd arrived at some hard truths.

His back couldn't stand another night on the sofa. He'd never bring himself to sleep in the downstairs bed without Kat. And hell would freeze over before Kat agreed to join him there.

So he was going to head into town. She could join him, she could wait for him to come back with transportation, she could finish out the weekend in expectation of the return of their cars. Whatever she chose to do, his choice was clear — get out of the cabin or end up in a rubber room.

He stepped inside, ready to deliver his manly decision, to announce his course of action. The downstairs was empty. He listened for a sign that Kat was stirring on the second floor. Silence.

Taking the stairs two at a time, Mark hurried upstairs. Kat's bedroom door was open. The room was tidy, the bed had been neatly made and Kat's suitcase sat at the foot. A piece of paper leaned against the pillow. It was a sheet from the CLR packet and she'd written something on the back.

Mark, Decided to go into town after all.
— Kat.

Outrage welled in him that she'd trumped his course of action. Worry followed on the heels of that emotion. Kat might be one of the most capable women he knew, almost scary in her determination and competence, but they were pretty much out in the middle of nowhere here. Anything could happen to a woman alone.

He'd have to go after her. She'd been conscientious enough to scribble the time at the top of the note. She had less than a half-hour head start on him. He could catch up with her, no sweat.

As he headed for the stairs, curiosity got the best of him, and he flipped over the pale lavender sheet. She'd written the note on the back of "List ten qualities* that first attracted you to your partner." She'd doodled on the paper, drawn curlicues along the margins, and he wondered if she'd thought about filling it out before writing the note on the back. Not likely.

Realizing his own list would be pretty incriminating if she stumbled across it, Mark retrieved it from under the sofa and crumpled it in a tight ball. He deep-sixed it in the kitchen trash with Kat's note, then grabbed his wallet on his way out the front door.

Two miles down the private gravel road and Kat was rethinking her rash decision to walk to town. Exhausted by her race-walk pace, her heels raw and blistering, her waist pack digging into her back, she had to face facts — thirty minutes on a tread-mill three times a week was no preparation for this kind of real world punishment. She was no foo-foo female, but right now, bon-bons and a dunk in the hot tub sounded mighty appealing.

It had just been too, too pitiful, lying there on the bed, hugging Mark's pillow. The scenarios running through her mind when he returned grew uglier by the moment, devolving into X-rated fantasies of her jumping him the instant he walked in the door. Running away seemed the best course to preserve her pride and self-respect.

Of course, right now, with her muscles screaming, her lungs puffing like bellows and her aerobic shoes whining they were never intended to walk on actual dirt, she was beginning to think self-respect was highly overrated. The thud of running foot-steps behind her clinched her suspicions.

Kat's heart, no doubt certain it would be safer outside her chest, pounded in panic. She was too damn tired to escape. If the owner of those footsteps had evil deeds on his or her mind, she was a goner. She creaked to a stop and turned, figuring she ought to at least confront the instrument of her demise, then sagged against a nearby cedar when she saw it was Mark.

He trotted up to her, barely out of breath. "Hey."

She nodded, too busy gasping to speak. When oxygen flow resumed in her brain she managed a few words. "Thought I'd go into town."

"Sure." His cocky grin gave her laboring heart an extra squeeze. "I'll come with you."

She should have been too worn-out to react to him. She should have been too mortified by what had happened on the cabin's front lawn to face him. But despite her better judgment, she was so happy to see him, she nearly threw her arms around him in gratitude. For the second time that day.

She wouldn't, of course. She'd play it cool even when she felt so hot for him, images of naughtiness sparking in her mind. Her back against the cedar, her legs wrapped around his hips. Him inside her, his face burning with ecstasy.

Lord, he'd read her mind. His smile faded and his blue gaze fixed on her, so intent she had to suppress the urge to squirm. He stepped closer, one hand reaching toward her. The two hours between the lawn interlude and now might never have passed.

Just before he would have touched her, she ducked out of reach. Fumbling in the pocket of her sweats for the water bottle she'd slipped there, she gulped a slug of water. Should she dump the remainder on her head? Better to keep some in reserve in the event she boiled over again.

"We ought to get going." She started down the road. Minced, really, as her left shoe sent a stabbing pain into her arch.

He fell in beside her. "Your feet okay in those shoes?"

Her heels were on fire and she'd started to limp. "They're fine."

He stared down at her, scowling. After a few more aching steps, he grabbed her arm. "Don't be an idiot."

She should have taken offense, but when he urged her toward a chunk of granite beside the road and sat her down, she couldn't summon the will to complain.

He pulled his wallet from his pocket and

flipped it open. "There's a couple bandages in here somewhere."

She gingerly untied her Avias and scooted them off her feet, wincing as they scraped over her blisters. Mark crouched on one knee, then sorted through a stack of business cards and plastic. As he dug out the bandages, he dislodged a folded bar napkin which fluttered to the ground. Kat got her hand on it first.

She read the flowery script. "Bambi. Four-six-one-eight-three —"

He snatched it from her and stuffed it in his pocket. "That's private."

"How could you even consider dating a woman named Bambi?"

"I was going to throw it away."

"She put a lipstick kiss below her phone number. How sick is that?"

"She didn't kiss it. She wiped her mouth before she wrote the number."

"Yuck." Kat wrinkled her nose. "That's even worse. Was she drunk?"

He lifted her left foot and propped it on his knee. "I didn't keep tabs on her alcohol intake."

"Where'd you meet her?" Kat sucked in a breath as he peeled her white ankle sock from her blister. "Was it O'Malley's?"

"No." He nudged up her sweatpants, his

181

fingers warm against her calf. "Drop it, Kat."

"Hennesy's?" She squeaked the last syllable when his palm brushed too close to her throbbing heel. "I can't see Thomas letting someone named Bambi into his bar."

He repositioned her leg so her sole rested against his thigh. Angle her foot a bit to the left, wriggle her toes and she'd be massaging a very interesting part of Mark's anatomy.

"This is a mess, Kat. You wouldn't have any antibiotic ointment in that bag, would you?"

"I have a tube of lip gloss." Just as a trial, she squirmed her toes against the soft knit of his sweats. Mark nudged her foot closer to his knee. Thwarted, she continued her inquisition. "Don't tell me it was Frank's."

Pay dirt. She could see it in the way his mouth tightened and the little lines grooved in his brow. She knew those little lines.

He stared so intently at her foot, you'd think he studied medicine instead of microeconomics at Cornell. "I can't just put a bandage on this. There might be debris in the wound."

"You said you hated Frank's. You said it was cheesy."

"I went in for a glass of water." His mouth tightened even more. "You can't walk to town like this."

"Did you call her? Is that why you still have her number?"

"We need a better first-aid kit." Grabbing her sock from the dirt, he shook leaf litter from it, then eased it back on her foot.

"You did call her, didn't you?"

He straightened and stuffed the bandages in his pocket. "Some antiseptic and antibiotic cream."

"Did you go out with her?" She hopped toward him on her right foot. "For God's sake, her name is Bambi!"

He spun on his heel so fast she nearly tipped backward in reaction. His face wild, he grabbed her shoulders, fingers digging into her. She thought he might swallow her whole or, at the very least, kiss her again. She tipped her face up toward him.

She thought he was going to kiss her. As if. Of course, that exact impulse was zinging around inside his crazed mind, urging him to accept the invitation.

Instead he bent and grabbed her around the middle, folding her in two before she could resist. Hoisting her over his shoulder in a fireman's carry, he pinned her legs with one arm and felt her dangling hands slap his butt.

She tried to twist loose, but he just held her tighter. "Lie still," he growled. Locating her abandoned sneaker, he hooked a toe in it and tipped it up.

"What are you doing?"

"Getting your shoe." Flipping the sneaker into the air, he caught it on its upward arc.

"With me. What are you doing —"

He reached behind him with the shoe. "Carry this."

As she took the shoe, it crossed his mind that now she could use it as a weapon. "You can't carry me all the way to town."

He turned and headed back toward the cabin. His teeth were clenched so hard, his jaw was cramping. "Yes, I called her."

She tensed in his arms. "This is really none of my business."

So now she didn't want to hear it. Tough. "Yes, we dated." He shifted her weight a little so her hip snugged against his neck. "I took her to Papa Gianni's." Take that, Kat.

He felt the reaction in her, the way her body sagged and her lithe legs drooped down his chest. "That's good, then. That you're getting out and seeing people."

Now he felt like a louse. "It was just that one time," he admitted. "She cried all during dinner about her cheating husband and their nasty custody fight. I referred her to a divorce lawyer and the local mental health clinic."

He waited for her to make hay with that. Instead she said, "Good for you," and Mark was tempted to set her down to make sure he still had Kat in his arms.

About a half-mile from the cabin, she torqued her body in an attempt to face him. "Are you going to leave me and go into town?"

"Lie still. Your water bottle is digging into my collarbone."

She flopped down again. "Are you going to walk to Ashford without me?"

That was his plan. He'd take care of her blisters, set her up on the sofa with something to eat and his deck of cards to pass the time, then head to town. The quicker he got them transportation home, the quicker she'd be out of his hair.

Damned if his traitor mouth didn't have other plans. "Do you want me to stay?"

She spoke so quietly he could barely hear her. "Yes."

"Then I will."

"You could go tomorrow, if the cars aren't back by then."

"Sure."

Around the last bend of the gravel road, the cabin came into sight. He crossed the lawn and climbed the porch steps. At the top, he bent and eased her down to the wide wooden deck.

He kept hold of her hand. "Can you make it inside?"

"If you help me get the other shoe off first."

She leaned against the cabin door and he knelt to unlace her right shoe. Her fingers dug into his shoulder when he nudged the shoe from her foot. When he peeled away her socks, she sighed with relief.

"Thanks."

Rising, he tucked her arm around his waist, supporting her as they went inside. After all, she could stumble on the rag rug in the entryway or smack her sore heel on one of the side tables. Better to hang on to him, prevent a mishap.

She didn't pull away, even when they got to the sofa, even when he turned her toward him. Then when he put his arms around her, tugged her even closer, she yielded, her face upturned, her chocolate brown eyes wide with anticipation.

Kissing her again was out of the question. Of course it was. If she needed CPR, maybe he could justify putting his mouth on hers. But she was breathing just fine and he could see her pulse leaping in her throat. She obviously didn't need resuscitation, not with her skin so warm and the way her chest rose and fell, her breasts pressing against him.

He had to kiss her.

But he shouldn't. He wouldn't. He'd already skied down that slippery slope and it left him with a hard-on and near cardiac-inducing sexual frustration. There was no reason to think Kat would go any further now than she had earlier. No matter how delicious her lips looked, their pale pink the color of strawberry cream fondant . . .

Okay, maybe just one kiss.

He brushed his mouth against hers and she shuddered, her response ratcheting up the heat in his body. In some circles, that might qualify as one kiss, but it was really just the start of a kiss and he couldn't leave it unfinished, could he? So he angled his head more comfortably and slanted his mouth against hers with more pressure, sliding his tongue across her soft lips.

His hands had no business being anywhere except where they were, pressed against her back, the thick sweatshirt a barrier to her soft skin. But somehow they started roving, drifting lower to the hem at her waist, his fingers burrowing under it. As he continued his one, long kiss, his palms skimmed up along her sides, thumbs tracing her rib cage, stopping just below the tickle spot below her arms.

Most men would have gone straight for the breasts, but he had more self-control than that. It was a bit dicey when he remembered she wasn't wearing a bra, and when she moaned into his mouth he thought his one kiss might segue into two. But he kept his hands right where they were, just beside her breasts, itching and burning with temptation.

Until she grabbed his wrists and shoved them over. Who was he to say no to Kat? He covered her breasts with his hands, enjoying the slight weight of them, the hard tips that rubbed against his palms. They were so perfect, so hot and silky.

"God, you feel so good." He kept his lips against hers as he spoke, technically a continuation of kiss number one.

She squirmed against his touch. "Too small," she murmured into his mouth.

"Perfect," he assured her. "Just right."

Her head fell back and it took some

skillful maneuvering to keep his mouth in contact with her. He explored her cheek, her jawline, her ear.

"Your ears are perfect, too," he whispered, drawing his tongue along the whorls.

Her gasp jolted through him. "Stick out."

"Do not." He moved one hand down to her hips, pulled her against his too-tight flesh. "Your breasts —" He thrust against her. "— are perfect. Your ears —" Another thrust. "— are cute. Your butt —" He couldn't help himself; he ground against her. "— is just the right size. Not too big."

Suddenly, she stiffened against him and for one wishful-thinking moment, he thought maybe she was about to come again in response to his masterful love-making. But he knew better. That wasn't Kat bracing for climax. That was Kat a heartbeat away from pulling out of his arms.

What the hell had he done this time?

As wrong as it felt, he let go immediately, stepping back. An appealing rose still colored her cheeks, but the flame of anger in her eyes threw a cold shower on any hopes they might resume his interrupted one kiss.

"You read it," she hissed.

Like his life flashing before his eyes, a bibliography of everything he'd ever read scrolled in his mind. Then he said the worst thing possible. "Read what?"

Her ire seemed to inflate her, adding a good two inches to her height. "My list!"

Although relieved to have his lifelong inventory of reading material narrowed down to lists, he was still completely baffled now. And said the second worst thing possible. "What list?"

Mistake number one — implying that, despite his innocence, he might have read, at some point in time, something objectionable to Kat. Mistake number two — implying that the offending reading material might not actually exist.

And when her anger dissolved into tears, her wet eyes and damp cheeks stabbing at his heart, he understood the magnitude of his error. Even though he still had no clue of how, exactly, he'd screwed up.

Backing away from him, Kat rounded the sofa, picking up speed as she headed for the stairs. When the door slammed upstairs, he figured it might as well be a guillotine plummeting toward his sorry neck. At least he'd be put out of his misery.

~ 9 ~

Kat stared down at the ball of crumpled pink paper in her hand and felt like the biggest fool in the world. She'd found it right where she'd stuffed it a couple hours ago — in the depths of her suitcase, shoved into the toe of her panty hose. While there was still an infinitesimal chance Mark had located the wad of paper in her Gucci carry-on, fished it out of her panty hose, uncrumpled it, read it, then reversed the process to hide it again, it surpassed even her finely honed sense of paranoia that he'd actually done it.

Now what? Climbing out of the bedroom window and across the porch roof to escape wasn't practical and was very likely hazardous. Especially since she'd have to do it barefoot. No way was she squeezing her feet back into her Avias.

She could stay walled up in her room the rest of the day. She had a bathroom, she had water. She'd downed an apple and her last two chocolate coins before she left the cabin. She could tough it out until morning.

Her stomach rumbled to let her know it was not on board with her plan. It reminded her all the food was downstairs with Mark and, except for the antacid tablets swimming in the bottom of her purse, she didn't have so much as a calorie to her name.

With a hiss of frustration, Kat buried the ball of paper back in her suitcase and padded into the bathroom. Once she'd taken care of nature's call and tidied up her hair and face, she headed resolutely for the door.

Mark sat slumped on the sofa, head tipped against the back. Despite her quiet footsteps, he sensed her, turning his head as she reached the bottom of the stairs. She hesitated there as his blue gaze fixed on her.

"I'm sorry," he said. "For whatever I did."

She started toward him. "You didn't do anything."

"Then consider it a universal apology." He waved a hand at her. "For future transgressions."

With some trepidation, she settled on the far end of the sofa. He kept his arm along the back, his fingertips inches away from her. He stared out into the middle distance. "Did we ever get along?"

Bringing up her knees, she hugged them to her chest. "I don't know."

"When we were kids . . ." He shook his head. "Not even then."

"You teased me."

"And you'd scream at me."

"Or cry." She felt a little like crying now. "Or punch you."

The pain only dug deeper in her heart at his faint smile. "You had a hell of a right cross."

"You never hit me back."

He looked at her as if she was crazy. "You were a girl. You were smaller than me. I would never —"

She covered his hand with hers. "No, you'd never."

The always-present heat between them blossomed in her palm where it lay against the back of his hand. He surely felt it — how could he not? — and for a moment she thought he'd pull her toward him.

But he tugged his hand out from under hers. "Let me do something about those blisters." Pushing up from the sofa, he headed for the downstairs bathroom. He came back with a first-aid kit.

He ministered to her gently and efficiently. When the antiseptic towelette burned against her broken blisters, she bit back her reaction, shutting her mind against the sting. When his fingers cradling her calf generated hot sensual images, she blocked them ruthlessly.

He set down her bandaged foot, then busied himself with restoring order to the first-aid kit. She touched him on the shoulder. "Thanks."

"Sure." He snapped the lid shut on the white case. "Are you hungry?"

"A little," she lied. She'd been ravenous a few minutes ago. Now a tight knot rested in her stomach. "Mark —"

He nearly jumped to his feet. "I'll fix us something."

More comfortable with her heels bandaged, she followed him into the kitchen. "I can help."

"Go sit down." He wrenched open the refrigerator. "I'll do it."

"Let me give you a hand." She stepped closer to him.

"I don't want your help!" He slammed the refrigerator door. "For chrissakes, Kat, would you just sit down!"

Backing away, she yanked a chair out from the dinette table. "Fine. I'm sitting."

His back to her, he looked ready to yank the handle from the refrigerator. His voice was taut with tension. "If you're near me, I want you. Hell, if you're in the next room, you make me so damn hot —"

He tugged the refrigerator door open. "We can't be friends, Kat. And I damn well won't let us be lovers. I just can't stand to —"

He started grabbing items from the refrigerator shelves and drawers — lunch meat, lettuce and tomatoes, jars of condiments. "What do you want?"

I want us to stop fighting. She locked the words in her throat. "Whatever you're having is fine."

"Sandwich?" He set everything on the counter and looked back at her long enough to catch her nod. "Ham or turkey?"

"How about both?" Their mundane conversation stabbed at her heart. How did they get so far apart?

Maybe they'd never been close. Maybe she'd just imagined they once had been.

She watched him work, his economy of movement as he assembled their sandwiches and arranged them on plates with some chips he'd found in the cupboard. He set hers in front of her. It was stacked high with meat and lettuce, cut into four neat triangles. That he'd remembered she liked it that way stabbed a little further into her heart.

When he turned to get his own plate, she expected him to sit down opposite her, but he started toward the door. "I'm going to eat on the porch."

She couldn't stand to have him leave her. "Mark —"

Halfway out the door, he stopped. "Yeah?"

Come sit with me. Come talk to me. She held back the selfish words. "Thanks for making lunch."

A nod, then he shut the door behind him. Appetite lost, her stomach rebelling, Kat picked up one neat triangle and forced herself to take a bite. It might as well have been sawdust in her mouth.

She rose and picked up her plate, intending to hide her lunch in the trash before heading upstairs. But she caught a glimpse of Mark through the front window, swaying on the porch swing. Loneliness shot through her, and her feet moved of their own accord toward the front door.

He didn't look up when she stepped outside, just kept up the porch swing's rhythm, forward-back, forward-back. A little like their relationship, except they always took twice as many steps back as forward.

Plate biting into her hand, she blurted out, "It was never you."

That got his attention. He turned toward her.

She forced herself to move closer, stopping just beyond the swing's arc. "The problem's always been me, not you."

"Kat —"

"No, let me talk." Her trembling hand threatened to shake the sandwich from her plate. "There's something wrong with me, something mixed up. I don't know how to get along with people." She gasped in a breath. "With you."

The distance in his blue gaze melted away. "Oh, Kat . . ."

His gentle tone was her undoing. Tears tightened her throat, brimmed in her eyes. She blinked them away. "Truce, okay? Until Kandy for Kids is over."

"Sure, Kat," he said quietly.

"When I want to fight you, I won't. I'll just keep my damn mouth shut."

His gaze searched her face and she couldn't bear the softness in his eyes. She wanted to yell, tell him to stop being so nice, because it just made her heart hurt more.

She didn't yell. She swiped her eyes with her sleeve and took a deep breath. "Can I sit with you?"

"Yeah." He smiled, and the urge to cry washed over her again. "Please."

He moved the plate he'd set beside him to his lap and patted the cushion. Once she'd seated herself, he sent the swing rocking again, the rhythm soothing. As the creek burbled and the wind whispered secrets in the trees, they ate together in a rare companionable silence.

In her car just out of sight of the cabin, Norma waited as Fritz finished the night's skullduggery. It had been just past midnight when they secreted Kat's Camry in the carport and now the hour was yawning toward one a.m. Norma hadn't stayed up so late since she was a teenager.

She rolled down her car window and listened. The engine of Mark's BMW rumbled softly in the distance for a few moments before it cut out. Fritz would be climbing from the car, shutting the door as quietly as possible, then walking the quarter-mile to where she was parked. Anticipation bubbled up inside her as she watched for him in the faint moonlight.

She heard his footsteps before she saw

him. Switching on the Metro's dome light, she waved at his silhouette. She felt goofy as a schoolgirl when he reached the car and climbed inside. A breeze had tossed his sandy brown hair and a glow of mischief lit his blue eyes. He seemed a little too thin in his mint green cashmere sweater, but her heart sang just looking at him.

A shocking impulse burst inside her, to throw her arms around him and kiss him in welcome. She discovered she'd started to lean toward him, to reach toward him. Stopping herself just in time, she dropped her hands in her lap. "Any trouble?"

"Nope." An odd look flickered in his eyes and she suffered a bout of mortification wondering if he knew what she'd nearly done. "The cabin was dark. I think they were already asleep."

"Good." Not quite able to resist touching him, she gave him an awkward pat on the shoulder. "Mission accomplished, then."

"Yeah," he said, still with that peculiar expression on his face.

"Is something the matter?" She shouldn't have asked; she was terrified to hear the answer.

His bright blue eyes pierced her heart.

"Just not ready to go home, I guess."

She wasn't, either. There were plants to water and a lonely Yorkie to pick up at the pet hotel. But given the choice, she'd just as soon stay a week up here with Fritz.

The temptation to put her arms around him rose up inside her again. The wanting set off a yearning inside her, but she kept her hands to herself. Entirely inappropriate feelings for a matronly forty-eight-year-old toward a young sprout like Fritz.

But the weekend had been so much fun, first the adventure of stealing cars, then last night at the inn when they sat in the lobby and laughed over each detail of the caper. They'd both been bleary-eyed at breakfast, but when Norma had suggested they take a drive to scout out wildflowers on Mt. Rainier, Fritz was as excited as she was at the jaunt.

Now the last thing she wanted was to return to the inn and have it all end. She sighed, toying with the strap of the seat belt. "We ought to get back. Get some sleep."

"Yeah."

She waited for him to turn, to pull on his seat belt. Instead he kept his blue gaze fixed on her. He reached across the center console, his fingers tentative on the back of her hand. "Norma . . ."

He tipped toward her so slightly, she wondered if she'd imagined it. His quick glance down at her mouth sent a shiver through her. Good Lord, was he going to kiss her?

On the heels of that jolt of delight, disappointment stumbled in when he sat up straight again and grabbed a tissue from the box at his feet. "You've got a little left over from that chocolate cake."

Mortification blossoming inside her, she took the tissue and flipped down the visor mirror. There was a spot of chocolate at the corner of her mouth, so small she just about had to press her nose to the mirror to see it. Dabbing the tissue on her tongue, she tidied the spot.

Still embarrassed, she looked sidelong at Fritz, unwilling to face him. The intensity of his gaze stole her breath. He turned away the moment he realized her eyes were on him, then fumbled with the seat belt. He pulled it out so quickly it jammed, then it took him two more tries before he could tug it around his slight body.

He stretched his mouth into what looked like a mighty fake yawn. Speculation tickled Norma, but she wasn't ready to give the wild fragment of a notion any credence.

Flipping off the dome light, she pulled on her own seat belt and started the car. They bumped along the gravel road back to Highway 706, the darkness putting a lid on harebrained ideas and crazy imagination.

Still, Norma couldn't quite erase that image — Fritz's gaze on her as if she was the most fascinating woman in the universe.

Kat peeled her eyes open as the brilliant morning sun pierced a gap in the bedroom's shut curtains. The twinge of pain in her heels brought back yesterday's events, her escape attempt, her meltdown and Mark's unbearable empathy. Weakness threatened to steal back inside her at the memory of his kindness, his gentleness, but she squelched the softness.

Kneeling on the bed, she drew the curtains and squinted out at the green lawn and burbling creek. She took another blow to the chest when she spotted Mark sitting beside the creek, a mug of coffee cradled in his hands. She wanted to rush downstairs and across the lawn to be with him, to let him wrap his arms around her, let his warmth soak into her.

She shook off the wrongheaded impulse. Scrambling from the bed, she took care of the morning necessities in the bathroom, then pulled on a comfy pair of stretch jeans and a soft angora turtleneck. Her feet were chilly, but she wasn't ready to pull on shoes. Instead she dug out the fluffy backless slippers she'd brought, then stowed everything else in her suitcase.

Downstairs, the coffeemaker had switched off, and the inch of French roast at the bottom had cooled enough it needed nuking. So Mark had been up a while, despite the late hour when they'd parted company last night.

The harmony between them might have been as fragile as soapsuds, but it held. After they finished their late lunch, Mark excavated the fishing poles from the storage shed and they spent the last of the day's light out by the creek. Mark snagged one tiny trout that he released back into the icy water; Kat's line spent more time tangled in trees than dipped in the creek.

Once the sun went down, they returned inside, threw together a snack, then spent the balance of the evening playing poker and cribbage with Mark's deck of cards. On the surface, they were friendly, cordial, courteous: two good friends spending an evening together. Just below that civilized skin, Kat felt ready to explode.

The microwave dinged and Kat took her mug outside, taking care to close the door quietly. His back toward the cabin, Mark didn't see her as she crossed to the far end of the porch to check the carport. There were her Camry and Mark's BMW, side by side. Nothing keeping her at the cabin now.

As she descended the porch steps, Mark turned toward her, his smile faint. "Cars are back."

"I saw." Hands wrapped around the mug, she held it close. "I'm all packed. I thought I'd head back."

Rising, he downed the rest of his coffee. "We could stop in Ashford for breakfast."

His well-worn henley hugged his body, the pushed-up sleeves giving her a nice view of the ropy muscles of his arms. She wondered if the faded cornflower knit felt as soft as it looked.

She gulped hot coffee, burning her tongue. "I thought I'd just grab something from here. Save time."

She wanted him to argue with her, tell her he wasn't ready for her to leave. Which was nutty since she'd been hankering to get away from here from the moment she first found Mark in her bed. Her psyche needed some serious reworking.

He started back toward the cabin and she fell in beside him. "How are your feet?"

"Better. Should be fine by tomorrow."

"Good." He opened the front door, stepping aside to let her go in first. "Give me a few minutes to get my things together. I'd feel better if I could follow you back to Seattle."

"Sure. I'll just take my bag out to my car."

"I'll get it for you."

She waited by the front door, feeling awkward and anxious. The studied politeness between them was ten times worse than the incendiary friction they usually shared. She was teetering on a tightrope made of eggshells — one step out of line and she'd be in free fall. No telling where she'd land when she hit bottom. Or what harsh and prickly emotions would be waiting for her there.

Mark backed his BMW from the carport, pulling in behind Kat's Camry where it waited on the gravel drive. The Camry jounced into a pothole, swerving a bit before Kat got the car straightened out again. A little more time and the proper tools, and he could have repaired some of the gashes in the gravel drive. It would have been an appropriate thank-you to the Roths for the use of their cabin.

Although he couldn't really say he felt particularly grateful for the last two days here. Kat had turned him upside down, inside out and shaken the heart straight out of him. He hadn't felt run so ragged since his honeymoon, which at least had the upside of four straight days of sex.

He supposed what had happened yesterday on the lawn with Kat qualified as half-sex. No satisfaction for him except for the electric charge of seeing her come in his arms. That was an image seared in his brain, filed away with all the other spectacular fireworks he and Kat had shared.

He followed Kat onto Highway 706 toward Ashford. He had to admit Phil Roth's shenanigans this weekend had been masterfully executed — what with getting them both here, stealing the cars, leaving them with the CLR packets. Of course, his ex-father-in-law couldn't control the most crucial element — getting Mark and Kat to play along. A shame, really, because it might have been useful to know what ten things made her fall in love with him in the first place.

If she'd ever been in love with him at all. A weight settled in his stomach, a heaviness barbed with bad memories. Had she ever said the words? Just then, as he kept his eyes focused on the red taillights of Kat's car, he couldn't remember. She'd been happy with him from time to time, but he couldn't seem to dredge up even one instance when she smiled and kissed him and whispered in his ear, "I love you."

He held on to his sour mood until they'd passed through Ashford, then decided if he didn't change his nasty attitude he'd never get through the rest of the Kandy for Kids campaign. He'd have to stick to what worked this morning — that neutral Kat-proof veneer that protected his tender male ego from her indifference. If he let her in at all, he'd only want her again, and when he was hot for Kat he was at his most vulnerable. Better to keep her skidding on his surface.

Storm clouds gathered as he rolled along behind Kat, an appropriate finish for the weekend. When the fat drops hit his windshield, blurring his view of the Camry ahead of him, he figured that was just as well. The sharper his image of her and the closer she was to him, the harder it was to protect himself.

And he was determined to protect himself at all costs.

★ ★ ★

The sofa's askew pillows, rumpled blankets and abandoned tube sock told the story clearly. Mark had slept here, not with Kat. Norma had already reported on the room upstairs — by all accounts only Kat had used that bed. Fritz had to admit his elaborate plan had failed.

He hadn't thought Mark and Kat would be completely ready to kiss and make up. He'd hoped for the kissing part, though, and had his fingers crossed it might go further than that. If he could have gotten them in bed together, that might have been enough of a catalyst to set them on the path Fritz had signed on to send them.

The weekend would have been a total waste if not for the time spent with Norma. The sweet glow of that bonus still warmed him.

She came downstairs with her arms full of sheets. "I remade the bed and put up fresh towels. The caretaker will pick up the dirty laundry when he comes to clear out the fridge."

Fritz folded the blanket Mark had used, then set the sofa pillows in order. He plucked the lone sock from under the end table. "Toss it?"

Norma dumped the sheets and towels by

the door. "Probably best. We can't exactly return it."

Carrying the sock to the kitchen trash, he stepped on the lid release. Just as he let the sock go, he spotted a crumpled ball of pastel green paper half-hidden by a coffee filter. Taking care to keep from dislodging the wet mass of coffee grounds, he saved the wad of paper from its trashy grave.

Norma came up beside him. "What did you find?"

Fritz unwrinkled the green sheet and spread it flat on the counter. " 'List qualities* that first attracted you to your partner,' " Fritz read aloud. "Is that Kat's handwriting?"

"Has to be Mark's," Norma told him. "Kat's isn't nearly so neat."

A quick glance down the list and Fritz realized that maybe the weekend hadn't been such a failure after all.

~ *10* ~

Early Wednesday evening Kat opened her condo door to a *High Noon* standoff between Rochester and Fritz. Rochester had Fritz pinned against the kitchen stove, his tufted ears back flat, body in a crouch, tail whipping like an agitated snake. Fritz gripped a rolled-up copy of the *Post-Intelligencer*, no doubt ready to fend off Rochester's attack.

As she entered the kitchen, Fritz kept his gaze fixed on her beefy cat. "I've been here nearly three weeks. Why does he still hate me?"

"He doesn't like competition." Dropping the lacquered black and silver bag from Sweet Elizabeth's, Kat grabbed the mass of threatening fur and set him by his food bowl. She filled it with an ample supply. "He's afraid you'll steal his crunchies."

"Yuck." Fritz set the newspaper on the kitchen counter. "Did he treat Mark this way?"

For a moment, she couldn't answer.

She'd spent most of her waking hours the last few days trying hard not to think about Mark. "He and Rochester had a gentlemen's agreement."

Fritz shoved his hands into his pants pockets. He was wearing the gray pin-striped slacks today with the white dress shirt. His entire wardrobe seemed to consist of two suits and three dress shirts. She'd given him one of Mark's old T-shirts that her ex had somehow left behind and a pair of men's jeans she didn't wear anymore.

She much preferred conjecture over Fritz's state of affairs to contemplation of her own and Mark's. "Have you gotten that replacement Visa card yet?"

Fritz wouldn't make eye contact. "Not yet."

"How long since you reported it stolen?"

"A while." He stared down at his toes. "I'll call them again."

"Has your dad cleared up that problem with your trust yet?"

He looked a little terrified by the reminder of his dad. "Not yet."

"I don't mind you staying here." Fritz's presence distracted her from her Mark obsession. "I just thought you'd be more comfortable in your own place."

He shrugged, then glanced up at the kitchen clock. "You're home early."

"The benefit concert's tonight. I wanted some extra time to get ready."

Fritz smiled. "Mark will be there."

"I suppose. I hadn't really thought about it," she lied.

"Uh-huh." Fritz obviously wasn't buying her B.S. "Any chance you could front me a few bucks for a tux? I keep forgetting to pick mine up at the dry cleaners."

Now who was lying? Kat considered calling him on it, but then her conscience would demand she come clean with her own tall tales.

She dug in her purse for her wallet, then handed Fritz her Visa. "Knock yourself out. Just leave me the receipt."

As he took the card she saw the color rising in his face. "Could I borrow your car, too? Mine's still in the shop."

Any more fibs between them and they'd both be sporting ten-foot noses. That might make it tough to maneuver in the condo.

She tossed him her car keys, grabbed the black and silver bag, then headed for her bedroom. She had a date with a hot bath and a blow dryer, and only two hours to gussy herself up for the benefit concert.

She longed to look like hot-to-trot dyna-mite, to be a drop-dead gorgeous knock-out. She'd have to be satisfied with not too skanky.

Upending the silver and black bag, she dumped the contents on her bed. It was slithery and slinky and a cobalt blue so vivid it made her eyes ache. It covered ev-erything decency demanded while baring a shocking amount of skin. If only she had the body to wear it.

With any luck, Mark wouldn't laugh at her. Surely he was enough of a gentleman he would bite his tongue, hold back the kind of commentary that had danced in her head when she tried the dress on at Sweet Elizabeth's. While the salesclerk raved over how absolutely stunning she was in the brilliant drape of cobalt lamé, Kat had been counting the number of fashion rules her body violated — bones poking everywhere, boobs nearly nonexis-tent, arms like skinny spaghetti.

She sighed. It was a beautiful dress. Such a shame to waste it on her.

As tiredness washed over her, she rubbed at her eyes, wishing the shopping trip had provided the distraction she'd hoped. Roth Confectionery's balance sheet seemed to be in free fall with no way to turn things around. Sales of their longtime favorites like the sizzling cinnamon suckers and dark chocolate liquor cups had plummeted in the last four quarters. Everything new they tried stumbled out of the gate.

Piled on to the rest of the bad news, she'd heard through the grapevine that Denham Candy was developing a top-secret new treat they'd be rolling out in time for Halloween. They predicted huge sales for the innovative new product.

If they could just pin down the Chocolate Magic formula. If they could just find the perfect sales program to boost their numbers. If pigs would only take wing . . .

Stuffing the tissue paper back in the black and silver bag, she arranged the blue lamé dress full-length on the bed, then noted with chagrin that even the bed looked better in it than she did. Her flats toed off her feet, she tugged off her gray, cowl-necked sweater and matching slacks, stripping panties, bra and knee-high hose on her way to the bathroom. A yank on the hot water faucet to start the bath, then she kept her back on her reflection in the mirror. No need to demoralize herself further with a clear-eyed view of her naked body.

She poured too much bubble bath into the tub, then eased herself into the steaming water. Almost too hot, she luxuriated in the silky feel of the rising bubbles, relaxed for what seemed the first time since she returned from the executive cabin. She'd probably end up lobster-red and her skin tone would clash hideously with the cobalt blue dress, but at least this part of her day was going right.

Damn her father for calling her this morning. Already ticked at him because he'd refused to admit his complicity in the cabin plot, she'd nearly told Norma she wouldn't take the call. But then guilt nibbled at her and she'd relented. She should have listened to her instincts.

Her father only had more heartbreak to offer. He hit her with the worst first — he and Patti had met with her mother and Tony to discuss some hard truths. They needed an infusion of capital, and quick. If they couldn't find an investor soon, they'd have to consider selling the company.

As she struggled to come to terms with that potential disaster, her father moved on to the personal arena. Just thought I'd let you know, honey, he told her. Mark's bringing a date tonight.

The right response had rattled around in her brain. Gee, thanks, Dad, but it's really nothing to me. Not sure why you thought it would matter, Dad, but it's good to hear he's dating again.

All lies, of course. And you'd think after all that practice during her teen years fibbing to her dad, it would have been a piece of cake to prevaricate as a grown woman. But somehow, those glib replies got stuck in her cerebellum.

Oh, she'd said. Just, Oh.

Then she'd hung up, told Norma she was taking an early lunch and spent the next hour and a half at Sweet Elizabeth's. She'd wriggled into one killer dress after another, wincing at the multitude of reflections in the three-way mirrors, doing her best to ignore the gadfly sales associate who must have been short on his sales quota that month. He was a fabulous liar, effusing ever more ebulliently with each gown, insisting she would stun every man at the concert. He was so convincing an actor, she nearly asked him to go along as her date, but he was as flagrantly gay as he was flattering and therefore a non-starter in the "making Mark jealous" department.

So she was on her own. She'd just keep her fingers crossed that Mark's companion wouldn't be too dazzling. There was at least an even chance she wouldn't be the most revolting woman there, not if that stringer from the *Post-Intelligencer* wore her circa-1970s, should-have-been-burned hippie regalia.

With a groan, Kat sank to her chin in the fragrant, foamy bubbles. Lord, it was going to be a long night.

Mark stepped into Benaroya Hall's vast Grand Lobby, Lydia from the sales department clinging to his arm like a blonde tick, his cummerbund like a vise around his waist. The tux he'd unearthed from his closet seemed to have shrunk since he last wore it. It gripped his shoulders like a straitjacket, the bow tie a garrote around his neck.

God, he wished he was anywhere but here. The glitzy and the overdressed packed the stunning, circular Grand Lobby, most of them more obsessed with showing off their high-priced finery than taking in the spectacular view of Seattle's skyline through the lobby's massive bank of windows. Although he wasn't the symphony's best customer, he was a big booster of Benaroya Hall. Denham held their annual sales recognition celebrations right here in the Grand Lobby.

Lydia scanned the room, no doubt

searching for admirers. "Let's go up on the promenade."

They headed toward the staircase, Lydia digging inch-long red fingernails deep into his arm. Seattle notables greeted him as he and Lydia ascended the stairs and meandered along the promenade. He smiled and nodded to each one until he felt like a bobble-head doll, Lydia nattering in his ear, her endless monologue pulverizing his brain cells.

This was the perfect topper to an absolutely rotten day. It started with a nine a.m. call from a staff member he'd terminated a week ago. The bozo ranted on and on about how unfair it was to be fired for a little pilfering — when he'd walked off with whole boxes of printer paper and cases of assorted chocolates. Then the Denham payroll software upgrade had gone belly-up, spewing out paychecks with garbled payees and astronomical payout amounts.

And now, this — a long tedious evening at the symphony with an annoying woman who scarcely paused for breath. He was a man of the world and as cultured as the next guy, but his idea of entertainment was Bruce Springsteen or the Dixie Chicks. Not Prokofiev's Symphony No. 5 in B Flat

Major — hell, even the title was sleep-inducing.

Late that afternoon, when he and the programmers were elbow-deep in software bugs, he'd toyed with the notion of asking his assistant, Rod, to go in his place tonight. Used to dress uniforms and high-octane military soirees, Rod could have certainly held his own in this crowd. But then Mark would have been deprived of the only high point of the evening — a chance to see Kat.

Over the past few days, they'd engaged in a few polite phone calls, had exchanged several E-mails back and forth, all the communication squarely focused on Kandy for Kids. He'd asked after her feet, given her sage advice on continuing to apply ointment and keeping them bandaged, to consult a doctor if they didn't improve.

He'd bitten back the questions he really wanted to ask — did she miss him, did she want him, was she burning up at night aching for him. He couldn't let her know how crazy he'd been the last few days, spending the weekend close to her, then separated from her, cold turkey.

As Mark searched for Kat in the teeming crowd below, Lydia nattered on, her blood-red nails clutching tighter, sharing every detail of her weekend trip on her fiancé's uber-yacht. Lydia had snagged herself a Microsoft gazillionaire and she made sure everyone within earshot knew it. Frankly, if Mark heard one more accolade about her paragon fiancé, he'd probably run screaming from Benaroya Hall.

In self-defense, he shut out Lydia's drone and kept his eye on the shifting crowd. Just as he despaired of spotting Kat's familiar tall, slender body, her sleek cap of dark chocolate hair, a flash of blue caught his eye.

The crowd below shifted, as if everyone had stepped back to give passage to the woman in blue. Lydia's interminable flood of words faded to a buzz as the parting wave of humanity stepped clear, giving him his first glimpse of Kat.

A lightning bolt would have struck with less power. She lingered beside one of the bars set up in the lobby below, her face lifted as if she was searching for someone — him, maybe? Her willowy body snatched the air from his lungs and stopped his heart dead. A roaring sound — no doubt all the oxygen leaving the room — pounded in his ears.

He shook free of Lydia's grip and walked away without so much as a glance back at her. As he moved along the promenade toward the stairs, Kat found him, her gaze locking with his. She followed him with her eyes until he stepped out of sight at the staircase, then found him again when he neared the bottom of the stairs.

As he drew nearer, he could see what she was wearing and it stole his breath all over again. A silvery ring around her throat was all that held up the narrow blue triangle of the gown's front. Her shoulders and arms were bare, her slim hips hugged lovingly by the glimmering blue dress that draped in a glittering waterfall to her ankles.

Then someone caught her attention and she turned away from him. The dress plunged in the back, exposing creamy skin from shoulders to just above her derriere. Any lower and she'd be indecent. A slit from the hem to her knees gave him a tantalizing glimpse of her taut calves.

Now that was a dress. Completely out of character for Kat, but perfect for her nonetheless, slinky as hell and a blatant invitation to touch her.

He couldn't resist; as she exchanged pleasantries with a dainty elderly woman at the other end of the bar, he laid his fingertips along Kat's spine. She didn't pull away, but he felt a tremor of reaction. It was all he could do to keep from pulling her into his arms.

Finally the older woman said her good-byes and Kat turned toward him again, dislodging his arm. She fussed with the silver ring around her neck, in the process pulling the shimmering blue fabric tight against her breasts. It wasn't polite to ogle, but his eyes had a will of their own when Kat's nipples made an appearance under the midnight blue knit.

Someone behind her, pushing toward the bar, nudged her toward him and he put his hands on her shoulders to steady her. He asked her, "Did you want something?" nodding his head toward the bar.

"If you're down here to get drinks for your date —"

"I don't have a date."

"Who's that enraged blonde you left on the promenade?"

He risked a glance up at Lydia. Her glare was palpable, even at this distance. "She's not enraged." Just ticked that she'd lost her audience.

While Lydia shot twin blue lasers at him with her eyes, Mark quickly reconnoitered the crowd. Jim from the *Business Journal*, good-looking, conveniently single and no more than ten feet away, stood gabbing with Alicia, one of the local news anchors. Mark threaded through the crowd and pulled Jim aside.

"I need a big, big favor."

Jim smiled and gestured apologetically to Alicia. "You're disrupting my rhythm here. I've just about got her softened up enough to ask her out."

"You're a friend, man. And friends help friends."

With a sigh, Jim tore his avid gaze from the shapely anchorwoman. "What?"

"I need you to baby-sit someone." Mark pointed up at the irate blonde on the promenade.

"Not Lydia." Jim shook his head and would have backed away if Mark didn't still have a grip on his arm. "Anyone but Lydia."

"A year's supply of free chocolate."

Jim gave him a savvy look. "For both my nephews."

That would put a serious dent in his discretionary fund. "Deal."

They shook on it, traded ticket stubs, then Jim went to give his apologies to Alicia. From the intimate way he whispered in her ear, Mark had no doubt Jim would get his chocolate and a night out with the anchorwoman.

Unencumbered, Mark turned back to Kat and discovered she'd escaped. It took him ten minutes to locate her over by the string quartet performing some warm-up adagios, or whatever it was string quartets played. Before he could get close enough to claim her attention, the lobby lights flashed, signaling the start of the concert.

She'd already entered the auditorium, a stream of people following her, before he could elbow his way inside. By the time he spotted her again, she'd found her row and was scooting past a well-dressed power couple on the aisle to the fourth seat over. Plowing through the crowd, Mark edged his way into Kat's row and plopped himself down in the empty seat next to her.

She looked ready to jump from her seat again. "That's not your seat."

"Sure it is." He made a show of checking Jim's ticket; the reporter's seat was up in the third tier, so far to the back of the auditorium the seat probably came equipped with an oxygen mask.

She grabbed for it. "Let me see."

Mark held it out of her reach. "Don't you trust me?"

She started, actually jumped in her seat. Then lifted her chin and turned away. "Whatever."

What the hell was that all about? He would have taken a moment to ponder it, but caught sight of a gigantic guy in a black pin-striped suit standing in the aisle, quizzically studying his ticket. He looked over at Mark, then back down to the ticket, then back at Mark.

Mark brushed a hand on Kat's bare shoulder, enjoying her shiver of reaction. "Be right back."

The couple on the aisle glared at him as he sidled past, obviously pissed at having to pull their well-groomed knees out of his way for a second time. The guy standing in the aisle, towering a foot and a half above Mark, seemed a bit peeved at having his seat stolen. When Mark saw the size of the hands gripping the ticket, then took another look at the movie star–handsome face towering above him, he recognized Mr. Pinstripe as the Seattle Supersonics star forward.

"Hey, Reggie. Mark Denham. We met at Hoops for Kids."

Reggie's hand swallowed Mark's as they shook. "Good to see you."

"If you could do me a huge favor . . ." Mark saw Kat scrutinizing them and he nudged Reggie aside. "I'd be glad to make another donation to your program."

Reggie smiled. "My wish is your command."

Mark could still feel Kat's stare between his shoulder blades and he urged the forward a little farther up the aisle. "We need to do a quick trade."

Reggie laughed. "Like when I came over from the Kings?"

"Something like that. See the guy over there in Row D?" Mark pointed to Jim on the other side of the auditorium. "You give me your ticket, give him my ticket, he'll give you his."

Peering across the auditorium at Jim, Reggie frowned. "Is that Lydia next to him?"

"Pretend you're from Croatia and don't speak English."

Reggie turned his all-American black face toward Mark. "Croatia. Right."

"She can't talk once the concert starts." Mark traded stubs with Reggie. "Whatever you do, don't ask about her engagement ring."

As Reggie ambled off toward the doors, Mark hurried back to the empty seat next to Kat. He caught sight of Reggie on his way down the aisle toward Jim just before the lights dimmed.

Kat gave him a poke. "That isn't your seat."

"Hush. The concert's about to start."

She jabbed him harder. "Why won't you leave me alone?"

The violins squealed as the symphony tuned up. "Friends don't leave friends alone."

"But we're not friends!" With the first notes of "The Star-Spangled Banner," the crowd rose as one.

"Oh, say can you see . . ." Mark knew he wasn't much of a singer, but he felt particularly patriotic tonight, what with Kat beside him in a slinky dress. ". . . by the dawn's early light . . ."

Kat dutifully belted out the words beside him, delivering with special fervor the phrase about "bombs bursting."

The audience screeched out "land of the free" in off-key but enthusiastic unison, then everyone took their seats. With barely a moment's rest, the symphony launched into the overture or opening or kickoff, filling the auditorium with sound.

Kat wasn't finished with him, but the volume necessitated her leaning so close she could have tongued him in the ear. That was an image to cherish.

"Mark," she whispered, sounding a little desperate now, "why won't you leave me alone?"

He would have answered her, but the music swelled, making conversation impossible. That is, he would have responded if he'd had an answer. In the two years since their divorce, he'd done everything he could to keep his distance from her out of self-defense. A few weeks ago, if he'd known they were both attending the benefit concert, he would have been grateful to have half the auditorium between them. Hell, he wouldn't have been here at all, would have sent Rod in his place.

He glanced over at her. She stared straight forward, the program in her lap morphing under the intense pressure of her hands clutching it. He couldn't quite make out her expression in the dim light, but that tortured program spoke volumes.

When he'd spent two years avoiding her, sidestepping her, why all the machinations now to be near her? The cabin hadn't been his doing, but even there, when he could have holed up in the downstairs bedroom, he couldn't stay away from her.

Physical attraction, that was all it was. Kat had always turned him on, whether in a knockout gown or a shapeless sweat suit. Her dark hair, chocolate brown eyes, lanky body — he'd never been able to resist that unconventional combination.

Nothing more to it than that. If he seemed so keen to keep her at his side, it was only because he enjoyed the picture of stripping away the clothes to the sleek woman underneath. For two years he'd only allowed those images in his dreams; now he wanted to enjoy them while he was awake.

But why Kat? The impertinent question nagged at him. Why not any number of other women, available women, interested women? Someone other than the ex-wife who had made it plain she had no inclination of taking up where they left off two years ago. He might have made her crazy with need at the cabin, but he didn't have a prayer of repeating that with her. He really ought to be moving on to someone willing to come out and play.

The blare of horns intruded on his turbulent thoughts, then the symphony segued into more strings. The music droned in his ears, a soporific for his sleep-starved brain. Another debt to lay at Kat's doorstep — her intrusion into his rest. If not for her teasing him with memories, he'd get a good night's sleep and wouldn't be persisting in this no-win obsession. He might have been able to resist her tonight instead of engaging in this crazy dance to keep her at his side.

More strings and the gentle rumble of kettledrums. It would be damned rude to fall asleep, especially since Denham Candy was cosponsor of this benefit concert. But with predictable ease, the blast of horns and thunder of kettledrums had its expected effect on him. Too many nights with insufficient sleep added to his languor. He was going, going, gone . . .

When Kat first felt the weight of Mark's head leaning against her shoulder, she tried a gentle shrug to dislodge him. He didn't budge, letting out a short, snorting snore before settling more heavily against her. She wondered if his zonked state was an act, but then he started to drool a little on her arm. Even Mark had more self-respect than that.

Besides which, she knew the effect classical music had on him. The louder the concerto, the sounder he slept. He could sit through an opera as long as the actors kept singing. But instruments only sent him straight to la-la land.

It wouldn't be too hard to push him off her, maybe over to that type-A harridan sitting with her tight-ass husband on the aisle. But that would cause more of a ruckus than simply letting him snore away the hour or so until intermission. He'd wake the moment the lights went back up. If he wasn't willing to go back to his own seat by then, she'd fabricate some excuse to leave.

Except she didn't want to leave. Not because she was such a fan of Prokofiev or Debussy, but because the feel of Mark's head resting on her shoulder sent such sweet memories rushing through her. Nights spent watching old movies until the wee hours when they'd both drift off to sleep on the sofa. That weekend he'd been slammed by the latest flu and she held him as he shivered with fever. Then it was his turn to comfort when she caught the bug.

It hadn't all been awful. They hadn't sparred every moment of their short marriage. She tended to focus on the altercations, the vicious, biting words exchanged. But there were tender, calm interludes between the storms.

Mark shifted, nestling his head more securely onto her shoulder. Like a throb of pain, her heart contracted and she thought she might cry. This was why she'd married him. There were a thousand reasons for their divorce, but there was one crystal-clear justification to unite them. No matter how much he riled her, how bitter their battles, she couldn't deny it — he touched her heart.

If only that was enough.

~ 11 ~

Kat stood outside Benaroya Hall, searching for a cab, shivering and cursing her vanity. The only jackets she owned were either down or fleece pullovers, none of them appropriate evening wear over this glitzy blue dress. She'd chosen glamour over practicality for once, and now she was paying for it.

Mark had finally repositioned himself halfway through the Debussy piece and she'd taken the coward's way out, sneaking past him and earning the everlasting ire of the power couple on the aisle. With her luck, the fierce-looking woman and her beetle-browed husband were joint CEOs of some high-flying new corporation seeking out a company to provide gourmet candy as executive and client gifts. When Mark woke up at intermission, he'd charm them into placing a gargantuan order of Denham truffles and she'd be out hundreds of thousands of dollars.

It would have to be millions to make any difference. Even a high six-figure sale wouldn't be enough. They were too far in the hole for that.

If she'd thought a pretty dress or a night at the symphony could distract her from the impending doom Roth Confectionery faced, she'd been sorely mistaken. She wanted to crawl into a dark cave and wail, stomp her feet and pound her fists at the injustice.

"What the hell are you doing out here alone?"

Could it get any worse? Kat turned to see Mark descending on her like a conquering angel. A conquering angel with a sleep crease on his cheek and hair sticking up to one side.

The urge to laugh welled up, but she stifled it, too afraid she wouldn't be able to stop. "The concert can't be over yet."

"The shrew sitting next to me elbowed me." He swiped a hand over his face. "I think she broke a rib."

A cab pulled up and Kat raised her arm to signal it. "If you'll excuse me —" She took three steps toward the waiting cab.

Mark grabbed her, warm fingers wrapped around her upper arm. "I'll take you home."

She ought to shake off his importunate grip, hurry over to the taxi at the curb. Instead she let his hand stay right there, his touch intimate no matter how impersonal.

The cabbie tapped his horn. "Hey, lady, you want the cab or not?"

Eternal damnation, she shook her head. "Sorry. Thanks anyway."

A light, cool breeze skimmed her shoulders and she shuddered. Mark's hand moved to her back. "Where's your jacket?"

"I don't have one." Shiver, shiver. "I'm not cold."

With a huff of impatience, he took off his tux jacket. "It's a shame to hide that dress," he said as he dropped the jacket around her bare shoulders.

She sighed with pleasure at the sudden warmth, his heat and scent suffusing her. "You can still see the dress."

"But not the good parts." His hand on her back again, he guided her up University Street. "I'm in the lot over on Fourth Street."

"I arranged parking for the concert in the University Street lot."

"Lydia wanted dinner at that French place on Fifth."

Insecurity stabbed her at the reminder of the paragon blonde bombshell. "And whatever Lydia wants —"

"She's self-centered and a bore and all night I was desperate to get away from her."

She still felt peevish. "So being with me was an act of desperation."

"Knock it off, Kat." He sounded tired and not a little irritated.

They reached Fourth and stopped to wait for the light. Her mind took the opportunity to refocus on something he'd said. "What good parts?"

The walk sign flashed and Mark urged her across the street. "You lost me, Kat."

The heat of embarrassment rose in her cheeks. "You said you couldn't see the good parts."

"Ah." She didn't have to look at him to know he was smiling. "Are you angling for a compliment?"

"My arms are skinny, my legs are toothpicks, there's nothing to fill out the top of the dress . . ."

He was staring down at her as if she'd grown a second head. "What the hell are you talking about?"

Damn his Denham charm. "Please, don't."

He looked utterly confused. "Don't what?"

"Don't . . ." Don't pretend I'm beautiful. Don't act as if I matter to you. "Just don't." She reversed direction, heading back toward Puget Sound Plaza. "I need a drink."

The Starbucks in the plaza was closed and Kat had to suppress the urge to pound on the door. "It's only eight-thirty. How can a coffeehouse close before eight-thirty?"

"This is downtown, everything closes early."

Kat glared at him. "If I wanted a sensible, logical answer, I would have asked for one." She continued down Fourth Street toward Seneca.

When she found the Starbucks there closed, she could have wept. Instead she turned to Mark and clutched his ruffled shirtfront. "Caffeine! Now!"

If his jacket felt luscious on her shoulders, her hands on his chest were downright seductive. As many times as she instructed herself to never touch Mark, she did it anyway.

It would be so easy to tug him down to her, to tip her mouth up to his. Then maybe the constant jangle of her nerves would quiet and for a few short minutes, the calamity of her life would recede.

A faint smile had curved his lips. "The Elliot Hotel."

"You want to get a room?" She ought to be outraged, but at the moment it sounded like a damn good idea.

He laughed, low and sexy. "The Starbucks at the hotel stays open late."

Starbucks. Right. "Lead on."

He took her arm and directed her back up Fourth toward Pine. A breeze gusted along the downtown Seattle street, sending her burrowing deeper into Mark's jacket. Almost like snuggling in his arms. She tried to squelch the image, but it kept popping up like an unwanted bloom on badly tempered chocolate.

When they reached the Elliot Hotel, Mark opened the lobby door for her, then took her arm again when they'd both stepped inside. She ought to shake him off, ought to give him back his jacket; it was certainly warm enough in the expansive lobby. But she couldn't bring herself to surrender it and didn't want to consider why.

She zeroed in on the Starbucks outlet and made a beeline for the counter. The baby-faced barista, a young man who'd nearly so-lidified with boredom, stared idly at the clock behind him as it ticked off the minutes until closing.

Kat slapped a hand on the counter, no doubt knocking a decade off the young man's life. "Venti double latte with a shot of caramel."

As the barista hopped to, Mark gave her shoulder a shake. "Maybe you ought to re-think that beverage choice."

"You have a point." She barked at the young man, "Better make that nonfat."

"It's not the calories, Kat. God knows you could use a bit more meat on your bones —"

She planted a hand over Mark's mouth. "Not another word. Not another commentary on my skinny, nothing body, my non-existent boobs . . ."

Damn, she felt like crying. In her mind's eye, the events of the last few weeks toppled domino-like in a serpentine line, closer and closer. The last one teetered above her head, ready to squash her flat with some final catastrophe. She couldn't do anything to stop the inevitable collapse, but she could distract herself from the calamity.

No more safe choices. It was time to be wild and reckless. She snatched her hand from Mark's hot, sensuous mouth and speared the barista with a steely gaze.

"Make that a double double."

The fresh-faced young man's jaw dropped. "Four shots of espresso?"

"You got a problem with that?"

The barista flicked a questioning glance at Mark, but Kat elbowed her ex aside. No one was speaking for her tonight. "He's not my keeper. Start brewing."

The young man shook his head, but he did as he was told. One tiny silver pitcher after another was upended into the venti cup, the steamed milk darkening with each addition of thick black Colombian. The last time she mainlined coffee like this, she'd been pulling an all-nighter at USC before her graduate macroeconomics class.

The barista handed over the high-test latte. The paper cup just about vibrated with java-fueled energy. Even the foam was brown.

Mark stared down at the witch's brew in her hand. "You realize there's enough caffeine in that drink to reanimate the dead."

She fumbled under his jacket for the minuscule purse she had slung over her shoulder. Before she could get it open, Mark had his wallet out.

"God forgive me," he muttered as he fished out a five, "I'm enabling an addict."

She let him pay, too far gone to object.

Wending her way through the tables arranged around the counter, she found a spot at the far edge of the seating area.

Maybe Mark would just go away now. He'd escorted her here, he'd bought her a latte with a near-illegal caffeine content, maybe she could convince him to order her a cab and send her on home.

Except, of course, she didn't want him to leave. She wanted to climb into his lap and squirm, tongue his ear and touch him where it wasn't polite to touch in public. The heat was so overwhelming she thought she'd explode with it, start tearing off her clothes as she ran like a madwoman through the hotel lobby.

With a quaking hand, she set down the latte. She looked up to see Mark standing over the table and her heart sank when she thought he might be leaving after all.

But then he pulled out a chair opposite her and lowered himself into it and a terrible mix of gratitude and outright horniness assailed her. God, she was a mess.

He stared at her a long time in silence, then said finally, "You drink that, you won't be able to sleep for a week."

She slammed down a long, rebellious slug of coffee, then another, nearly half the cup. Foam smeared her nose, her poor tongue whimpered at the scalding and her heart lurched with the caffeine overload.

A powerful hiccup jostled her hand and she sloshed a bit of latte on his jacket. "Sorry." She took another sip, but another hiccup hit before she could finish swallowing and she nearly choked.

Mark pried the cup from her hand. "What is going on?"

Caffeine screamed along her veins, loosening her beleaguered tongue. "I am so damned hot."

He nudged the cup farther out of her reach. "I don't doubt it, gulping all that coffee."

"You don't understand." She grabbed his hands and tugged them closer. "You were supposed to stay gone. Why the hell won't you get out of my life?"

"Kandy for Kids —"

"No-no-no-no-no . . ." She shook her head until she was dizzy. "See, you never left. You're jumping up when I least expect it. Some guy who looks like you, but isn't you. Sometimes it is you, but then I think maybe it isn't, that I'm just imagining . . ."

Now she was dizzy without the head-shaking. "So now here you are, big as life. Bigger —" A broad gesture of her hands nearly swept the half-full latte cup from the table. Mark rescued it just in time.

He set the cup on another table. "You want me to leave?"

"Of course I do! But I don't want you to leave here." She pointed an emphatic finger on the table in front of him. "I want you to leave here." Her fingertip tapped her temple.

She leaned toward the latte, but he captured her wrist before she could get her mitts on the cup. "I don't control your thoughts, Kat."

"Neither do I," she said mournfully. "Or my mouth, for that matter." A twist of her wrist loosened his grip, then she took his hand in both of hers, yanked it toward her. "I want you. I'm burning for you. I am so hot for you, I can't sleep, I can't eat . . . anything but chocolate, anyway. I can't think of anything but scht —" She cut off the pithy Yiddish word. "Anything but sleeping with you. Many times. All night long."

"Okay," he said slowly, drawing out the syllables. "This is the caffeine talking. Tomorrow, once you've slept this off —"

"I'll still want to jump your bones." Her nerves jittered in syncopation with her stuttering heartbeat. "This can't be a complete surprise."

"We're not married anymore, Kat. We don't love each other anymore."

Damn. Why did that feel like a knife plunged in her chest? "It's sex, Mark. Just sex."

He disentangled his hand from hers. "So do we get a room?"

A proposition like that ought to sound inviting and sexy. But he might as well have suggested they go purchase a socket wrench for all the sensuality in his tone.

"Not necessarily," she hedged.

"Why tell me this, Katarina?"

He was mad at her. He always used her full name when he was mad. That had been the first clue they were heading into argument territory.

Sudden exhaustion slumped her shoulders. "I don't know." Now she felt on the edge of tears again. "I want to go home."

He reached across the table, laid his warm palm against her cheek. "I know you're hot for me, Kat. Sometimes I want you so bad I can't stand it. But that's all there is between us anymore."

She squeezed her eyes shut as the stones of his words crashed on her in an uncontrollable landslide. Grief welled up inside her, and like a drunk who gets sappy when the alcohol wears off, she wallowed in a post-caffeine nosedive.

She chanced a quick look up at him and saw something flickering behind the bland neutrality of his face. His expressive blue eyes held a question and she wanted to answer it, but she was simply too tired to think.

He rose and took her hand. Kat dumped the rest of the latte on their way out of the lobby, then walked outside with Mark. The downtown streets seemed deserted and lonely and Kat felt a crying jag coming on. Gritting her teeth, she smothered the impulse.

The short walk down Union Street seemed to stretch into a silent eternity, although it couldn't have taken more than a few minutes to reach the parking structure and his BMW. If there was a sense of purpose to her life anymore, she didn't know what it was. Once it had been Roth Confectionery, once it had even been her life with Mark. Now her foundation seemed as porous as chocolate-covered honeycomb.

The leather seat in Mark's BMW seemed impossibly soft and comfortable. She nestled into it, his jacket pulled around the front of her, her cheek resting against the seat belt. "Could you just drive all night? I could sleep here forever."

"I'd have to fill the tank first."

He sounded perfectly serious. She turned her head to look at him. "I was kidding."

"Yeah," he said with a sigh as he started the car. "I know."

The drive to her condo wasn't nearly long enough. He pulled up to the garage and used her keycard to open the gate. The BMW made its way through the rows of cars to the elevator.

She didn't want to leave. Not because she didn't want to leave him, although she still fought the urgency to touch him, to kiss him. She didn't want to step from the car because then she'd be walking back into her life and all the disasters lurking there.

She unsnapped the seat belt and the jacket slithered into her lap. He was watching her, his blue gaze intense with those same secret messages that had begged for translation earlier. Damn him, why couldn't he just say them out loud?

"We're in trouble," she blurted, without realizing she was going to.

His brow furrowed. "You and I?"

"Roth. The company. We're in trouble."

She shoved the car door open and ran for the elevator. Punching the button, she prayed it would come before Mark thought to press her for more information. He was the enemy, damn it, the competition. How could she have said such a thing to him?

He was half out of the roadster. "Kat —"

Salvation arrived in the form of the elevator and she stepped inside before he could catch her. The doors slid shut as he rounded the front of his car. With a lurch, the elevator rose.

She stumbled along the corridor to her condo, then fumbled the keys before she got the door unlocked. Fritz was not in residence; just as well, she'd had enough of those damn Denham blue eyes staring at her. Shimmying out of the glitzy blue dress, she raced through her evening routine so she could hide in bed that much quicker.

Zapping the television on with the remote, she paced her room, channel flipping while she contemplated which was the worst cataclysmic misfortune. That she'd admitted to Mark her lust for him? That she'd let slip Roth was tanking? Or the fact that the company she'd invested her life's blood, her entire being, into was quickly going down in flames under her stewardship?

You can cry now, she thought. No one will see.

But her eyes were dry and her grief had faded to numbness. Good Lord, she was so inept, she not only couldn't manage the corporation entrusted to her, she couldn't even muster a decent catharsis.

Digging in her nightstand, she unearthed a bar of bittersweet chocolate and climbed into bed. A truly awful movie on the satellite, pillows plumped up behind her, she munched chocolate and winced over bad dialogue until the less-than-stellar third act when she drifted off to sleep.

Fritz snoring softly on her shoulder, Norma glanced at the clock on the DVD player and saw it was nearly eleven. The benefit concert was long over and with any luck, Kat and Mark had spent some quality time together tonight. If not, she and Fritz still had the ace in the hole he'd found at the cabin.

Turning her head slightly, she looked down at his slight body nestled beside her. She ought to wake him and send him home, but he felt so wonderful snuggled against her neck. His hair brushed her ear and it took everything in her to resist burying her face in the soft sandy curls.

One slender hand lay against her arm and she wanted so badly to link her fingers in his.

She tried to tell herself Fritz reminded her of her grandson, Travis, when the youngster lost the valiant fight to stay awake during a late movie. It had happened often enough when she'd had six-year-old Travis and his older sister, Brittany, over for the weekend. It was an inside joke between eight-year-old Brittany and her — how long before Travis slumped against her, snoring.

But the feelings bubbling up inside her were anything but grandmotherly. The temptation to brush aside one sandy curl that had fallen across Fritz's brow had nothing to do with keeping him tidy. She longed for the sensation of that dark honey-colored lock of hair sweeping against her fingertips. Would it be silky or crisp? Would it tickle her palm or stroke it?

Heat rose in her face at her wandering thoughts. This was entirely inappropriate. Fritz was younger than both her daughters and should be nothing more than a friend to her. She had no business mooning over him the way she did. But when he was, oh, so near, his hand so intimate on her arm, the most improper images danced in her head, images that just wouldn't go away, no matter how often she scolded herself.

Her long, heavy sigh must have roused him because he stirred, shifting against her shoulder. His hand flexed, then his fingers curled, his thumb stroking her arm through the sleeve of her cotton knit sweater. Norma froze as his hand moved up, palm against her upper arm, the back of his hand alarmingly close to her breast. Sensation shot through her as his face turned and his mouth pressed against the point of her shoulder.

If she didn't know better, she'd think he was kissing her, caressing her. But he had to still be asleep, still lost in some dream of a cute little twenty-something girl in his arms. Any second now he'd wake and be completely mortified that he was touching matronly old Norma instead of that sweet young thing in his dream.

"Norma . . ." Her whispered name shot through her like a jolt of electricity. "Oh, Norma . . ."

Okay, his dream girl had the same name as her; that was the only explanation. In his sleep-befuddled brain, he held taut young flesh, not forty-eight-year-old flab. And she had to put a stop to it, to save them both horrible embarrassment.

Then his hand on her arm moved higher, his knuckles grazing ever so slightly against her breast on the way to her shoulder, then her throat, before his fingers curved around her jaw. Before she could so much as take another breath, he'd turned her head toward his and pressed his mouth against hers.

He was kissing her! Oh, dear heavens, he was kissing her!

She had to push him away, had to shake him awake. This couldn't go on another moment. Not another second. Not another . . .

His tongue flicked lightly against her lower lip and her heart just up and stopped beating. Thankfully, it started right up again, although it beat about a million times a minute and would probably fly out of her chest anytime now. But, oh, heavens, what a way to go.

He only tasted her that little bit before he slowly pulled away, his hand still curved around her cheek. Now she'd see the mortification, the horror that the sexy little sylph of his dream had transmogrified into dumpy old Norma. She'd see it in his eyes anytime now.

But she saw nothing of the kind in his clear blue eyes. What she did see — heat, smoldering sensuality — she could barely understand, although it warmed her from toes to thudding heart.

He smiled slowly. "Hey."

"Hey." The word squeaked out. "You kissed me."

His smile broadened. "Yeah."

"I know you didn't mean to."

He laughed. "The hell I didn't."

She blinked at his emphatic statement. "I mean, you must have been dreaming and you thought you were kissing —"

"I was dreaming of you."

Shock stunned her into silence. She shook her head.

Fritz's thumb skimmed along her cheek. "Yes."

"No!" She jumped to her feet. "You can't."

"Can't dream about you? Why not?"

"Because . . . because . . ." It should be obvious, shouldn't it? "I'm old. You're not."

"You're forty-eight, Norma. That's not old."

This was crazy. Yes, she'd been longing for exactly this kind of thing, but that had been a fantasy and a wrongheaded one to boot. She had to squash this looniness before it went any further.

"Fritz . . ." His sharp blue eyes fixed on her, and emotions muddled inside her — yearning, hope, wanting and down-and-dirty desire. She had to nip all of it in the bud. "You are simply too young for me. You . . . you . . . remind me of my grandson."

It was a terrible lie and she saw its impact in his face. She spent enough time around Fritz to know how fragile his ego was and how easily it would be to wound him. Color stained his cheeks a moment before he turned away, then pushed to his feet.

"I'd better go." He grabbed his worn denim jacket from the hall tree by the front door. "Call you later."

"Fritz! Wait!"

But he didn't. He had the door open and hurried through it before Norma could so much as make her way around the sofa. By the time she got her door open, he'd reached the sidewalk and was jogging up the street.

"Fritz!" she shouted.

She thought she saw him hunch his shoulders when he heard her call his name, but he didn't slow his pace. In another moment, he'd disappeared around the corner, headed for the nearest Metro bus stop.

Tears pricking her eyes, Norma shut the door again. How could she have botched things so badly? Fritz kissing her was all wrong, and she needed to make that clear to him, but she didn't have to hurt him.

Guilt digging deep, Norma plopped back on the sofa and dropped her head in her hands. There had to be a way to fix this. If she had to stay up all night finding a way, she'd make things right.

~ *12* ~

"There's no way around it, Kat. We have to sell the company."

When her father dropped the bomb, Kat had been leaning back in her cushy conference room chair, caught up in the usual, plaguey daydream about Mark, the one that for the past three weeks wouldn't leave her alone. Last Wednesday's debacle had only intensified the X-rated images and on a dreary Monday morning, it was so much more pleasant to focus on a truly fine picture of Mark naked between her legs than whatever further bad news her father planned to deliver.

When her father's pronouncement registered, Kat jolted upright in her chair, gaping like a fish. The other members of the Roth Confectionery board seated around the conference table — her father, her mother, her stepparents — met her openmouthed stare with varying degrees of sympathy and concern. The only face missing from the tableau, the only one that would truly have offered comfort, was her Nana Ruth, now living full-time at the care home. Kat was just as glad Nana wasn't here to witness this heartbreak.

She gripped the soft leather arms of her chair, no doubt leaving fingernail impressions. Groping in her now vacant brain for a response, she mustered a query for her father. "No other choices . . . sell the company or go under?"

The room fell into an uneasy quiet, her stepmother Patti's gaze fixed on her hands folded on the table, her mother Rose punctuating the quiet with an occasional heavy sigh, her stepdad Tony holding his coffee mug without ever drinking from it. The morning gloom hanging over Lake Union was a perfect counterpoint to the nasty business inside. That roiling cloud of white lurking over the lake might as well be hovering over their heads.

His brown eyes soft with empathy, her father nodded somberly. "That's it in a nutshell, Kat."

She couldn't quite get her mind around the reality of it. "But when all the Mother's Day sales figures are in —"

"They're in, Katarina." Worry lined her mother's usually cheerful face. "And they all tell the same story."

An image of a cartoon sales chart danced in her mind — a big jaggedy black line plunging precipitously down. "What about another loan? Until we can roll out Chocolate Magic."

Her mother and father exchanged telling glances and a heavy weight thunked in the pit of Kat's stomach. "What?"

The sympathetic look on her mother's face tightened the knot inside. "Chocolate Magic is a sinkhole, Kat. We've been pouring all our discretionary funds into that one project for too long with no results."

"But the team is almost there!" Kat protested, the plush comfort of her chair suddenly suffocating. "In another few days, a week tops —"

Her stepdad Tony clunked down his coffee mug. "They've been promising that for months."

Patti threw in her own dire two cents. "We've just been hit with a double whammy — sales of the old favorites have dwindled and our new products just haven't caught on. Coffee Pals were an expensive mistake."

Patti's words struck like a stake to the heart. Coffee Pals had been the first project she'd devised and championed after the divorce. She'd heard through the grapevine about Denham's Coffee Buddies, knew they would be using the whimsical cartoon Buddy to sell the line. She'd thought she had a better idea — grown-ups drank coffee, why not a mature, sophisticated sales program?

Who could have guessed Coffee Buddies would go so well in hot chocolate? Kids clamored for them, snapped up the blasted Buddy dolls as if they were the Cabbage Patch Kids of the new millennium. Denham responded quickly to the craze, selling family packs with an assortment of flavors sure to appeal to both kids and adults, complete with a goofy-faced Buddy doll.

With a groan, Kat dropped her head in her hands. "I'm sorry, I'm sorry. It's all my fault." Honey, I tanked the corporation.

Her mother jumped to her feet and hurried to Kat's end of the table. "No, sweetheart." Her hand stroked Kat's bowed head gently. "These problems started long before your tenure as CEO."

Now her father put a supportive arm around her slumped shoulders. "The whole industry is in a downturn. You couldn't have controlled that."

Kat shrugged off her parents' comfort.

"Denham's not in a downturn." The petulant whine in her voice was not attractive. "Denham's doing just fine and dandy!"

Even more telling glances around the table. Tony mouthed something at his wife that looked like "Tell her," but Kat's mother shook her head vigorously. Patti raised her brows at Kat's father with a not-so-subtle gesture in Kat's direction.

"What?" Kat asked, not even wanting to know. No one at the table would meet her gaze.

Her father patted her on the shoulder, a suspicious smile on his face. "It's just a little idea we've been throwing around."

Kat gritted her teeth. "What?"

Her mother sat up straighter in her chair. "It would really be the perfect match."

Now that Kat knew where this was heading, she really didn't want to hear more. "No way."

Patti took on her let's-be-reasonable tone. "It just makes good business sense."

Kat slapped a palm on the table. "Absolutely not!"

Tony harrumphed. "It's not as if we'll have any other suitors."

Kat surged to her feet. "I won't marry Mark!"

As they all gawked, Kat did a little rewind in her mind of the last ten seconds. Damn. "We're not merging with Denham." She sank back into her seat.

She had a microsecond respite before they all started in on her. Her father played the practicality card, rattling on about how well-acquainted Denham and Roth were with each other's businesses. Her mother hit the emotional notes, reminding her of the long friendship between the families. A fellow MBA, Patti filled her patter with business-speak, extolling synergism and strategic partnerships. Bottom-line Tony simply stated the obvious — Roth Confectionery was dead-broke.

"Okay, okay!" Kat shouted above the cacophony. "We're out of options. We need a buyout."

Her mother and Patti smiled, no doubt in expectation of complete capitulation. And there was a part of her that wished she could sell the damn company to Mark and just walk away. Open a Starbucks downtown, one that would stay open past six o'clock on a weekday.

Even worse, there was a more insidious, secret little smidgen of herself that still longed, against all logic, to do more than merge Denham and Roth. That little speck inside still mooned over a much more personal merger. Wished there was a way they could be together. Wished Mark still loved her.

Her jaw tightened until her TMJ screamed with tension. "Any company but Denham. Hershey's, Mars, Tootsie Roll for God's sake. Anybody but Denham."

Shoving her wheeled chair back, Kat pushed to her feet. "I'm going down to R&D. The Chocolate Magic team has something new to show me."

That was a lie, but ridiculous tears burned in her eyes and she wasn't about to let them see. She race-walked out of the room, ignoring her mother's importunate "Kat!" and her father's pleading "Sweetheart, please!"

She kept going until she reached the elevator, punching the down button with a vengeance. Damn, damn, double damn. Mark had her life upside down and inside out and he wasn't even here. She'd gone back to dodging his phone calls and E-mails since Wednesday night and had thought she was doing a pretty good job of ignoring his existence. She even had a date tonight, dinner with her dad's estate attorney, Greg. Or was it Gary?

What difference did a name make, anyway? What's-his-name was so drop-dead gorgeous women swooned and drooled when he walked into the room. His smile just about knocked the wind out of her. Of course, the moment he opened his mouth, he was so deadly dull he made her teeth ache, but they didn't have to talk all night, did they?

Yet all the while she'd been busy making other plans, Mark had been busy burrowing into her subconscious. She'd like to blame it on him — maybe he was employing some weird psychically influencing voodoo device. But that didn't change the inescapable reality — she was obsessed with her ex-husband.

Sell the company. Her gut burned at the thought. That was bad in so many ways. She could have accepted her Mark obsession, might have even enjoyed it, trotting it out in her most private moments. If all had worked the way she'd hoped — the rollout of Chocolate Magic a brilliant success, sales climbing to dizzying heights. But who could enjoy the occasional sexy ex-husband fantasy in the face of the desperation of Roth's financial situation?

The elevator arrived just as she had her leg primed to kick the doors and probably break her toes in the process. As it was, the forward arc of her foot sent her stumbling into the elevator car just as a woman from FedEx was exiting. Kat danced around the FedExer with a clumsy little side step, muttering an apology under her breath. She sank against the elevator wall as the doors shut her in with her solitude.

When the car didn't move, she remembered to push the button for the seventh floor. She was setting herself up to add insult to injury by visiting R&D, but she might as well get all her disasters over with in one day.

When she stepped into the experimental kitchen, her first shock was when the usually staid lead chemist, Tess Nguyen, made a mad dash toward her and grabbed Kat up in a breath-stealing hug. When the three other team members closed in, whooping and hollering and slapping Kat's back, she wondered if Tess had added a little something extra to the weekly batch of brownies she brought into work.

Then Tess said those miraculous words. "We've got it, Kat. We've pinned down Chocolate Magic."

Tess's pronouncement was almost harder to accept than her dad's dire declaration. "You're sure? You've run a test batch?"

Tess gave her another ebullient one-armed hug. "Ten test batches, all with the same results. We've had the formula since yesterday, but I didn't want to give you any more false hope."

"That's great. That's fine." Kat was shaking, her fingers numb. "I want to see. Make a batch for me."

Terrified her presence would somehow jinx the process, Kat followed Tess into the nearest kitchen station. Her team had set out the ingredients — a large stainless steel restaurant square piled high with what looked like chocolate crumbs, another square filled with what looked like vanilla pudding. Crumbles and custard, sales called them, the mystical components for Chocolate Magic.

Tess pulled out a disposable plastic bowl. "We only have the one flavor so far — basic chocolate. We'll want to add mint, peanut butter, walnut — all the varieties you suggested when you first developed the concept."

This had been her second big project — and the one unique, innovative idea of her life. Mark had always been the one with the stunning brainstorms, the leaps into the extraordinary. Her skill was the dogged work of bringing an idea to fruition.

And yet in this, her moment of glory, her

one phenomenal epiphany, an ache settled in her heart. When she should be chortling with glee, looking forward to gloating to Mark about her coup, a more soft-centered longing nagged at her — to share her triumph. Instead of imagining Mark green with envy, she could all too clearly envision him smiling, happy for her, glad that she'd succeeded, business rival or no.

Damn. She couldn't win even when she won.

Now she realized Tess had been standing there for far too long, holding out the empty plastic bowl. "I assumed you'd want to do the honors, Kat."

"Yes, right." Kat took the bowl and dragged over the square holding the pudding-like mixture.

Tess handed her a two-ounce measure. "For the trials we've tried to be as precise as possible."

Kat spooned the custard into the measure. "There'll be some wiggle room with the proportions for the finished product?"

"Sure." Tess gave her a rubber spatula to scrape the measure clean into the bowl. "Lose a few crumbles and the customer can still have a good finished product."

As she swiped the spatula clean on the side of the plastic bowl, an annoying thought niggled at her — Mark at her side, enjoying the anticipation with her. She redirected her focus. "Marketing has packaging designed, ready for production."

"They demoed it for us." Tess nudged the crumbles closer to Kat. "An all-in-one unit was smart."

That had been her idea as well. The molded plastic bottom included a two-ounce reservoir for the custard and a one-ounce for the crumbles. Once the consumer tore off the colorful plastic cover, the divider between the chambers slipped out, allowing the custard and crumbles to mix.

Kat meted out the required amount of crumbles with a one-ounce scoop. Kat held the scoop over the bowl of custard as the ghost of Mark Denham seemed to hover at her elbow, encouraging her to proceed.

Kat set her jaw. It was time for an exorcism. She upended the crumbles scoop.

"You have to combine them quickly." Tess handed over a wooden stick the size and shape of a tongue depressor. "The reaction is fast."

Kat swirled the stick through the mixture, stirring in rapid strokes as the chocolate crumbles dissolved into the custard. The pale creamy custard grew darker, thicker. Kat had to use a little more effort as the mixture firmed up. In less than ten seconds, she had the finished product — creamy chocolate fudge. Chocolate Magic.

Kat poked with the stick. "It looks good."

"It tastes better," Tess said. "Feel the bottom."

Kat lifted the bowl and rested it against her palm. "Warm."

"That's the chemical process. Took some doing to dial down the heat."

Scooping up a generous dollop with the stick, she offered it first to Tess. The chemist shook her head. "Go ahead. I've sampled so much of that stuff, I'm ready to pop."

Kat took a nibble, scraping a bare morsel off with her teeth. The delectable richness melted on her tongue and she almost groaned in ecstasy. She took the rest of the lump of fudge off the stick and sank against the kitchen counter with a long, appreciative "Mmmm."

The stuff was fabulous. Ten times better than what she'd expected. Nearly as good as the carefully handcrafted fudge her Nana's mother had made that had started Roth in the first place.

Kat scooped up another helping. "I was

never much on science, but now I'm a true believer."

Tess laughed. "Believe it or not, we're using all-natural ingredients as much as possible. There's just a little something extra to make all the magic work."

"We're still in lockdown on this, aren't we?" That level of secrecy had been Kat's directive. "I wish I could take this up to the board." Or to Mark. She could rub it in his face. Or on his chest . . . his legs . . . his . . .

"Invite them down here." Tess yanked Kat back from her reverie. "We've got plenty to sample."

"I almost can't believe it." Kat chased the last of the fudge from the bowl with her finger. "We've finally got it."

"There's still the process timing. We get some pretty nasty results if the mixture isn't stirred the moment the components are combined."

"We'll work that out." Nothing could discourage her now. Setting aside the bowl, she started for the door. "I'd like an up-to-date report by the end of the week. For myself and the rest of the board. We'll want a top-notch presentation for the bank."

Sated with chocolate and buzzing with

sugar, Kat did a jig up the corridor on her way to the elevator. On the twelfth floor, she danced to her office, alarming the temp admin from accounting who'd come up to deliver last week's payroll report. As she stepped into her office suite, she was a bit disappointed to see Norma's chair empty. Her first instinct might have been to tell Mark the good news, but her second was to share the excitement with Norma, her most faithful friend at the company.

Number three, and most crucial, would be her father. She might be CEO, but since Nana's health forced her to step down, Phil Roth was the member of the board with the longest tenure. He carried more weight than even her mother and his vote of confidence would go a long way.

As she seated herself behind her desk, she rehearsed the announcement in her mind. We've got it, Dad! Chocolate Magic is a reality.

A fist of doubt squeezed her belly. Even if Tess and her team worked out the last kink, even if they rushed it to market, the product wouldn't be on the shelves for at least a couple months. Roth Confectionery's problems couldn't be put on hold during that time. They still would need a bridge loan or some other kind of financing to keep them going.

They'd find a way. Once her father knew that Chocolate Magic was truly just behind the finish line, he'd throw his support behind her. She'd make sure of it.

She picked up the phone, fingers ready to dial her father's extension when a familiar male voice spoke on the other end of the line. "Hello?"

With a shriek, she fumbled the receiver and it clattered across her desk like a beached fish. Grabbing it up, she gasped out a greeting. "Mark?"

His deep voice caressed her ear. "Did I catch you at a bad time?"

For a moment, her brain crossfired and she couldn't gather a single coherent thought. Too much fudge and unsettled emotions.

She laughed, a jittery sound. "The phone didn't even ring. I'd picked it up to make a call."

"I don't suppose you were calling me?" She heard the wry humor in his voice. "I was wondering if you were free for lunch. There's a wrinkle with the kayak race."

"Lunch." Preoccupied with an uneasy conglomeration of Chocolate Magic and sex, her mind raced. She fumbled for her Palm and checked her calendar. "Not today. I've got a Chamber meeting."

"How about tonight? Dinner?"

She nearly blurted out a yes, then remembered her tête-à-tête with George. Garth? "I have a date tonight."

Kat had to wait so long for a response, she thought the call had been disconnected. Mark finally spoke, so softly she could barely hear. "Not tonight, then. Lunch tomorrow?"

She knew that tone. He was ticked. Tough patoots if he didn't like her dating other men. Besides, there could only be other men if he was the man, which he wasn't. For all he knew, her date was the man, which would relegate Mark to the position of other. Her back molars twinged at the thought of Garth, the gruesomely tedious estate attorney, as her one and only.

With impatient stabs of her thumb, she scrolled forward in her calendar. "I can do lunch at one."

She imagined Mark flipping through his PDA. Dueling Palms. "Works for me. That Thai place downtown?"

"Sure. Fine." Suddenly her mind whirled with the aphrodisiac qualities of Thai food. "See you then."

The moment she hung up, her heart sang a joyful aria and her libido did a happy dance. Disgusted with herself, she grabbed the receiver, intending to call Mark back and cancel. When the phone burbled its summons, she startled, launching the receiver off the desk. The phone's base nearly followed and it took a quick lunge to keep it on her desk.

She reeled in the receiver by its curly cord, wincing as it clattered and clunked on the modesty panel. She heard the buzz of conversation when she brought the handset to her ear. "Hello?"

Another mutter of sound, then her father snapped, "Kat? What the hell was that?"

"Dropped the phone. I've got fantastic news." She gave him a quick rundown of the triumph in R&D. "This changes everything, Dad."

She expected his immediate agreement and her heart stuttered at the silence on the other end of the line. The muted exchange that followed, no doubt filtering through his hand covering the mouthpiece, increased her alarm. She could have sworn she heard Mark's name mentioned more than once, certainly not a good sign.

Finally her father came back on. "You're absolutely right. It changes everything."

After a quick assurance that he'd begin exploring bridge loans, he signed off, leaving Kat with the nagging sense she'd missed something in their brief exchange. And had she truly heard Mark brought into their discussion? Unease settled in her stomach.

Then she reminded herself that Chocolate Magic was an easy hurdle away from complete success and her spirits rose again. Her life was on the right track again. Damned if she'd let doubts or ex-husbands knock her off her stride.

As Phil Roth hung up the phone, his expression worried, Fritz had to shake off the urge to take Norma's hand for moral support. When he'd been brought into Phil's office to strategize about the Mark and Kat situation, Fritz had cajoled Norma into coming with him, using the excuse that they made such a great team. Now he just wanted the reassurance of a connection with her. God, he was such a wimp.

Phil relayed Kat's message about Chocolate Magic and Fritz felt doom gathering overhead again. He looked over at Norma and her sweet face showed none of the anxiety burning inside him. Her gaze went from him to Phil. "I don't understand. What's the problem with a Chocolate Magic success?"

Phil gestured at Fritz to answer Norma. "First, when Kat's feeling cocky, she's that much more certain she doesn't need anyone, let alone Mark. Second, it makes the excuse of the company's failing fortunes that much less believable."

Norma's soft brown eyes widened. "You mean Roth isn't failing?"

Phil cleared his throat. "We're in trouble, sure enough. We do need a quick infusion of capital and a merger would be the most cost-effective way to do that. However, our straits are not quite as dire as we've led Kat to believe."

Ideas bounced like popcorn in Fritz's mind, but he couldn't sort the crazy notions from the sound concepts. If there was anything but junk floating around in his brain, that is. He wished again for the anchor of Norma's hand, wished he had her steadiness to clear the clutter in his head.

But he had to stand on his own two feet. Take responsibility, his father had lectured him time and again. Be a man. If only he knew what that meant.

The most insistent notion rattling around in Fritz's mind elbowed its way out of his mouth. "Let's do an end run," he told Phil. "Force Kat's hand."

Phil's brow furrowed. "Meaning?"

"Put the Roth-Denham merger into motion. Don't tell Kat until it's finalized."

"I don't know, Fritz," Phil said doubtfully. "Kat won't like us dealing behind her back."

"It's for her own good," Fritz said, then winced when he heard his father's autocratic tone in his voice. Damn, when did he start sounding like his father? "She'll thank us later." God, that sounded even worse.

Norma's worried look almost had him recanting his suggestion. It suddenly seemed crucial that he convince her, even more than Phil Roth.

"The merger is a no-brainer." Fritz focused on Phil, but was all too aware of Norma beside him. "The Roth and Denham businesses complement each other perfectly and Kat knows that as well as you do, Phil."

"But to force her hand . . ." Phil said.

"Present Kat with a fait accompli and her emotional objections to a Denham merger vanish. They're no longer a stumbling block to rekindling a relationship with Mark."

He sounded like his father again, cold and businesslike, and the realization put a nasty taste in his mouth. Ned Nichols didn't believe in love, thought marital alliances could be negotiated like business deals. No wonder Fritz's mother left him five years ago.

And yet . . . a tiny little grain of instinct buried deep inside told him this was exactly the correct course of action. Not because it was logical or sensible, but exactly the opposite — it felt right.

Fritz turned to Norma. "Kat's so mixed up right now, I don't think she knows herself what's best for her. This might just clear the way for her."

Norma's expression turned thoughtful. "You know, I think you're right." Her smile warmed Fritz clear to the core. "You're brilliant."

"I agree." Phil rose from his desk and thrust out his hand to shake Fritz's. "I'll set the wheels turning with the Roth executive board. We already have a detailed proposal the Denham folks submitted two years ago. I'll talk to Ian Denham about an update."

As glad as Fritz was for Phil's vote of confidence, Norma's admiration puffed him up until he felt ten feet tall. Success was at his fingertips for the first time in his life and he owed it all to Norma.

As they left Phil's office and headed for

the elevator, the flush of triumph still across his shoulders like a mantle, Fritz got another incredible idea. Norma had been such an essential part of this coup, it was time he trusted her with the one secret in his life he'd kept from everyone. He'd once had the temerity to reveal to his father the slimmest sliver of his aspiration and had been slammed so hard he'd never mentioned it to another soul.

But maybe it was time he shared it with Norma. He risked her disapproval, even her derision, but it was time he took that chance. To be a man. To stand on his own two feet.

They reached the twelfth floor and headed toward Kat's office. Before Norma could open the door, he put a hand on her arm to stop her. "Are you busy tonight?"

She blinked in surprise. "I'm taking my grandkids out to dinner."

Sudden doubt seized Fritz and he felt like a complete coward. "Never mind then."

"Travis and Brittany have to be home early, so I won't be out late." Color rose in her cheeks and he realized she was embarrassed. "But I guess you can't —"

He squeezed her arm to reassure her. "I'd like to come by."

His heart winged skyward when she smiled. "I'll probably be home by eight."

He shouldn't touch her, had no reason to, but somehow his hand lifted and laid itself on her cheek. Her hazel eyes softened in response and he wanted desperately to kiss her, almost couldn't hold himself back. It would have been crazy, stupid, even without the witnesses roaming the busy hallway.

He dropped his hand and stepped back. "See you tonight." He turned and headed toward the elevator, his mouth stretched in a smile impossible to quell.

As Norma watched Fritz step inside the elevator, she tried to quiet the excitement bubbling up inside her. She'd been allowing her imagination far too much free rein lately when it came to Fritz. Just now, for instance, when he touched her cheek, she was sure he was about to kiss her.

Her fantasies had gotten entirely out of hand. An attractive young man like Fritz would never contemplate smooching a middle-aged lady like herself. She had to put an end to such nonsense.

But she'd be seeing him tonight. No doubt to discuss their next move in bringing Kat and Mark together. If she had secret hopes there might be a more personal reason for them to meet, she'd just sweep those wishes into a dark corner. And drat her heart if it insisted on pulling those dreams back out from under the rug.

~ *13* ~

Mark felt twitchy all afternoon long and as explosive as a lit stick of dynamite. He'd be seated at his desk, struggling to focus on a sales report or contractor's drawings of Denham's latest build-out, and he'd suddenly lunge to his feet to pace his office. The sandwich he'd picked at random from the vending machine sat vilely in his stomach and the Diet Coke he'd washed it down with left him with an edgy caffeine high.

This afternoon was just the culmination of five days of madness since Kat's crazed admission last Wednesday night. *I want you. I'm burning for you.* Her words had rolled around in his mind, thrummed in his body, sang along his veins. She might as well have dropped a live grenade in his lap.

Now as the clock crawled toward five, he'd completely abandoned any pretense at work. With reports and folders and rolled-up drawings littering his desk, he sat rigid in his chair clutching his phone, battling the urge to call her. The litany that had haunted him all afternoon rolled through him.

Kat had a date. Kat was having dinner tonight with some lecherous gigolo who would sweet-talk her into a compromising situation. Of course, the last person she let talk her into something was the doctor who'd sworn to eight-year-old Kat the tetanus shot wouldn't hurt. The MD had been lucky to escape without any broken bones.

So her date tonight wouldn't persuade her to do anything she didn't want to do. The thought of that was even worse — Kat going willingly to another man's bed. That precious gift of Kat's cataclysmic climax in another man's hands, another man swallowing her cries of passion.

He hurled his phone across the room and it snapped from the tether of its cord to smash against his office door. He stared unbelieving at the wreckage — the cordless receiver half-hidden by his bookcase, the base unit in pieces against the wall. He'd committed phonocide in a fit of jealous rage. He was one sick puppy.

A rap on the door brought him out of his daze. "Yeah?" he called out, his voice raspy.

The door opened and Rod stuck his head in far enough to check for another possible missile attack. "You okay?"

Not even close to okay. He felt ready to kill someone. His volatile state probably merited a two-rosary penance at confession.

Rod slipped inside, got a good look at the rubble strewn on the carpet. "I'll order you a new phone."

"Whatever." He still had his cell in his jacket pocket. Kat's number was still programmed in the number two spot. "Can I be done for the day?"

Rod bent to pick up the scattered pieces. "Considering you blew off the two-thirty sales meeting and the four o'clock interview with the chemist you flew in from Denver, leaving early sounds like the perfect follow-up."

Mark pushed his chair back and grabbed his leather bomber jacket. "Forward calls to my cell."

"I'll send them to voice mail," Rod said as Mark walked past him. Mark was nearly out the door when Rod added, "Except for Kat."

Rod might as well have slammed him in the chest with a fifty-pound box of bittersweet chocolate. Kat wouldn't call. She would be too busy being wined, dined and charmed by her mystery suitor.

Rod followed him from his office, dumping the trashed phone on his desk before dogging him to the elevator. "Since when did you become such a damn wuss?"

Mark reached for the elevator call button. "Did the chemist go home?"

Rod slapped a hand over the button. "Not yet. I told him you took sick."

Mark tried to wedge his hand under Rod's square, blunt-tipped fingers. "Reschedule the interview for tomorrow morning."

Rod's hand stuck like a tick. "You going to have your brain back by then?"

Changing tactics, Mark used Rod's hand to call the elevator. "I'll be in by nine."

Rod scowled as Mark stepped into the elevator. "Just call her, you idiot."

Mark let the doors shut without comment. His cell sat like a lead weight in his pocket, taunting him. Instead of pulling it out, he grabbed a Coffee Buddy from his other pocket and unwrapped it with methodical care. As he let the hazelnut mocha cube melt in his mouth, the chocolate seeped into his wounded being, rejuvenating him, anointing him with a flash of brilliance. Was he the idea guy, or what?

Fishing his cell phone from his pocket,

he dialed a familiar phone number. She answered after one ring. "Roth Confectionery, Norma Wilson speaking."

His incredible idea hit a snag. He couldn't extract the information he wanted from Norma without a plausible excuse. He could throw himself on Norma's mercy and admit he wanted to spy on Kat, but he had a little more pride than that.

"Hello?" Norma prompted. Then she lowered her voice to a surprisingly intimate tone. "Fritz, is that you?"

Norma and Fritz? As he rolled that little tidbit around in his mind, brilliance struck again. Why not recycle the excuse he'd given to Kat?

"Norma, sorry. Mark Denham. I'm up to my ass in alligators today." Holding the cell at arm's length, he barked at an imaginary minion, "Give me twelve copies of that!" just as the elevator door opened on the third floor. A pair of young administrative aides sidled inside, keeping their distance.

He brought the phone back to his mouth and tried to look like a busy executive. "Kat and I have a lunch date tomorrow to discuss the kayak race, but something more pressing came up. I'll have to talk to her sooner."

"She's still in her office," Norma said

helpfully. "I'll put you through."

"No, no, no!" Hell would become a winter wonderland before he'd beg Kat for her dinner destination. "I'm on my way out right now, shouldn't even be making this call." When the elevator opened on the ground floor, he stepped aside to let the admins out. "She mentioned a dinner date tonight. I don't suppose she told you where?"

He prayed his rushed query would translate over the phone as harried, preoccupied CEO instead of desperately jealous ex-husband. Then pure panic hit him when it occurred to him Norma might have to go ask Kat at what restaurant she'd be meeting her stud du jour. No way would Kat simply answer the innocent question; she'd press Norma for why.

"Ma Petit Aubergine at seven-thirty," Norma finally said. "Took me a bit to find it. She had password protection on that calendar entry."

It crossed Mark's mind to wonder first why Norma had Kat's password and, second, why she was so cavalier about using it. He decided it was better not to look too closely at that particular nag's teeth.

He thanked her for the information as the elevator doors slid open on the parking

285

garage level. Now he knew the when and where, he'd have to devise an appropriate disguise. Something unobtrusive, subtle yet impenetrable. There was a funky little costume shop downtown that catered mostly to the theatre crowd; maybe he'd find just the right thing there. He'd slip in and out of Ma Petit Aubergine and Kat would be none the wiser.

Kat nestled more deeply into the sinfully comfortable bucket seat of Garret Neidenmeier's Mercedes E320, the rich notes of Rachmaninoff's Symphony No. 1 in D Minor drifting from the Blaupunkt. She still tingled from her bath, the pale rose silk of her dress yummy against her skin, the ribbon-thin strap of a minuscule purse looped over her shoulder. She could spend the rest of her life gliding around in this car carrying nothing but a credit card, the key to her condo and, God love her, one foil-wrapped prophylactic.

That is, if Garret Neidenmeier didn't speak. He'd been kind enough to keep mostly mum when he'd picked her up at her condo, had let Rachmaninoff do the talking for him as he navigated his Mercedes through the downtown traffic. Once they arrived at the fussy French restaurant he'd selected, he'd probably expect them to converse. But in the interim, his silence afforded Kat ample opportunity to gaze in undisguised admiration at his truly stunning profile, his impeccable features.

When he pulled up to Ma Petit Aubergine, Kat sighed with regret that the blissful interlude had to end. She considered locking the door so the parking valet couldn't open it, but that would just arouse Garret's curiosity. He'd probably want to know why she preferred to stay alone in his Mercedes rather than spend the evening with him. Lawyers were nosy that way, always asking questions.

So she let the valet open her door, even took Garret's hand when he offered it. His palm was damp and his grip was too tight; she thought her fingers might pop off if he didn't let go soon. Just as she was considering a karate self-defense move to extricate herself, Garret seemed to realize his transgression. He dropped her hand as if she'd burned him.

He choked out an apology, then put a tentative hand on her shoulder to escort her to the restaurant door. A wet spot formed at the point of contact. His other hand shook as he reached for the door handle.

As they stepped into Ma Petit Aubergine's tastefully subdued lobby, she smiled up at him. "Hey, nothing to be afraid of, Garret. I consumed my mate just yesterday. Won't need another for at least a week."

When he stared at her in abject terror, she realized he didn't have a sense of humor. Probably surgically removed in law school. "That was a joke, Garret."

He gave her a sickly laugh. "Yeah, knew that. Let me see if our table is ready."

He swiped his palms on the back of his slacks as he stepped up to the Valkyrie-proportioned hostess, drawing Kat's gaze to an exquisite pair of buns. That tush would give even Mark's derriere a run for its money.

But she wasn't thinking about Mark tonight. Tonight was all about her and the gorgeous hunk at her side. Lust and libido, not pain and heartache. Eye candy and boy toys, not love and forever.

When Garret returned to her side, the palm moisture syndrome had migrated to his head, drawing beads of sweat across that magnificent brow. She supposed a sweaty gorgeous guy could still be sexy, but the ick factor provided a definite challenge. She'd have to imagine him slick and wet in the throes of passion to make it work. As long as passion didn't involve him opening his mouth to speak.

Physical contact with him was losing its appeal, however, and she was just as glad when his hand hovered over her shoulder rather than actually touching her. The hostess, no doubt an understudy for Wagner's Brunhilda, seated them at a secluded table near the back, its locale made all the more intimate with its proximity to the kitchen. No one else was sitting anywhere near them.

Garret looked behind him to the swinging kitchen door, then at the Eva Braun look-alike holding the menus. "I'm not sure . . ."

"We're busy tonight," the hostess snapped, gesturing imperiously at the dozens of empty tables. "Take it or leave it."

Stunned as a deer in the headlights, Garret gulped and nodded. "Sure, sure, this is fine."

The hostess tossed down the menus. Garret tugged out Kat's chair, colliding with the swinging kitchen door when a plate-laden waiter hurried out to his customers.

Kat surveyed the distance between the

door and her chair and realized she'd get creamed every time an order came up. "Grab the other end of the table."

Garret gave Brunhilda a fleeting glance, but he helped Kat move the postage stamp–sized table into the clear. When Kat sat down, he stood for a moment in flustered confusion before easing himself into his chair.

A quick glance at the menu told Kat she wouldn't get anything as plain and simple as a plate of food in Ma Petit Aubergine. The chefs didn't cook, they presented, and every sauce listed included mysterious substances not actually intended for human consumption. She knew for a fact huitlacoche was a fungus that grew on corn plants, and why was a French restaurant throwing Central American mold into their capon crepes anyway?

As she searched the menu in vain for something edible, the restaurant door opened, a gust of outside air ruffling the vase of weedy wildflowers on their table. Kat caught the new arrival out of the corner of her eye, then did a double-take. From the neck down, the guy was a ringer for Mark. The same nicely muscled biceps and broad shoulders, slim hips that fit so nicely between her legs. But if everything below the Adam's apple was Mark's double image, everything above was a weird parody, complete with long Simon Legree mustache and black cowboy hat.

The waiter arrived, cutting off Kat's view of the strange male conglomerate. She ordered at random, hoping she hadn't selected deep-fried hippo schnozzes in a pomegranate reduction. She'd be so busy admiring Garret's glorious face, she'd never notice the drek on her plate.

Bereft of his menu, Garret sat with fingers locked in a strangler's grasp on the mauve linen, looking everywhere but at Kat. Finally, she risked the damp and covered his hand with hers. His heart-stopping green gaze zeroed in on her.

Damn, he's good-looking. His perfect face stunned her into momentary silence before she could muster speech. "Garret, I get the feeling you'd rather be anywhere than here."

"No, no," he squeaked, his appeal slipping another notch. "I've been looking forward to this." The busboy arrived with glasses of water and Garret slammed back the entire contents of his.

No wonder he sweated so much. All that water had to leak out somewhere. She gave his soggy hand a squeeze. "I have, too," she lied. "But you might want to relax a teensy bit."

This was exactly what she'd prayed for — a night with the dazzling Garret, shared in non-sleep-inducing silence. But the poor guy looked so pitiful, sitting there like a perspiration fountain.

"I never relax." He shook his elegant head sadly. "Not on a date. Oh, get me talking about work and I'm quite the conversationalist."

Kat's eyes crossed and her tongue suffered as she bit it. "Of course you are."

"But I'm a complete failure at social interaction." His chin hit his chest. "I go out with a woman and all that great conversation about living trusts and estate planning just flies out of my brain."

"Such a pity," Kat said in a suitably somber tone.

"The funny thing is . . ." He forced a garish grin. "Most women seem to think I'm kind of cute."

Cute wasn't even in the same universe as Garret's perfection. But, alas, there was no substance under the surface.

She patted his hand, the sensation akin to stroking a frog. At least his skin wasn't green. "You must have a hobby," she prompted.

A bit of a hullabaloo at the door distracted her again. Brunhilda waved her arms imperiously at Mark's doppelganger, objecting furiously to the hat, the black T-shirt, probably even the mustache. Kat strained to hear the man's voice, but the nasal twang wasn't the least bit familiar. A buzz in her ears reclaimed her focus.

"Zeppelins," Garret said.

She stared, sure she'd missed some crucial thread of the conversation. "Zeppelins."

"Model Zeppelins," he clarified. "I build them."

"Uh-huh." Kat hadn't a clue what he was talking about. Zeppelins were . . . what? An Italian squash? The spear used in pentathlon? Maybe it was some kind of ancient structure like the Coliseum. "Sounds like fun."

"Mine are strictly for display, not for racing." He laughed, his luscious mouth widening into a smile. "Some of the fellows in the ZUG are, well . . ." Leaning across the table, he whispered, "A little on the nutty side."

Kat blinked, resisting the impulse to guffaw. "Really."

With the hostess on his heels, the mustached pseudo-Mark finally took a seat two tables over. He raised his menu, concealing all but the black hat and the odd-looking brown eyes. When he should have been reading the menu, he kept his gaze fixed on Kat.

She glared in response, and Black Hat ducked behind the tall menu. Now that Garret was in familiar territory, he was regaling her with Zeppelin stories, telling her tales of "those crazy guys in the ZUG," which she finally figured out was the Zeppelin User's Group and not some kind of Brazilian tree beetle. Her eyes glazing over, Kat nodded whenever it seemed appropriate and pinched her leg through the skirt of her silk dress whenever lethargy threatened.

The sort-of-Mark clone provided the only diversion from Garret's droning. His cowboy-hatted head would lift over the top of his menu and that oddly colored brown gaze would sneak a peek at her. Every so often he would rub at his eyes, wiping them as if they watered.

Despite the leaky eyes, he was good-looking in a rough-edged way — not in Garret's class certainly, but passably decent. If he offered to buy her a coffee at Starbucks, she'd probably accept — after all, who passed up free java? She doubted

she'd go with him to check out his etch-
ings.

The Markish fellow got into a bit of a
tug-of-war with the waiter over the menu,
finally relinquishing it with a scowl. Now
his acute interest in her was obvious
without the menu to hide behind and the
guy was starting to give her the creeps.
Real stalker material.

She was about to heave her water glass
across the room at him when he suddenly
froze in the act of rubbing his left eye. He
pulled his hand away, then with a frantic
expression started a mad examination of
his table.

He paused, looked up at her, eyes wide.
With a shock, she realized his brown left
eye was now brilliant blue. Denham blue.

Damn. Damn, damn, damn, damn.

Mark scoured every square inch of the
puke-pink tablecloth, searching for the
brown contact lens he'd just popped out of
his eye. Across the room, Kat glared at
him, her baleful gaze penetrating his carefully crafted disguise. He could almost feel
his eyebrows and fake mustache singeing
under that infuriated glower.

The Adonis with her chattered on,
oblivious to the impending implosion. His

nattering trailed off when Kat pushed to her feet and made a beeline for Mark. The delectable pale pink silk dress she wore hugged every slim curve, made him itch to touch her. The thin fabric would be warm, permeated with Kat's scent.

She slammed her palms on the table, jolting him out of his musing. "What the hell are you doing here?"

There comes a time in every man's life when the gospel truth is more judicious than a lie. Face-to-face with an irate Kat was not one of those times. "Good to see you, too." He tried a smile, but the mustache's adhesive pinched.

That was nothing compared to the agony when she grabbed the stiff, itchy thing and ripped it off his upper lip. He yelped, felt for a bleeding gash he was sure was there. "Damn it, Kat!"

"You have no right!" Every head in the place swiveled toward her. She snatched out the chair opposite him and sat, the shifting silk of her dress diverting him momentarily from his pain. "You have no right to spy on me," she hissed.

"I'm not spying." He checked his hand. No blood, but he might never grow a natural mustache. "I'm having dinner."

She stabbed a finger at him. "You hate

French food. You hate foo-foo restaurants."

"Maybe I'm trying to broaden my horizons."

She flung the mustache across the table. "Why won't you leave me alone?"

"Because you don't want to be left alone!" He didn't realize he'd shouted the words until he saw every face turned toward them, including Pretty Boy. To hell with them all. "Because you want me."

She started to shake her head. Mark jumped to his feet, knocking his chair back. The table tipped perilously as he pushed past it to grab Kat's arm. He yanked her toward him. "You want me."

Then he kissed her.

Stop, her wussy, weak-willed mind murmured. Don't. Stop. Mark's tongue slipped inside her mouth and her body hummed. Don't stop.

She had a brief, fanciful notion that the glue from the fake mustache might permanently join them lip to lip. Another bout of tongue wrestling and she realized that would be an ideal scenario.

He pulled back finally, his mismatched eyes wild, the black hat askew on his head. She could see from the way his dark curls were mooshed on one side he'd have a serious case of hat hair when he took off his cowboy chapeau. But who the hell cared about that?

"Come home with me," he whispered.

Her libido had her nodding before her brain could muster so much as a protest. There was nothing right about this and everything wrong, but she was so damn tired of saying no.

A hand fell on her shoulder, one that wasn't attached to Mark's wrists. She turned to see the godlike Garret behind her, looking just a wee bit peeved. She supposed she owed him some kind of explanation.

"Sorry," she gasped out. "Have to go. Pressing business."

Mark tugged her out of Garret's reach. "Do you need to get your purse?"

"Got it right here." She lifted the business card–sized silk envelope.

He steered her toward the door. "What the hell can you keep in a purse that size?"

A condom, she thought, then decided discretion was the better part of valor. "Just cab fare home."

Once they'd exited into the cool night air, Mark put his arm around her, pulling her close to his side. His hat brim brushed the top of her head with each step. When they reached the corner, Mark shoved it off and dropped it in a trash can.

The walk sign flashed and they took one step off the curb before Mark yanked her back. He turned her toward him, hands on her shoulders, a lunatic with skewbald eyes. "We're going to my place."

"That was the plan."

"Okay, good." His eyes widened and his fingers tightened a bit. "To have sex."

"Always the romantic, Mark." At least he didn't say "screw" or that other word that rhymed with fire truck. "Yes, sex is in the program."

He nodded, but he still looked dazed and crazed. "And you won't change your mind halfway through."

She would have laughed if not for the exquisitely clear memory of what had happened at the cabin — her riding him on the lawn, screaming into orgasm. She grabbed his black T-shirt and pulled him closer. "This time we go the distance."

~ 14 ~

Norma loved dinners with her grandkids and usually the time flew by, six-year-old Travis and eight-year-old Brittany enthralling her with the details of their lives. She liked to indulge them, letting them pick whatever they wanted on their pizza, promising them ice cream after, dropping quarters in the big gumball machine so they could watch the sugary sphere wind its way down a spiral path to drop in their hands.

But tonight she couldn't sit still, couldn't focus on Travis's cheerful chatter or Brittany's big-sister wisdom. All she could think about was the clock and how close it crept toward eight.

"Grandma, are you listening?" Travis finally asked imperiously as they left Chuck E. Cheese's, his hands full of skeeball prizes.

She bent to give him a hug and a kiss. "Sorry, I was daydreaming." She stole a look at her watch. Seven-fifty-five. "Tell me again."

Travis chattered on, words streaming out a mile a minute, his conversation as energetic as his wiry six-year-old body. Norma met Brittany's gaze and her granddaughter gave her a very grown-up sigh and shrug of the shoulders. As Travis ran ahead to Norma's Geo, Brittany said with just the right touch of amused tolerance, "Boys are so weird."

Norma tried to hold back her impatience as she seat-belted her precious cargo in the backseat, then quickly got behind the wheel. Travis's rapid-fire monologue continued until Norma pulled onto the 520 freeway, then abruptly cut off when he zonked out as usual from the car ride. When Norma met her granddaughter's gaze in the rearview mirror, the little girl smiled and rolled her eyes.

In the ensuing silence, Norma's mind strayed again and again to Fritz, waiting for her at her house. It was well after eight. Would he wait for her? Maybe he'd figure she'd forgotten and he'd head back home. If he had a cell phone, she'd give him a call when she got to Lisa's, but Fritz seemed to be the one person in greater Seattle without a cell.

If he wasn't there when she got home, she'd call him at Kat's. Just to make sure everything was all right and to apologize for being late. She'd looked forward so much to seeing him tonight; it would be a big disappointment if he'd gone home, but she wouldn't let on . . .

"Grandma?" Brittany's sweet high voice snagged Norma from her frantic mental gyrations.

Norma headed north on the 405, glancing at Brittany in the rearview mirror. "Yes, sweetheart?"

"Do you have a boyfriend?"

Warning bumps rattled under her tires. Norma yanked her car back into the proper lane. "Oopsey. Did I wake up your brother?"

"Do you?" Brittany persisted.

"Grandmas don't have boyfriends."

"Why not?"

The exit for Lisa's house in Kirkland was just a half-mile ahead. She needed only a couple more minutes to stall and she could escape Brittany's third-degree.

"Because they don't, Brittany." She took the Eighty-fifth Street exit. "What made you ask such a crazy question, sweetheart?"

"Your face looked funny during dinner," Brittany said. "Like the goo-goo eyes Daddy makes at Mommy."

Goo-goo eyes. The way she felt about Fritz was so obvious even an eight-year-old could see it. Dear Lord, what if Fritz could see it?

Norma laughed, but it came out as a breathy titter. "That's quite an imagination you have, Brittany." She pulled into her daughter's driveway and jammed the Geo into park.

"But, Grandma —"

Before Brittany could finish another awkward question, Norma hopped out of the car. Lisa had come out onto the porch and held her arms out to Brittany as the little girl ran across the lawn. Travis woke from his nap cranky, clutching his Skeeball prizes as he slid from the backseat.

Norma was nearly bursting with eagerness to get back in her car and return home, but she couldn't just dump the grandkids and run. Travis's crossness saved her. He was so whiny and grumpy Lisa begged off inviting her mother inside, since she had her hands full placating her son.

Back in her car, Norma zipped across Lake Washington to Seattle, grateful the light traffic made the trip a quick one. It was twenty to nine by the time she pulled onto her street and she was absolutely certain Fritz wouldn't still be waiting. When she slowed to turn into the driveway of her darkened house, she saw only shadows on her wide front porch. But when the Geo's headlights strafed the porch, they illuminated a slight figure seated on the top step, hunched over something bulky cradled in his arms.

Fritz.

She was so overjoyed that he was still there, tears gathered in her eyes. Happiness flooded her, and she sat there a moment, trembling, struggling to get herself back under control.

Fritz rose, both hands clutching the handle of a battered suitcase. For a single, crazy instant, she thought maybe Kat had kicked him out of her condo and he was here to ask if he could stay. That only increased the fountaining excitement inside her.

He set aside the suitcase and started toward her as she climbed from the car. He stopped a decorous two feet from her and she had to fight back the urge to throw her arms around him.

She hooked her purse strap over her shoulder with shaky hands. "Sorry I'm late."

With the headlights off, Norma could

barely see Fritz's face. "If you're too tired —"

"No!" She put a tentative hand on his shoulder. He seemed too thin under the polo shirt he wore. "Come on inside."

Fritz retrieved his Louis Vuitton suitcase as they climbed the steps, and held it close to his side, wishing for the hundredth time he hadn't brought it at all. He'd seen Norma's curious glances at the shabby valise, the questions in her eyes, and the handles dug into his hand as if the case contained a two-ton boulder.

She smiled, but there was a strange edge to her voice when she asked, "Planning to move in?"

If God had any mercy at all, He'd strike him down with a lightning bolt right then and there. If He didn't, Fritz would probably die of mortification, anyway. He squirmed at the reminder of his deadbeat status, that he was virtually homeless, and if the suitcase didn't currently weigh more than a neutron star, he would have flung it across the lawn into the street.

She must have seen his anguish in his face because she let go of the keys in the front door lock and turned toward him. "What did I say?"

"Nothing. I'm sorry. I shouldn't have —"
He edged off toward the stairs.

She grabbed his arm and waited for him to face her. "Fritz . . ." Her voice trailed off to a whisper. "There isn't much that can distract me from my grandkids. But you . . ." She ran her hand lightly over his arm and the sensation jolted straight to his toes. "I've hardly been able to think about anything but you waiting here for me."

Okay, this was good. The way she touched him, the look in her sweet brown eyes, that wasn't exactly grandmotherly. A tiny speck of hope sparked inside him. The Louis Vuitton suitcase suddenly seemed lighter than a soap bubble, skipping along across the sky hand in hand with his heart.

He shook off the bizarre image. "Can we go in?"

She giggled, an endearing sound, and unlocked the door. Flipping on the porch light and entryway lamp, she stood aside to let him in. He shut the door, but still gripped the suitcase, still unsure of whether he should open it.

Her hand fluttered toward the vintage Louis Vuitton and he could see she was nervous. "So if that's not all your worldly goods, what is it?"

The gentle light of the entry softened the

lines of her face, made her smile, her hazel eyes, impossibly beautiful. Her generous curves filled out the gray sweater she wore, drew his gaze to the row of pearly gray buttons that ran from throat to waist. Suddenly the contents of his suitcase lost significance. If he didn't touch her, kiss her right now, he might just die from wanting.

"Norma . . ." Her eyes widened as he put down the suitcase. "I have to . . ."

His first step toward her, his toe caught in the tile of the entryway and he tripped, nearly stumbling into her. She grabbed his arms to steady him, then quickly let go. He felt like a clumsy idiot and had to fight the urge to turn tail and run.

But he was tired of giving up, tired of being such a coward. Norma was more important than his trivial fears. He would damn well touch her, caress her, kiss her, and if she didn't like it, she'd let him know, out loud or with her reaction, and he'd stop. But if he wimped out like he always did, he'd never know.

His palms curved around her face and her skin was so warm, so soft, it took his breath away. He was nearly eye level to her, just a smidge taller, just enough to have to tip her head back to kiss her. His few girlfriends had always been taller than he was and he'd always felt a little stupid leaning back to kiss them. Norma felt just right.

He'd given her plenty of time to pull away and she hadn't. He brushed his mouth lightly against hers, melted at the contact. She still stayed right where she was and so he kissed her again. This time he tasted her lipstick, a flavor he could only describe as pink, and the heat inside him burned a little hotter. Deciding he'd gone too far to retreat, he slipped just the tip of his tongue across her lower lip and nearly imploded when she opened her mouth.

Okay, this was good, really good. He dropped one hand to the small of her back and pressed her tightly against him. Despite the pounding in his ears, the racing of his heart, he was ready to let her go if she gave him the slightest indication she wanted to call it quits. But she wrapped her arms around him, holding him just as close.

Now the problem of his age came pretty clear. She was probably used to an older man with some self-control, who could take his time with a woman. But his body was on immediate overload, a thermonulear device about to reach crisis point. He was pretty sure if they took this kiss a whole lot further, he would completely embarrass himself.

He let himself taste her one more time, then relaxed his arms, not enough to let her go, but enough to get a safety zone between the monster between his legs and her sweet body. He saw the question in her eyes, the first trace of concern that maybe something was wrong.

"Not your fault." He gasped for breath. "Just a little . . . hair-trigger here."

When she understood what he was saying, she smiled, color rising in her face. "That was a pretty good kiss, then."

"You crazy woman." He shook his head. "That kiss was amazing. Phenomenal. A bigger explosion than the Death Star."

She giggled. "No explosion yet."

Now he felt his own face get hot. "Premature discharge is not what I had in mind with you."

She grabbed the collar of his polo shirt and tugged him closer. "We can always relight the fuse."

Could a guy die of arousal overload? His skin felt suddenly way too tight, especially south of the equator. When she brushed his mouth with hers he was ready to chuck circumspection and carry her off to the bedroom.

But in his periphery, he saw the suitcase sitting on the tiled entryway floor. Yeah, he could tell her what was in it after the fact, reveal his secrets later. But although he might be a loser, he had a conscience and, before they went any further, he wanted to make clear to her who he really was — and wasn't.

"Time-out, love." He took her hands, pressed a kiss into each palm. "I have something to tell you."

"Fritz, you don't have to —"

He put a finger against her lips. "Yeah, I do."

Retrieving the suitcase, he took her hand and led her to the living room sofa. The suitcase on the coffee table, Fritz's fingers trembled as he unzipped it. He pulled open the top, revealing rumpled wads of tissue paper.

Norma's brow furrowed. "What's in there?"

For the moment, Fritz sidestepped that question. "I'm not what you think I am." Admitting it didn't seem as hard as he thought it would be. "First, I'm dirt-poor."

She still looked confused. "I thought your father —"

"He kicked me out. Disowned me. Dis-avowed any knowledge." Fritz dragged in a breath. "Got tired of my million failures and cut off the trust fund."

Her hazel eyes flashed. "You're not a failure."

"Tell that to the twelve colleges and universities I flunked out of."

"Not everyone's cut out for college. My older daughter barely made it through two years. Now she runs her own business from home."

"The thing is, I don't seem to be cut out for anything." A weight settled in his stomach. "I've failed at every entry-level position within Denham. Made expensive mistakes, alienated co-workers, nearly set one of the test kitchens on fire."

"But you're doing great with Kandy for Kids."

"Mark and Kat are doing all the work. And Phil Roth is pulling the strings in the background." He held her hand between his. "Besides, Kandy for Kids is just a front. The real job is Mark and Kat, and I haven't done a damn thing right with them."

"You've done the best you could," Norma protested. "You've had some great ideas — the cabin, the concert. You've done everything to nudge them closer."

"Fat lot of good that's done." He felt

himself sinking into his usual funk over his misguided life and realized he was pretty sick and tired of being sick and tired. "Forget Kat and Mark. I have something to show you."

He reached for the Louis Vuitton bag, his stomach in knots. He still remembered his father's scorn when he'd finally worked up the nerve to reveal what he'd hidden so long. Norma didn't have a mean bone in her body and would probably try to conceal her disappointment in him. But even the slightest indication from her that the one little scrap of talent he thought he had was just as trivial as he suspected, he might just die on the spot.

"It's really just a hobby," Fritz warned her in a preemptive strike.

Pulling out the topmost clump of tissue paper, he carefully unwrapped it under Norma's interested gaze. He kept his own eyes on the precisely carved wooden train engine in his hand, terrified to see dismissal in her face. Her reaction — an Oh! of wonder, the enchanted smile he dared to take a peek at — filled him with undiluted joy.

"My God, Fritz, this is more than a hobby." She stretched tentative fingers toward the glossy painted wood toy. "Can I hold it?"

He passed the engine over to her. "There are four more cars and the caboose." He took another mass of tissue paper from the bag. "They hook together and make a clacking sound when you roll them. Put a little baby powder in the engine and it puffs out smoke."

Before long, he had the entire train set unwrapped and laid out on the table, the cars and caboose hitched to the engine. "I've been trying to figure out how to incorporate a windup mechanism in the engine, but I haven't quite got the details worked out."

Norma rolled the train across the table. "You carved these? Painted them?"

"Yeah." Warmth glowed inside him at her obvious admiration. "I did the engine first, after a few trial runs I had to trash. The caboose came last, so it's got the fewest mistakes."

"What mistakes? They're perfect."

"The black smeared a little on the engine's wheels." He pointed out a blot in the paint. "There's a gouge in the smokestack."

"That just shows it's handcrafted." She unhooked the caboose and turned it over in her hands, examining it. "Not turned out by a machine."

His father had seen every error, every flaw. But Norma saw only perfection. He struggled with an entirely unmanly urge to shed a few tears.

She set the caboose back with its mates. "What else do you have?"

He emptied them all from the suitcase — an elephant that shook its head from side to side as it rolled on its wheels, the carousel horse that rose and fell on its pole with the touch of a lever, the collection of garishly decorated tops that clattered and jingled as they spun. Norma oohed and aahed them all until he felt as puffed-up with pride as a rooster.

"You should have shown these to your father." She stroked the soft strands of leather of the carousel horse's mane. "Shown him how talented you are."

"He's . . . seen them." He could still picture his father's face when Fritz had opened up this bag, unwrapped the toys. The anger, the disappointment.

Norma's hazel eyes met his and her gaze roamed his face for a long quiet moment. Then her mouth tightened with determination. "Don't take this the wrong way, Fritz. But your father's a complete ass."

There they were, past nine in the evening in Norma's living room, but the sun rose right over Fritz's head. Angels sang, heaven opened and the weight of twenty-six years of being the one failure of his father's life vanished in an instant.

Tears stung his eyes and, although he felt a little foolish, he let them gather. "You are a miracle," he told Norma, then he pulled her into his arms.

Before long, the feel of her close to him brought him back to where they'd been in the entryway. Now that he had his secrets out of the way, he intended to follow through on an entirely new matter.

He kissed her cheek, inhaling her perfume. His mouth close to her ear, he whispered, "I want to take you to bed."

"Yes . . ." she sighed back.

They rose together and Norma led the way. He wasn't sure if he'd manage much more than a heated rush the first time, but he'd learned a few tricks in his twenty-six years he was pretty certain would prove satisfactory. And he had one advantage over an older guy — excellent recovery time.

In his nervousness, his elbow jostled her bedside lamp and it nearly toppled before he could catch it. But she just laughed, sounding jittery herself as she helped him right the lamp. She slipped out of her shoes, the simple act impossibly erotic. He kicked off his loafers, cringing a little when one crashed on her dresser. But she ignored whatever he might have broken, instead urging him toward the bed.

As he lay with her, the soft light golden on her face, his happiness was tempered by the failure of his matchmaking project. He sighed, guilt weighing on him.

"What?" she asked, her fingers toying with his hair.

Her touch made it hard to frame a response. "Kat and Mark."

She nodded, her thumb grazing his ear. "They should be perfect together."

"But they hate each other." Fritz ran his hand down Norma's arm, then fingered the bewitching line of tiny gray buttons. "Too bad."

"Yes . . ." She moaned as he kissed her throat, arched back as he released the top three buttons and dipped his fingers inside. Suddenly Fritz didn't give a damn about Kat or Mark or anything except the woman in his arms.

~ *15* ~

Mark burst through the door of the Denham estate's guest cottage, stumbling backward as he pulled Kat in after him. She kicked out behind her to slam the door shut, then continued to pull at his T-shirt, fumble with the button of his jeans, all the while driving him insane with her mouth and tongue. He'd nearly crashed his car on the way to Mercer Island, Kat's hands all over him, her tongue in his ear, her voice whispering all the things she wanted him to do to her.

Their awkward tango collided with an end table and he heard the sound of breaking glass as a lamp toppled. She had his T-shirt off one arm and bunched at his neck; he'd gotten the buttons of her silk dress undone, but probably half of them were scattered in the front seat of his BMW.

With a four-legged swoop around the living room sofa, Mark took the navigator's position and aimed Kat toward his bedroom. Her dress was bunched at her hips, the last button too stubborn to release from the buttonhole. Leaving the dress for the moment, he unhooked her strapless bra with an impatient jerk of his fingers, then stripped it from her. She yanked his T-shirt over his head, catching an ear, but he didn't give a damn about the momentary pain. With his T-shirt on the floor and her bra gone, he could finally hold her hot, satiny skin against him.

He nearly exploded from the feel of her breasts, nipples hard, her chest heaving. Her hands on his zipper didn't help matters and he would have pushed her clever fingers away, but she'd finally achieved her directive and had his jeans unzipped and sliding down his hips.

While she worked on his briefs, Mark sent the last button of her dress to its death on the bedroom carpet and the dress followed it to the floor. While ridding her of panty hose and panties, his hand tangled in one of the stretchy legs and she had to help him work it free. She still had one sandal strapped around her ankle and she broke the buckle clean off the strap in her effort to get it loose.

They fell to the bed, blessedly naked, and Mark shot straight to heaven with

Kat's soft, lithe body above him, straddling his. Something kept tickling him each time she bent to kiss him and at first he thought it was her hair trailing across his chest. But Kat's short-cropped hair barely brushed the tops of her ears, so whatever it was that kept dancing across his chest and belly, it wasn't hair.

The next time it skittered over his abs, he grabbed it. It took a moment to parse out the tiny square of satin, then he remembered Kat's ridiculously minuscule purse. The satin cord suspending it was still slung across her body.

He pulled it over her head, then made to toss it off the side of the bed. She stopped him, gasped out, "Just a sec."

Unsnapping the tiny purse, she retrieved a small foil packet from inside it. Mark's lust-riddled brain could still add two and two and come up with the requisite answer.

"You and that beef-brain —"

She put her hand over his mouth and his wounded male pride sank without a trace in a sea of erotic images — sucking on Kat's fingers, licking her palm, her wrist, the crook of her arm . . .

Then she ripped open the foil packet, and he didn't give a damn about what she might have thought she would do with the goon at the restaurant. Because she never would have. Never.

Her hands unrolling the condom over him punched the breath from his lungs and he thought he might die from the pleasure. But then she took him inside her and pleasure leapt into an entirely new universe. Her body arched back, her head tipped up, eyes closed. Then he reached for her, pulling her down, slender form pressed against him.

Through some miracle of self-discipline, he didn't come in the three seconds he'd feared he would. It helped that Kat just lay there at first, shuddering, breathing ragged. Then when he tilted his hips up at her, she matched the motion, so that each thrust brought him deeper.

He'd never made love to her in this bed, had bought a new one after their divorce. But Kat in his arms was exquisitely familiar, a paradise he thought he'd never again possess. He must have done something good — beyond good — to deserve this second chance.

The moment Kat came, her body pulsing around him, pulling him even deeper, a realization burst inside him in the scant second before his own climax. His mind didn't even have a chance to register the epiphany before his body took over, waves of sensation crashing over him and washing away everything that wasn't Kat's touch, Kat's scent, Kat's heat. In the aftermath, he was so addled, he wasn't sure which way was up, let alone what great insight had just crystallized in his brain.

It wasn't until later, as Kat fell asleep in his arms, her body half covering his, her soft breath curling against his face, that it hit home. He lay frozen for a moment, scared to death, his heart slamming against his chest. Bit by bit, he let the understanding creep inside his head.

He loved Kat. Thoroughly, completely, overwhelmingly. He loved his ex-wife, no doubt never stopped loving her. It just took these moments in bed, when everything had been wrenched away except his and Kat's essence, when only souls remained, that he let himself recognize the truth. He loved her.

And damned if he knew what he was going to do about it.

As dawn crept in through the plantation shutters in Mark's bedroom, Kat lay there with a goofy grin on her face, her body in a state of post-ecstatic bliss. Mark snored softly beside her, one arm covering her breasts, a leg pinning her to the bed. She felt sore in places she'd forgotten got sore after a bout of sex and scrumptiously sensitive in just about every square inch of her body.

During their marriage, she and Mark had pulled some all-nighters in the bedroom, but none of them compared to the last several hours. The weeks of temptation, her heightened awareness of him, the unavoidable proximity, all conspired to turn her into a sex-mad lovin' machine. She'd never come so often in such a compressed period of time, even in the heady first days of their marriage. She'd definitely achieved a personal best.

Would it be too pushy to wake him up for another go-round? She took a peek at the clock — nearly six-thirty. She dimly recalled an eight o'clock meeting with the CFO, but she could just blow it off. After all, she had a couple of years of restraint to compensate for. Surely, her chief financial officer would understand.

Before she did any ravishing, though, she'd better visit the bathroom and take care of the usual morning routine. She struck gold when she rifled through Mark's medicine cabinet, finding a toothbrush still in its packaging and a stash of condoms. They'd exhausted the supply from the nightstand drawer and would need re-inforcements if they were to continue their bedroom activities.

It crossed her mind to wonder who else Mark might have bought the condoms for, but imagining him with another woman hurt so badly, she pushed aside the image. She'd rather play ostrich and hide her head in the sand than contemplate something so painful.

Too nosy for her own good, she poked around in the cupboard under the sink and unearthed a dim memory. Hidden back in the corner was a jar of chocolate fudge sauce, its lid a bit dusty. She pulled it out and tried to unscrew it, but time and con-gealed fudge had glued the lid tight. This had been a honeymoon favorite, and she and Mark had found some imaginative places to smear it. She was tempted to bring it into the bedroom, but after two years of disuse, even chocolate turned. She shoved the jar back under the sink.

He was still asleep when she stepped from the bathroom. The light filtering in through the shutters turned him into a slumbering god, and she understood how Psyche must have felt seeing Cupid for the first time. An ache settled in her chest and for a moment she felt desolate. She wanted something, something she couldn't articulate, couldn't quite grasp. The closest she could come was an emotion she didn't want to let into her mind, not even for a heartbeat.

This had nothing to do with love. This was sex and heat and passion. Love was a damned slippery thing, fragile and insubstantial and impossible to trust. Her own parents had claimed to love each other once and look where they were now. She and Mark had thought they'd been in love, but it had only been a mistake.

She returned to the bathroom and replaced the condoms in the medicine chest. Then she quietly gathered her clothes, snagging Mark's T-shirt to cover the front of her buttonless dress. It smelled divine when she pulled it on over her head and she felt embraced by him. Plucking up the tiny purse with its house key and credit card, she hurried into the living room and made a quick call for a cab. With any luck, the Denhams wouldn't be up yet in the main house and she could escape unnoticed.

She couldn't resist — she took one last look at Mark before she left. Still deeply asleep, his subconscious seemed to notice she was gone because he groped for her, his hand moving across the sheet. Kat jumped back out of sight before he woke.

Barefoot and bare-legged, she ran up the Denhams' driveway and out to the street. It must have been a slow morning because the cab came quickly and she was gone before Ian or Mary Denham came out for their paper. The cabbie didn't comment on her eclectic attire, just asked for the address and drove on without comment.

The throbbing in her chest persisted as they crossed Mercer Island's floating bridge toward Seattle. Inexplicably, she felt close to tears. Maybe she should have just stayed until Mark woke, faced him, faced her feelings.

But then she might have found out something she didn't want to know. And damn her cowardly heart, she just couldn't bring herself to face the truth.

As full morning beamed through her lacy bedroom curtains, Norma stretched in her bed, wiggling her toes against the warm sheets. Next to her, Fritz was a one-man heat source, his slender body giving off waves of toasty comfort. He had his back to her, but she sensed he was awake and worry niggled at her that he had a mean case of the morning-after regrets.

Then he rolled over to face her, his face serious, his blue gaze shuttered. Now her heart really squeezed tight and for a moment Norma couldn't breathe. When he raised his hand to rest on her cheek, she thought she'd scream from the tension.

"Norma . . ." He stroked her cheek with his thumb. "This isn't just one night for me."

The hold on her heart eased. "Not for me, either."

"I . . ." He took a breath, and his shoulders rose and fell. "I . . ." He shook his head, shut his eyes. When he opened them again, they were clear as a sweet summer sky. "I love you."

"Oh . . ." English might as well have been a foreign tongue because she couldn't frame a sentence to save her life. "Oh . . ."

"You don't have to say it back." His throat worked as he swallowed. "You don't even have to feel —"

"I love you, too, Fritz."

Now he lay there in stunned silence. She would have laughed at his startled expression if she wasn't afraid he'd take it the wrong way.

Instead she smiled and rubbed her palm

across his cheek, rough with a morning beard. "It's crazy and nutty and probably entirely inappropriate. I'm more than twenty years older."

"That doesn't matter."

"It does," she told him, making sure she saw understanding in his eyes. "It matters because I'm not having any more children and you might want them. Because when you're my age, I'll be ready to retire. And even though women live longer than men, you'll probably have to say good-bye to me first."

"I love you, Norma." He said it with the fervency of youth.

"It matters," she said again. "But it doesn't change a thing. All the logic in the world won't stop my heart from feeling what it feels."

His smooth, unlined brow furrowed. "So you're not —"

"I'm not."

"But you are —"

"I am."

She saw the wheels turning in his head. "Just to get this clear," he said. "I love you, you love me. We're going to get married, hang out together, and live until we're both old and decrepit."

She laughed. "I hadn't thought as far

as marriage yet."

"Be prepared, I always say." He eased her back onto the bed, at the same time reaching for the small box on the nightstand. After an imaginative first round last night, he'd hotfooted it out to the local drugstore for enough supplies for the rest of the evening's activities. She might be forty-eight, but her ever-hopeful body was still launching those eggs.

After the long, busy hours of the night, their morning lovemaking was a quieter, more leisurely affair, but still extremely satisfactory. Fritz was the kind of lover her husband had never been — patient, inventive, eager to try new things. She felt absolutely spoiled.

As they snuggled together in the afterglow, Norma's thoughts drifted as she half-dozed in Fritz's arms. One interesting idea popped up and roused her awake.

"Your toys," she said, an image coalescing in her mind. "My grandkids would adore them. Fight over them probably."

Fritz went up on one elbow. "I'd love for them to have them. I can make more."

She put a gentle finger on his lips. "That's not where I was going. Your train, the cars . . . what if they were all filled with chocolates? What if you tied a cellophane bag of mint melties around the elephant's neck?"

"The carousel horse could pull a cart heaped with candy." Enthusiasm sparked in his bright blue eyes. "How about a puzzle box with candy hidden inside?"

"That would be marvelous." Taking his hand, she pressed a kiss to it. "You could make a bundle with these toys."

"But I can't build them fast enough. That's always been the problem." A trace of doubt flickered in his face. "Sometimes it takes me a week to carve and paint one toy. I couldn't possibly make enough to make the time worthwhile."

"Let's think this through." She gave his hand a squeeze. "What do you like best about making the toys — actually carving them or the design?"

He brushed her fingers back and forth across his lips. "It's fun enough to carve them, but I have to admit after I do one, I don't particularly want to do another just like it. That's why all my samples are different."

"Then you design and make the proto-types." Excitement built inside her. "Turn them over to a manufacturer to mass-produce them."

"I could do that. I could absolutely do

that." He slapped his forehead with the heel of his hand. "Why didn't I ever think of that?"

She planted a kiss on his nose. "Because you didn't have me."

"You are brilliant!" He pulled her into his arms for a breath-stealing hug, then lay back, the light of inspiration flaring in his face. "I could make that spider toy I've been wanting to do. And the cow . . . I could never quite work out the mechanism."

"Roth would jump at the chance for a product like this. Or Denham."

"They can do it together after the merger." He scooted from the bed, then came around to her side. "I'm starving. Let's get breakfast."

As Norma let him pull her up, she took a peek at the bedside clock. "Half past eight. Oh my heavens, I have to get to work." She raced for the bathroom, calling over her shoulder, "We'll get breakfast on the way!"

She heard his laughter through the door. Other than when her children and grandchildren had been born, she'd never in her life been happier.

Kat leaned a bit sideways at her desk, her neck cricked way to the right, and took another look through her open office door at Norma's empty chair. In the four years Norma had been working with her, she had never once been late. In fact, other than vacations, Norma had never been missing from that chair when Kat had counted on her to be there. Yet this morning, when Kat returned from her abbreviated but still depressing meeting with the CFO, with the clock ticking away toward 9:30, Norma still hadn't appeared.

Just as worrisome was Fritz's conspicuous absence from the condo when she'd arrived there after her flight from Mark's. She'd fully expected to have to dodge Fritz's curious inquisition as to her whereabouts last night and had ready a whole storehouse of clever evasions to sidetrack him, but her ex-cousin-in-law must have already left for the morning.

With her luck, Fritz would probably give her father a full report about how she'd stayed out all night and she'd have to try those clever evasions on a much harder audience — Phil Roth. She was thirty-two years old and hadn't had to ask her father for permission for a sleepover for fifteen years, but she still didn't relish his third-degree about why she didn't sleep in her own bed.

Was that the elevator bell? She leaned over even farther, the arm of her chair digging into her side, her aching legs reminding her that she'd done things last night that should only be done by gymnasts and contortionists. She'd just caught a glimpse of Norma stepping from the elevator when her chair wheels slid out from under her. She caught herself before taking a complete nosedive, whacking her elbow on her desk before gaining her feet. When the phone bleated she grabbed it savagely, in a mood to tear apart whoever it was on the other end.

"You left," Mark said in a gravelly, grumpy bear voice.

"I had a meeting." It wasn't even a lie.

"I overslept." He yawned, the loudest inarticulate noise known to man. "Should have woke me up."

"Sorry." Lord, she wanted so much to be back in his bed. "I had a meeting."

"Still having lunch?" Another ear-blasting yawn. "Thai place?"

"Yes." As she reached for her Palm to confirm, she saw the while-you-were-out note from Tess underneath it. "Can we meet at one? C.M. update." "Damn. Can't make lunch after all."

She pictured him stretching every lean,

luscious inch. "Dinner then."

She didn't even bother checking her calendar. If she had a conflict, she'd cancel. "Dinner would be perfect."

He hung up and she had a ridiculous urge to kiss the phone. Three hours ago, she'd run for her life. Yet she'd just blithely made dinner plans with him.

Why not? She was young and hungry; it was time she satisfied her appetite. It didn't have to mean anything.

When Norma hurried into her office a moment later, her usually impeccable hair looked slightly mussed, her color was high and her earrings didn't match. Even more peculiar, she couldn't seem to stop smiling.

"Everything okay?" Kat asked.

"Fantastic." Norma giggled, then her gaze narrowed on Kat's neck. "What did you do to yourself?"

Kat's hand flew up to check. The spot was tender and now she remembered Mark's beard rasping her there. "Allergic reaction."

"Uh-huh." Norma's fingers touched the side of her own neck, her expression thoughtful. Then shock seemed to set in. "Oh, no!"

"What?"

"Tell me it wasn't him."

"Him who?"

"Him," Norma answered without clarifying. "The one you went out with last night."

"Garret? Wait a minute, how did you know I went out last night?"

"Because . . . because . . ." Norma stared at her, a deer caught in the headlights, then insight lit her face. "Oh!"

"Oh, what?"

Norma clasped her hands in thankful prayer. "It wasn't him who gave you beard burn."

"Him . . . who . . . Garret?" The sense of Norma's bizarre statement sank in. "No! Yuck. That would have been . . ." She wrinkled her nose, remembering the gorgeous but slick-with-sweat face. ". . . icky."

Norma let out a whew of relief. "Of course not. Because it was . . . he did call, didn't he?"

"Who called? Norma, you're not making a lick of sense."

Her assistant smiled brightly, her attractive face now stunningly beautiful. Did she have a makeover? "Never mind. I have it all figured out now." She nearly skipped out of Kat's office.

Kat rubbed at her eyes, lack of sleep sitting like an evil elf on her shoulder. "Good. At least one of us has."

Kat's phone caroled, the bleating pattern telling her it was an internal call. Effing fabulous. It was probably her father calling to noodge her about where she'd spent the night.

She grabbed up the phone and said sweetly, "Hello, Dad."

A pause, then, "Kat. Hey, sweetheart. Have a good time last night?"

For a thunderstruck moment, Kat thought her father was asking about her mattress athletics with Mark. Then she remembered Garret. "Does everyone on the planet know I went on a date?"

"Garret called to ask if you like nouveau French. I told him McDonald's was more your style."

"At least Micky D's doesn't put corn fungus on their burgers."

"He dragged you to the French place anyway, didn't he?" Her father chuckled. "We've scheduled a Kandy for Kids status meeting with the Denhams tonight at Papa Gianni's. Are you free?"

"Yes. No." Remembering Mark, she allowed a few X-rated images to dance in her head. "Already have plans."

"Sweetie, you're not dropping the ball

on the Kandy for Kids project, are you?"

"I've got the ball firmly in my glove," she reassured him, although she hadn't a clue what game they were playing.

"The concert alone brought in over a hundred thou. We've got high hopes for the black-and-white ball."

"Me, too, Dad. Even higher hopes."

A moment of mutual silence in honor of their high hopes, then she heard her father's heavy sigh. "Sometimes, sweetheart, I wish I could have made things different for you."

Kat scrunched her brow, completely befuddled. "Kandy for Kids?"

"Your mom and me. Wish we could have found a way . . . but we always made better friends than lovers."

Kat's stomach tightened and she wanted to rewind the last few seconds. "Dad, this isn't really —"

"We knew it couldn't work between us. But you . . . you were so little. And we hurt you so much."

Her heart thundered in her chest. She didn't want to hear any more, had to stop the words, shut them out. Besides, she dealt with this a long time ago with the therapist, child of a broken home, yada yada yada.

"Geez, Dad, feeling pretty maudlin this

morning, are we?" She forced a laugh. "You and Patti have a fight?"

Silence ticked away. "I just worry about you, baby."

Eyes squeezed shut, she grit her teeth against the pain. "I'm fine, Dad. Completely, totally fine. It wasn't that big a deal." Another false laugh. "Besides, look what it got me — two extra parents to spoil me."

"We all love you, sweetheart."

And love hurt. That was the damn bottom line. She forced her thoughts in another direction. "Hey, what did you think of the Chocolate Magic report?"

He hesitated before answering. "The report . . ."

More unease bubbled up inside Kat. "You got your copy from Tess, didn't you?"

"Of course. Read it top to bottom. Very exciting."

"I'm wondering if we could put the merger on hold for now. See if we can scare up additional capital on the strength of Chocolate Magic's potential."

"Not a good plan, Kat. We're still in the same fix. Chocolate Magic isn't a cure-all."

"But if it can turn the sales picture around . . ."

"Let's just cover our bases, sweetheart. The merger . . . won't happen tomorrow."

"Right. There's still time. Hey, if you reschedule the Kandy for Kids thing for tomorrow night, count me in."

"Great. I'll see if I can get hold of the Denhams."

The I-love-yous and good-byes finished, Kat hung up the phone. Troubled by what her father wasn't telling her, she tried to parse out the meaning between the lines. Likely it was just his worry over Roth's bleak financial picture.

Which she couldn't do a damn thing about for the moment. Chocolate Magic might have a few kinks to work out, but Kat was bone-deep certain it would be the huge success she wanted it to be. The project just needed a little more time.

Just like Scarlett, she'd worry about that tomorrow. Today, she had the evening's entertainment with Mark to anticipate. That would soften any hard edges the day threw at her.

Sex with her ex-husband. What a brilliant idea. No muss, no fuss, no commitments. Just an enjoyable romp in bed.

But why Mark? a little inward voice had the temerity to query.

Because, she told herself, he's there. He's handy.

Then why not gorgeous Garret? Or the pediatrician? Or that muscle-bound guy from the gym? They were handy.

But Mark . . . Mark's familiar.

Nothing familiar in that little variation at two a.m.

He knows what I like.

But I thought you didn't trust him.

"I don't have to trust him to have sex with him."

She didn't realize she'd said it out loud until Norma poked her head in the door. "Were you talking to me?"

Now Kat felt like that antlered woodland creature staring down an oncoming car. "Just thinking out loud."

Kat didn't like that smug look on Norma's face before she returned to her own desk. It didn't help that the little voice in her head had had that same smug tone when it sneered, Yeah, right.

~ *16* ~

At 4:10 that afternoon, Fritz fidgeted beside Phil Roth's desk, torn by competing emotions. His new joy over recent events with Norma urged him to jig a fancy two-step across Phil's Berber carpet. His constant companion, doubt, nagged at him to run away and hide before disaster revisited and pointed its finger of blame at him.

But despite the current lack of progress in the Kat and Mark campaign, Fritz felt certain the Roth-Denham merger was exactly the right thing to do. It might not affect Kat's feelings toward Mark in the short term, but surely given time, Kat would realize she and Mark were meant for each other.

Just as he and Norma were a perfect match. His doubts on that score had vanished somewhere in the night in Norma's arms.

Fingers drumming on his desk, Phil stared at his phone as if he could will it to ring. His gaze would occasionally stray to the thick manila envelope on his desk and he'd stop his drumming to square the envelope on his blotter. When the phone finally bleated, Phil jumped, then snatched up the receiver.

"Send them in," he barked, then dropped the phone back on its base.

Excitement and alarm burst inside Fritz in equal measure as Ian and Mary Denham stepped inside Phil's office. They seemed just as edgy as Phil, although Mary smiled at Fritz reassuringly.

Phil lifted the envelope from his desk and held it out to Ian. "This is all of it. The Chocolate Magic formula, every report from day one to the most recent, including an addendum added just this afternoon."

About to take the packet, Ian hesitated. "You're sure about this, Phil? The merger isn't a done deal. It might be premature to reveal proprietary information."

Phil dropped the thick envelope into Ian's hands. "To tell you the truth, this merger is long overdue. And the contents of that envelope will boost Roth's value, so it's vital all the principals see it."

"I agree," Ian said. "Roth and Denham have pretty much been family for so long, it's time to make it official."

Mary pinned Fritz with her steady blue gaze. "You really think this will help with Mark and Kat?"

Doubt poked its ugly nose out, but Fritz shoved it aside. "Once Kat gets used to the idea, she'll come to her senses about Mark." He figured if he said it with enough conviction, it would make it true.

Mary gestured toward the envelope. "Mark will want to see a copy of this."

"Absolutely," Phil said. "But for his eyes only. It might be best not to take it back to the office."

Ian nodded. "I'll leave it for him at the cottage. He'll see it when he gets home tonight."

The Denhams left and Fritz was feeling pretty pleased with himself at the way everything was turning out. With the Roth-Denham merger in progress and the potential for a Kat-Mark reunion in place, he'd done a good day's work. And he had tonight to look forward to, when he and Norma would be together again. Life was good.

Damn, life is good.

Turned to face Kat who sat beside him in a vinyl booth at Lulu's Diner, Mark offered her another bite of banana split and watched her lap it from the spoon. Chocolate syrup smeared the corner of her mouth and whipped cream dotted the tip of her nose. He wiped away the dot of cream with his finger, sucking it clean. His tongue licked away the chocolate on its way into her mouth.

The kiss tasted of chocolate and cherry, with hints of pineapple and strawberry. He felt so hot, he thought he heard the ice cream sizzle, and when he drew back he was surprised to find it still frozen in her dish. Still hard. Just like he was.

They'd been on their way to the Thai place when they passed by Lulu's with its retro fifties look, all chrome and glass, its giant neon sign flashing red and yellow. Kat had a sudden compulsion for a banana split; to hell with dinner, she wanted ice cream first. Who was he to tell her no?

So now they sat wedged into the booth together, Mark with his back to the diner, Kat facing him, doing her best to drive him wild. She'd started by spooning him bits of banana, telling him she couldn't wait to eat his, then when he fed her, she moaned with each morsel he slipped into her mouth. If anyone else in the diner was watching, they were getting a hell of a show.

She nudged aside the half-eaten banana split and rested her hand lightly on his knee. With slow strokes, her hand moved to the top of his thigh, then down again. On a leisurely journey back up his thigh, she ran her finger along the seam of his slacks, hesitating at his crotch before meandering down to his knee. Then her trailing fingertip continued back up, to his crotch again, up his fly, over the hard ridge of flesh.

"Okay," he gasped. "You've got my attention."

She leaned close enough that her breath curled against his ear. "I want you inside me." Her hand tightened on him. "Now."

"Oh, dear Lord," he squeezed out, then decided a counterattack was in order. He wrapped his hands around her upper thighs, his thumbs meeting near their juncture. Turning his head, he whispered in her ear, "I can make you come. Right here. Right now."

Her hands retreated from his crotch, pushed against his chest. "Out, out." When he didn't move quick enough, she shoved so hard he nearly fell over backwards. She extricated herself from the booth, then slapped a twenty on the table and shooed him outside.

They made it as far as her Camry, conveniently parked in a secluded corner of the downtown parking structure. With headlights occasionally strafing the car windows, he stripped down her panty hose and put his mouth where his thumbs had been. It took all of twenty seconds before she climaxed, screaming.

Barely recovered, she fumbled for his zipper with one hand, pushed her panty hose off her ankles with the other. Grabbing his hips, she urged him to her.

"No protection," he gasped, then the breath left his lungs when she put her mouth on him. He broke a land speed record as he came, the windows of the Camry rattling with his roar.

He pulled her up and held her, her body a sweet weight against his. When she drew back to look up at him, her mouth curled like a Cheshire cat's, her cheeks flushed with her heat. God, he loved her.

He almost said it out loud, might have if she hadn't shifted to pull her skirt back into place and wad up her panty hose. Her fingertip grazed his cheek, her gaze dreamy. "Part deux at your place?"

"Yeah. Sure."

Once he was decent, they climbed out of the car in unison, then into the front. As she started the engine and pulled out of the parking slot, a strange dissatisfaction nibbled away at him. He'd just had some of the most incredible sex of his life, should be crowing his triumph, but something was missing. A piece had fallen out of place.

They had the rest of the night. Maybe in the dark hours, with Kat sleeping in his arms, he'd find a way to finish the puzzle.

Her body still shuddering from her last climax, Kat lay in Mark's bed, waiting for him to return from the bathroom. The only light in the room came from the glow of the usual electronics — the bedside clock, the DVD player, the recharger on the laptop sitting on the corner desk. Peering at the clock, she watched the time blip over to 2:35.

Light spilled from the bathroom as the door opened, then extinguished when Mark flipped it off. She could barely see the lines of his tall frame — the broad shoulders, narrow hips, long legs. As if they hadn't just had four rounds of sex already, her heart hammered faster, her body at attention. Not even when they'd been married had she been so hungry for him.

He lay beside her and immediately pulled her into his arms, hugging her tightly for several seconds before relaxing.

He settled her against him, from shoulder to thigh. His breathing slowed almost immediately.

The rat was about to fall asleep. Here she was, raring for round five and he was halfway to unconsciousness.

She drew her hand along his side down to his hip, his tight rear end, then around to the business end of things. When she wrapped her hand around him, his flesh stirred halfheartedly. A snore in her ear told her the rest of him was asleep.

And here she lay, jazzed-up and wide-awake, ready for action. It had been this way sometimes during their marriage — sex put him to sleep but stimulated her into full alert. Back then he didn't mind if she woke him up for one more time, but maybe she'd gotten all she was going to get tonight. She'd let him snore.

It felt pretty luscious lying there with him, his heat coming off him in waves, his arm heavy across her body. Even his snoring, which used to prompt her to give him a good hard nudge with her feet, seemed to soothe with its familiarity.

This had always been the good part of their marriage. They'd yell and shout and fight, angry at the smallest, stupidest things, but if they could just make their way into bed, all the problems seemed to resolve. It wasn't any way to run a marriage, but the times in bed made the rest of it tolerable.

She should have walked out with the first fight one month in. She should have listened to that little voice in her head, the one she so despised, when it told her people who fought as much as she and Mark did couldn't stay together. She'd witnessed her parents' conflicts, had seen them cling to their contentious marriage for seven long years out of deference to Kat. As much pain as their parting inflicted, their battles hurt Kat even worse.

But now Kat had the perfect solution. She'd separate out the good part of her marriage to Mark — the sex — and enjoy that without the commitment that had caused them both so much grief. Certainly Mark wasn't looking for anything more than a roll in the hay; this physical-only relationship would probably suit him just fine.

She ought to be feeling a little cheerier about this modest proposal of hers. All the sex she wanted, no pesky strings, no more dead-end dating. Their parents would be thrilled at the apparent reunion of their progeny and so preoccupied with drawing up guest lists for *Mark and Kat — The*

Remarriage, they'd quit with the match-making. Then when the sexual glow vanished between her and Mark, as it surely would, they'd say their good-byes, the last of the sensual spark stamped out forever.

Kat went up on one elbow and tried to judge just how deeply asleep Mark was. If she made another foray down to that little friend lying soft and relaxed against Mark's leg, would he wake up? It had been a good fifteen minutes since he slipped off to dreamland; surely that was enough of a nap to recharge the sexual batteries.

Before she could make a move, he growled out another snore and turned over, presenting his back to her. He scooted back into her warmth, but it was pretty obvious Mark wasn't in a mood to play.

With a sigh, Kat eased herself away from him and out of bed. If she couldn't get any action here, she'd go raid Mark's kitchen. A banana split didn't make much of a dinner.

Grabbing Mark's DKNY dress shirt from the corner where he'd thrown it, she pulled the still-buttoned shirt over her head. The kitchen light switched on, she opened the fridge and made a quick scan of its contents, shivering against the cold. A few cartons of Chinese sat beside a jug of expired milk. A grease-spotted cardboard pizza box took up the entire shelf below. The apples in the crisper drawer were as wrinkled and wizened as the ones in Kat's refrigerator, although she didn't have the sadly wilting head of lettuce rolling around beside them.

Grabbing the least aged apple, she gave it a spit bath in the sink and padded out to the cottage's cozy living room. A small dining table was set up at the end nearest the kitchen, its surface littered with unopened junk mail and back copies of the *Post-Intelligencer*.

On the one cleared space on the table sat a fat manila envelope. Munching her apple, Kat sidled over to take a look at the most interesting bit of flotsam on Mark's table. The illumination from the kitchen wasn't quite enough to make out the handwritten note in the corner, so she picked up the envelope and tilted it toward the light.

"Mark, Read ASAP, then call me. — Dad."

This was none of her business. This was obviously proprietary to Denham and she had no right to nose around. Her burning curiosity over what might be inside was no justification for invading Mark's privacy.

Besides, the flap was sealed with clear packing tape. No way to check out the contents without tearing the envelope open. Steaming probably wouldn't release the adhesive on the tape. If she peeled it off carefully then replaced it with a new piece, she might be able to sneak a peek then hide her tracks, but it really wouldn't be —

"Kat?"

Mark's sleepy voice from the kitchen jolted the packet from her hands. She repositioned it back where it had been on the dining table before he stepped through the kitchen doorway.

She gestured with the apple. "I was hungry."

He smiled, the curve of his mouth sweet and boyish, the jut of his erection anything but. "Come to bed."

He moved closer, pulling her into his arms. His kiss went from warm to scorching in seconds flat. The apple slid from her fingers and the envelope from her conscious mind as he carried her back to bed, her legs wrapped tightly around him.

It took Mark a week to open the packet from his father. A week filled with so much sex, he thought his nerve endings

351

would explode, leaving him in some kind of mindless nirvana. There wasn't a free moment he and Kat didn't fill with one adventurous experiment or another — intimate lunchtime interludes, pre-dinner bedroom bops, late-night risqué rendezvous.

The day they'd tested two-man kayaks at the paddlesports store had been a mind-blower all by itself. He'd lost count of the number of hours' sleep he'd forsaken, but by day six, Mark calculated they might have beat their record number of sexual encounters set on their weekend honeymoon.

It wasn't until this morning he finally got his head reseated well enough to notice the fat manila envelope buried by the week's mail. Kat had an early meeting and without her to wake him for another round of sex he'd overslept. He was nearly out the door when he caught sight of the thick manila packet.

He had to grab it and go and so didn't open the envelope until he'd arrived at the office. He took one quick look at the contents and his father's cover letter and saw red. His blood pressure rising as he stabbed out his dad's extension, he all but ordered his father to his office.

His mother came as backup. Behind his desk, Mark glared at them both, so pissed he could barely sit still. "Whose idiot idea was this?"

His parents exchanged a quick look, then his father 'fessed up. "Fritz."

"But we all agreed," his mother quickly added.

Snatching up the manila envelope, Mark thrust it at his parents. "This is industrial piracy. You've stolen propriety information."

His mother's eyes widened in shock. "We did no such thing. Phil Roth gave it to us willingly."

Mark dropped the envelope again. "To bolster Roth's value for the merger." He shook his head at his parents' lunacy. "Kat will go beyond ballistic when she hears about this. It's a damn good thing the paperwork isn't finalized yet."

"The deal is going through," his father said.

"It won't once Kat finds out it's in the works," Mark told him.

His mother pitched in her two cents. "She won't know until it's over."

"Oh, but she will," Mark told his mother emphatically. "Because I'm going to tell her."

His father crossed his arms and narrowed his eyes, the same steely blue gaze that used to scare the crap out of Mark. "I don't think that would be a good idea, son."

But Mark wasn't fourteen anymore and was pretty much immune to his father's disapproval. "I'm telling her. The moment you leave."

Another glance exchanged between his parents, but Mark had lost his patience for subterfuge and intrigue. "I do have work to do."

His mother put a hand on his arm. "Give us a chance to speak to the Roths first."

Mark might be able to stand up to his father, but he never could say no to his mother. "I'm seeing Kat tonight. You have until then."

His mother zeroed in on what she no doubt considered the most crucial bit of information. "You're seeing Kat?"

Yeah, I'm boffing her on a regular basis now. "The chocolate tasting, remember? Kandy for Kids fund-raiser?"

"Of course." She bent to give him a peck on the cheek, then mercifully they left. Leaving him to drop his head in his hands and contemplate the mess his life had devolved into.

He ought to be ecstatic. He ought to be executing handsprings and back flips across his office — figurative ones anyway, since the real deal would send him to the chiropractor. He was getting all the sex he could possibly want with the one woman who could pleasure him like no other and yet . . .

And yet he was miserable. Okay, not miserable in the midst of that great, wild sex. During those moments, he was absolutely with the program, completely focused on the task at hand. Kat would send him to heaven and he'd do his level best to do the same for her.

It was only afterward, when Kat left his bed, that the misery started eating at him. He loved her. He wanted her in his life, not just in his bed. He wanted to marry her, have children with her, enjoy forever with her. He wanted it all.

But he knew with a bone-deep certainty that Kat wanted none of that. She never let a word slip that touched beneath the surface, never let so much as a gesture expose what might be going on behind that hot-as-fire-but-distant-as-Pluto façade of hers. As much as he might wish and hope and ache for it, there wasn't a prayer that Kat felt for him even an iota of what he felt for her.

What was wrong with him, anyway? His parents made it look so easy. Fall in love, marry your beloved, live happily ever after. Never fight, never argue, never a word of opposition. Just smooth sailing from day one to what would soon be their thirty-eighth anniversary. That's the way it should have been with him and Kat.

But there was a defect in his character, a failing he couldn't pinpoint. Bliss had become bedlam in his marriage, the perfect harmony in bed impossible to match in their lives outside the bedroom. What he'd thought was love had obviously only been lust.

Maybe he was only fooling himself. He thought this was love pounding inside him, setting off the ache in his heart, stealing whatever sleep he could manage between bouts of sex. But maybe in reality it was just lust in a pretty package, his own guilt suggesting he felt something he didn't really feel. Didn't really understand.

Shoving aside the Chocolate Magic report, he pulled the latest Kandy for Kids spreadsheet toward him. So far, the program had been a smashing success and a boon for Denham's sales. The benefit concert had raised three-quarter-million between ticket sales and related donations, the kayak race was on track to generate another half-million in sponsorships, and the chocolate tasting tonight was long sold-out. Kandy for Kids might have seemed a goofy idea at the outset, but the money they'd raised would do a tremendous amount of good for the targeted child-centered nonprofits.

Line one on his phone flashed, then glowed a solid red as Rod picked up the phone. Even before Rod rang it through, Mark knew it was Kat. His body jolted to full alert, ready for another go between the sheets.

Her voice was throaty and sexy and melted over him like warmed honey. "Hey, hot stuff. Are you free for lunch?"

Yes jumped to the forefront of his mind, but then his gaze fell on the Chocolate Magic report. He'd promised his parents until the end of the day. To share his bed with her while keeping quiet about the upcoming merger seemed slimy and monstrous. He couldn't do it.

He checked his Palm and realized he had a valid excuse. "Damn, Kat. I have to attend a retirement lunch today."

"Oh," she sighed, the sound brushing

the hair on the back of his neck. "Then you'll have to wait to see what I bought at the Naughty Girl store."

Completely unfair. Now he'd spend the rest of the day hard as a brick. "Pick you up at seven?"

"Make it six. I might need help zipping up."

Erotic images cascaded through his mind. "What about Fritz?"

"Fritz seems to have moved out. All his things are gone."

Mark didn't like the idea of his cousin MIA. "Where's he staying?"

"Not sure," Kat said thoughtfully. "But Norma seems to be smiling more than usual."

He ought to be smiling, too, would be once he got past this funk. If he could either convince Kat she loved him or himself that he didn't love her. "Six, then."

"Sex at six." She laughed, the sound sending fingers of sensation up his spine. "Bye." She hung up and Mark dropped his phone back onto the cradle.

There wouldn't be any sex at six, not after Mark dropped the bomb about the merger. Just how pissed Kat would be and how much she would blame the course of events on him would determine whether there would ever be sex again, at six or any other time.

It might not even matter if she decided he was the evil instigator of the merger plot. They already toted an entire matched set of Gucci baggage with them whenever they climbed into bed. The old news, ancient wounds never had been resolved. They'd simply made a tacit, unspoken agreement that they didn't need to clear the air to roll around in bed.

It was every man's dream — sex without commitment or strings. All the pleasure and none of the pain. But why the hell did it hurt so much?

~ *17* ~

The slinky little dress in chocolate brown lay on the living room floor in a shimmering puddle of lamé. Kat had had it on her body less than ten minutes when Mark arrived, stripped it off her, ravished her on the couch. Now as they lay gasping for breath, Kat's gaze drifted to the clock on the DVD player and she pondered whether they had time for a second go.

Mark stared up at the ceiling, his chest heaving under her. He was still inside her, at half-mast now but still warm and welcome.

She nuzzled his neck. "How long to re-load the cannons?"

"Kat." He sucked in a breath when she scraped his earlobe with her teeth. "I have to tell you something."

Her tongue traced the whorls of his ear. "Tell me later."

He groaned, his arms tightening around her. "It's already later."

Her legs still straddling him, she levered herself up just enough to graze his chest with her nipples. He stirred to life inside her and she smiled in triumph.

To her great disappointment, he took firm hold of her shoulders and lifted her away from him. He sat up, easing her aside so he slipped from inside her. Her sharp regret distracted her momentarily from what she felt between her legs, then the wet warmth registered.

Disbelief stumbled along on the heels of realization. She dove for his lap, grabbing him, as if with her close inspection she could deny the truth. But his half-erect flesh sagged naked in her hand.

"Ohmigod, ohmigod," she chanted, staring at the one-eyed snake then up at Mark. "Where is it?"

"Where's what?" He looked down at himself, then understanding hit. "Ohmigod! It's not there!"

"Then it's in me. It must be in me." She groped between her legs and found the tiny scrap of rubber. She tugged it free, held it out. "We're okay, here it is. Everything's safe in —"

She watched in horrified awe as the remaining contents of the condom dripped slowly from the ragged tear in the tip.

"No," she moaned. "Oh, no, no, no."

Mark looked from the condom to the spent soldier in his lap. "We might still be okay. Do you have a backup plan?"

She shook her head, feeling queasy. "Abstinence has always worked just fine."

"Okay," he said, although his expression said they were anything but okay. "How's your timing? Do you think you're safe?"

She tried to count back, figure out the days since her last cycle. But it was all a blur. "I might be. I don't know."

He brought his hands up to cradle her face. They trembled as he leaned in to kiss her. "We'll get through this, sweetheart."

Tears threatened and she had to get away, get some space. "Excuse me." She pulled away and hurried to her bedroom.

She locked herself in her bathroom, dumped the condom in the toilet and flushed it. She cleaned herself up, then leaned against the sink, trying to get her mind around what she and Mark might have just done on the sofa.

I could be pregnant. A maelstrom of emotions clattered around inside her — terror, anxiety, panic. She felt both paralyzed with shock and frantic with fear. But not at the thought of a baby inside her, not at the prospect of her body changing and a tiny being growing inside her. What transfixed her with horror, left her thunderstruck with awe, was the immensity of the connection.

With Mark. With the ex-husband she never knew how to love. During their marriage, she couldn't find a way to link her heart with his because nothing she ever did would be right. But this, a baby, if it even existed, would be right without any effort on her part.

Damn, she was going to cry. She could feel tears grip her throat, burn her eyes.

A knock on the door jolted her upright. "Kat, are you okay?"

She cleared her throat. "Fine. Give me another minute."

A splash of water on her face, a drink from her cupped hands and she felt the sting of emotions subside. She retrieved her terry-cloth robe from the back of the bathroom door and buried her body in it. Armor on, she felt ready to face Mark again.

He stood just outside the door, dressed in briefs and the socks they'd been in too much of a hurry to remove. Kat pinned a bright smile on her face. "We'd better get going." She edged past him.

He followed her to the living room.

"What about —"

"We'll work it out." She snatched up her panty hose and leaned against the sofa to put them on. "Nothing to worry about until . . ." Her throat closed a moment. "Until we know for sure."

He took her arm, stopping her from reaching for her dress. "Kat, you wouldn't . . ."

"No . . ." She said the word slowly as the certainty sank in. "No," she said more emphatically. "If I am, we'll just . . ."

She didn't know what the hell they'd do. She only knew that she had to get dressed, get out of here, away from Mark. If she didn't, her heart, overloaded with emotion, would explode.

Hooking a finger in her dress, she backed away from him. "Hey, I was just thinking," she said as she shimmied into the chocolate lamé, "I need to stop by the office for something. We'd better take two cars."

In the process of buttoning his dove gray dress shirt, his fingers stilled. "Are you okay?"

"I'm fine, perfectly fine." Her voice seemed shrill to her ears. "I just need to drive to the party alone."

He slowly tucked his shirt into his slacks,

his gaze never leaving her face. She turned her back on him, but didn't ask for help with her zipper. Her arms pretzeling behind her back, she worked it up herself.

To the gold leather purse she'd left by the door she added her driver's license, a credit card and some cash, then she gathered up her keys. She waited for Mark to slip on his shoes and find his own keys in his pants pocket.

"We're going to have to talk," he told her, his face serious.

"Later," she said blithely.

It seemed to take an eternity to make their way down to the parking garage. At her car, Mark leaned in to kiss her, but she turned, his lips landing on her cheek instead of her mouth. Then as he headed for the guest parking on the other side of the garage, she climbed in her Camry.

He pulled out but waited for her to do the same before he exited the garage. Once she'd backed from her parking space, she waved him on, pretending to be busy with something in the car. When he was finally out of sight, she shut off the engine again.

Now she could let herself cry. Hunched over the steering wheel, head pressed against the laced cover, she felt despair lapping at her. But to her eternal misery, not one tear squeezed itself from her eyes.

Mark prowled the length of the hotel ballroom, the chocolate delicacies filling the linen-draped tables a blur. He hadn't so much as tasted a morsel in the thirty minutes he'd been here, so keyed up the thought of chocolate turned his stomach. All his thoughts centered on Kat, what had happened on her sofa, where she was now.

The room was packed with smiling, laughing, happy people. Long rectangular tables covered in crisp white lined every inch of available wall space, each one heaped with treats from Denham and Roth. Round tables dotted the middle of the room, offerings from some of the smaller, specialty candy makers arrayed across them. Swarms of people collected around the tables, filling small plates with chocolate, sampling the candy as they sipped champagne.

A stage had been set up at one end and a jazz band played Benny Goodman. Phil and Patti Roth stood near the stage with Mark's parents and Fritz and Norma, the lot of them thick as thieves.

God, she wasn't going to show. He never should have driven off without her. But he was just as shaken as she was at the realization that they'd had unprotected sex. The thought of Kat pregnant had utterly terrified him for the first fifteen minutes. It wasn't until he drove away that he realized how perfect it would be. He loved her. That she might have his baby seemed absolutely perfect.

Even if it was all a false alarm. It might not have been the right time of the month, his little swimmers might not have hit their target. Still, Kat expecting his baby was a damn good idea.

If she'd only show up. He reached the far side of the ballroom and turned back the other way. He still had the little matter of the merger to discuss with her. Until they cleared the air on that issue, they couldn't move on to their relationship. He should have told her at her condo, but she'd looked so delicious in that shiny chocolate brown dress, his mind surrendered control to Mr. BVD the instant he saw her. Next thing he knew, they were both staring at a broken condom.

He thought he caught a glimpse of Kat by the door, but the shifting crowd got in his way. Serpentining through the meandering bodies, he made his way toward the entrance, spying fractured images of sleek brown hair, a bare shoulder, a slender arm.

He was pretty sure it was her, but his tension didn't ease until the crowd by the door cleared, revealing Kat in her slinky chocolate gown.

She reached for him the moment she saw him. He took her hand and led her from the ballroom. In a quiet room next door, a few busboys cleared the tables from an earlier event. Mark drew her inside and back into a secluded corner.

He took her in his arms, his heart pounding as he held her slim body. Hard-as-nails Kat, who could chew up a business adversary and spit him out, seemed as fragile and vulnerable as spun sugar. She trembled under his hands and he pulled her even closer, wanting to cocoon her in his protection.

She finally eased back, a weak smile on her face. "Still a little shaky," she said, her fingers tight on his arms. "Probably worrying about nothing. I checked . . . My last cycle . . . I should be okay."

"Either way, sweetheart, we face it together."

"But if I'm not . . . you and I . . ." She looked away. "We wouldn't have to be together."

He cupped her face with his hands, waited until she met his gaze. "This isn't just about a baby."

She tried to pull away. "No. It's about sex."

He took her shoulders, keeping her with him. "You mean a hell of a lot more to me than sex."

"Okay, great sex." She twisted her body, trying to shake him. "Monumental sex."

He'd hurt her if he didn't let her go. He relaxed his hold. "It hasn't been just sex for a long time. Not for me."

He had to shout the last few words because she just about ran from the room to escape. I love you echoed in his mind, the unsaid words an ache in his heart.

He'd intended to lay out the facts of the merger, get all that nastiness on the table and out in the open before he said a word about a future for him and Kat. But he'd botched that. He hadn't had a chance once he saw her in that melted chocolate dress, felt her trembling body in his arms. Now he had to retrieve her from the ballroom again and take her to another quiet corner.

Back in the noisy, packed room, the multitudes seemed to have increased. He didn't immediately spot Kat, and for a brief moment of panic he wondered if she'd just gone home. He caught sight of her near the stage just as Phil Roth and

Mark's father stepped up to the mike.

An early warning system clamored in the pit of Mark's stomach and the urgency to get to Kat flared. But Phil and Ian up on stage had caught the attention of the crowd and the hordes seethed toward that end of the room, blocking Mark's way. He had to elbow his way through the sardine tin of bodies to make any progress at all.

He must have sent thought vibes Kat's way because she turned and her gaze locked briefly with his. Then Phil tapped on the mike and asked, "Can everyone hear me?" and she turned away again.

Disaster was looming and Mark faced a wall of humanity between him and Kat. Every route he took through the mass of people dead-ended and he had to continually backtrack, losing forward progress. But he had to get to her.

Phil Roth beamed up on the stage. "I'd like to thank you all for being here. Kandy for Kids has been a phenomenal success and with tonight's receipts, we've raised an incredible one point eight million dollars!"

Applause swelled in the room. Mark was starting to sweat under the heavy jacket, the heat radiating from so many bodies stifling.

Ian Denham stepped up to the microphone. "In addition to Kandy for Kids' spectacular triumph, Roth Confectionery and Denham Candy have another exciting, stupendous announcement to make."

Sweat turned to icy chill as doom walked fingers down Mark's spine. Kat was still a good twenty feet away and he didn't have a prayer of reaching her in time. His only hope was to be there to comfort her in the aftermath.

Phil smiled broadly at the crowd. "The Kandy for Kids campaign has demonstrated to the Roths and the Denhams the value of partnership and how two well-matched allies can join hands to create a whole greater than its parts."

Good, they were dragging this out, making a real show of it. Mark had advanced another five feet and he could just make out a path through the crowd leading to Kat. She seemed riveted on her father, her slender shoulders held so stiffly he could feel her tension.

On the stage, Ian Denham bounced on the balls of his feet, his excitement barely contained. "Kandy for Kids will be ending in a month's time, but it didn't seem right to terminate this temporary marriage between Roth Confectionery and Denham Candy."

Kat knew. If she'd only suspected a moment ago, now certainty had settled on her. Four or five people still blocked Mark's access to her, but he saw her sudden stillness, then her hand raised toward the stage as if to stem the tide of words.

"Kat!" Mark shouted her name. She flicked a glance over at him, then returned her focus to the impending car accident up on stage.

Phil Roth beamed. "Without further ado, we are thrilled to announce the merger of Roth Confectionery and Denham Candy."

Kat stumbled back as if her father had punched her in the gut. Desperate to get to her, Mark pushed past the last few onlookers between them. He took Kat's hand, but when she looked up at him, she stared as if she didn't know him.

Mark's father just rolled on. "And the first exciting new product to be released by the Denham-Roth Candy Company will be a wonderful new treat." He gestured to the drummer on stage who rattled out a drumroll. "Chocolate Magic!"

Kat sagged against him. "Oh, God. Oh my God."

Mark pulled her into his arms. "It's okay,

baby. Just hang on to me."

"How could he?" Tears choked her voice. "How could . . . ?"

He rubbed her back, tried to soothe away her shudders. "They wanted it a long time."

"But, I told him . . ." She took in a shaky breath. "Anyone but Denham."

He ignored the pain that stabbed through him. "I wanted to tell you. Prepare you."

She went rigid. "You what?"

Damn, he was an idiot. "It doesn't matter."

She shoved away from him. If her brown eyes had been lasers, he'd be a crispy critter. "You knew?"

The confession stuck in his throat. He squeezed it out in a wimpy squeak. "Yeah."

"You knew. You schtupped me and you knew." She nearly shrieked the words. "And you didn't bother to tell me."

"I meant to." The band had started up again and he had to shout to be heard. "I tried to."

"Not very damn hard!" She whacked her hands against his chest with surprising strength, then took off through the crowd.

"Uh-oh." Fritz grabbed Norma's hand.

"Trouble in paradise."

They watched Kat slam her fists against Mark's chest then make a mad dash for the exit. Mark went after her, a linebacker scattering the opposing team.

"This might not be a bad thing," Norma said hopefully.

Fritz tugged her after him. "Can't take the chance."

By the time they reached the parking garage elevators, both Mark and Kat were gone. An eternity later, they were racing for Norma's car.

"Where would she go?" Fritz asked as he climbed into the driver's seat. "Her condo?"

Norma shook her head. "Roth is home to her, more than the condo. I'll bet you ten pounds of chocolate creams she's headed for her office."

Neither Kat's Camry nor Mark's BMW were in sight when they pulled up to the attendant kiosk to pay their parking fee. "Let's hope you're right," Fritz said as he roared off in the direction of Roth headquarters.

When they arrived, Kat's Camry was in the CEO slot, Mark's roadster parked haphazardly beside it. Norma put a hand on Fritz's arm. "Park my car behind theirs. Block them in."

Fritz shut off the engine and they stepped from the car. He listened to the silence. "No shouting. They're not down here."

"Upstairs," Norma gasped, heading for the elevator.

They heard Mark's voice and his pounding on her door all the way down the hall. "Damn it, Katarina! Let me in!"

Norma didn't hesitate. She grabbed her keys from Fritz and marched to Kat's office door. Nudging Mark aside, she deftly unlocked the door and pulled it open. Fritz caught a glimpse of Kat inside, behind her desk, shooting daggers at them all as Mark entered.

The moment the door shut behind him, Norma locked it again then coolly turned to Fritz. "Help with that desk, please."

Fritz laughed as he understood her intention. "You are absolutely devious. And the most incredible woman in the world."

She smiled at the compliment, her cheeks dimpling. Then with a surprising strength, she hefted her end of her desk. Together, they moved it against the door, trapping Kat and Mark inside.

There he stood in her office, big as life, looking too damned delectable in his dark suit and tailored cream shirt. Kat couldn't believe the audacity of the man. Or the duplicitousness of her assistant, who had let him in. Her life was tumbling into chaos and she didn't have a friend left.

"Get the hell out," she demanded.

"No."

Rising from behind her desk, Kat headed for the door. She tried the knob. Locked. With impatient irritation, she retrieved her keys from her desk and unlocked the door. Now the knob turned, but the door wouldn't budge.

"It's stuck. It won't open."

"Never mind the door, Kat. We have to talk."

She rounded on him, hand clenched in a fist, fighting the urge to swing. "We have nothing to talk about. Traitor."

She went back to the door, throwing her body against it. "Damn it!" she screamed at the immobile hunk of oak. "Norma! Let me out!"

No answer from her faithless assistant. Mark took her arm, but she shook him off. "Fritz was right! The damn therapist was right!"

He reached for her again. "Kat —"

"I don't trust you." She wrenched away from him. "Because you're untrustworthy.

The lowest of the low. A snake!"

"Kat, I screwed up —"

"You think?"

"I found out about the merger this morning, I should have told you then. I shouldn't have let them —"

"Who knew?" She saw the reluctance in his face, took his arms and shook him. "How many knew?"

He put his hands on her shoulders, his touch so gentle her throat tightened. "Everyone, likely."

She blinked back tears. "Everyone but me."

He stroked her hair. "I didn't know either until this morning."

Face buried in her hands, she moaned, "Chocolate Magic was mine. How could they steal it from me?"

"No one's stealing it, sweetheart."

She backed away from him. "I'm not your sweetheart."

He moved toward her, implacable. She backed across the room, but he followed. "Denying it won't help you, Kat. Won't change how I feel. How you feel."

"No," she whispered. "You walked away. You didn't even try. I asked for the damn divorce and you just said yes."

"Because you were miserable. You hated

me. You hated the marriage."

"I didn't hate you. I mean, I did, but . . ." She shook her head, wishing she could shake away the pain as easily. "I won't revisit this. Not any of it."

"What do you want, Kat?" He grabbed her shoulders. "You want me to say it hurt to leave you? Yes, it hurt. It was agony."

She slapped her palms against his chest. "But you didn't fight. You just backed down." She slammed her hands against him again. "You let me go." A third blow stung her palms and she screamed, "You didn't even try to change my mind!" She dropped her hands, tears streaming, despondent as a lonely child.

He pulled away, crossing his arms over his chest. "It wasn't up to me to change your mind."

"But I wanted you to." She shook her head. "Damn, how childish is that?"

He stared down at the floor, shoulders slumped. He was a million miles away, lost to her. She'd finally done it — pushed him away, irretrievably, and her sense of desolation grew, threatening to overwhelm her. If the pain inside her increased another iota, she'd die, expire on the spot.

So immersed in her pity party, she almost didn't hear his softly spoken words.

"We fought so much."

They had. Screaming matches where angry words flew between them. Shouting through the walls of separate bedrooms when they couldn't stand to sleep in the same room. Except the passion would always flare, bringing them back together.

Now she felt sick at the rage they'd exchanged, the fury of their doomed marriage. It had been exactly what she'd witnessed as a child, had sworn she'd never do herself.

The enormity of what she'd destroyed overwhelmed her. "Oh my God." She sank against the edge of her desk.

Mark moved close enough to touch, but he kept his hands to himself. "I didn't know, Kat. I didn't know you wanted me to fight for you."

The insistent tears spilled down her face. "I didn't know, either. I just thought . . . my parents split when I was so young. I didn't know people could stay together."

He swiped away her tears with his thumb. "I didn't know people could fight and still stay together. My parents never did."

"Your parents fought." She met his gaze. "At least once. I heard them."

He shook his head. "You couldn't have."

"Your twelfth birthday. You were out by the dock and I went in for a soda. Your mother threw a coffee mug at your dad."

His mouth dropped open in shock. "They told me that mug fell off the shelf."

She shrugged. "Good thing your dad ducked."

A ghost of a smile curved his lips, then he sighed, staring out at the lights of Seattle beyond her office window. "Even so, they managed it, Kat. Staying together. Your own parents, too, once they found the right people."

"But they're different. Special."

"You're special, Kat."

"Not that way. They all know something, a secret or . . ." She grasped for the words. "All I know is it's something I'll never understand." She swallowed against a dry throat. "I'm not smart enough or . . . I just can't."

If he was distant before, now he was in another universe. He stood frozen a moment, then turned toward the door, covered the distance with two long strides.

Her heart thundered in her ears. "Where are you going?"

He rapped on the door, calling through the thick oak, "Let me out. We're finished."

She couldn't move, her feet rooted to the spot. She heard the sound of something heavy being moved on the other side of the door, waited for the turning of the lock. Damned coward that she was, she couldn't watch him leave. She squeezed her eyes shut.

But when she didn't hear the door, or hear his footsteps leaving, she opened her eyes again. Mark still stood there, a white envelope in his hand, a quizzical expression on his face.

"They pushed it under the door." He held it out to her. "It's for you."

In the aftermath of her terror that he'd leave her, Kat's legs had transformed into pillars of trembling jelly. "Can't move," she gasped out. "Sorry."

Two tentative steps toward her and he was close enough for her to take the white rectangle from him. "Th-thanks."

She nearly shredded the envelope as she tore it open. Inside was a rumpled sheet of paper in a familiar shade of lavender.

As she unfolded it, Mark grabbed for it. "Don't —"

She turned away, keeping it from his grasp. She read the printed title across the top. "List ten qualities* that first attracted you to your partner."

"Kat, don't —"

"Her sense of humor," she read aloud. "Her determination. Her generosity." She narrowed her gaze on Mark. "Who did you write these for?"

"Who the hell do you think, Kat?"

"You always hated my jokes."

He glowered, then flicked an impatient hand at her. "Just read the damn thing."

She continued. "Her kindness. Her sweetness. I'm not the least bit sweet."

He raised one brow. She tipped her head back down to the list.

Her wild temper. Her vulnerability. "I'm not —" She cut the words off, kept reading. Her strength. Her inner beauty. Her throat grew tight, but she forced herself to read the last one aloud. "The way she touches my heart."

Persistent tears brimming in her eyes, she lifted her gaze to his. "Mark . . ."

His blue eyes fixed on her face. "What?"

The air left her lungs, and she had to drag in breath to speak. "Don't leave me."

He didn't give any ground. "Why?"

"Because . . . because . . ." Her fingernails nearly tore through the lavender sheet. "This scares the hell out of me. I'm positive by saying it out loud I'll jinx it, now or later."

"Say it anyway."

"Because I know so many ways to screw things up. I probably won't even say it right."

"Three little words, Kat."

Three words. Piece of cake. She could do it.

It was the hardest thing she ever did. "I love you."

He grabbed her tight, squeezing the living daylights out of her. She was dizzy with elation, crazy with love. Until realization tapped on her shoulder and she wriggled loose.

He didn't quite let her go. "What?" He gave her a look of pure innocence.

Which she didn't believe for an instant. "Your turn."

"My turn, what?"

Growling, she gave him a hard poke in the ribs. "Give, buster."

"I really don't know what —"

A full-fledged punch cut off his wind. "Now. Or you're not getting any tonight."

"I love you," he gasped, then he pulled her back in his arms and just held her, rocking her gently. As she buried her face against his chest, she felt the doubt creep back.

"I still might mess it up." She held her

breath as she waited for his response. "I might ruin everything."

"You won't," he said with a steady certainty. "No matter what you do, how much you yell, what you say, this time I'll never let you go."

As his conviction registered, she didn't know whether to laugh or cry, so she did both, the tears making her hiccup so badly she could barely take a breath. Mark pounded on her office door, shouting through it, "Norma! Fritz! Let us out!"

There was a scuffle through the door, an exchange of voices. Mark squeezed her hand, then yelled, "We love each other. We're getting married again. Open the damn door!"

The screech of something heavy being moved, then the door edged open. Hand in hand, Kat and Mark squeezed through past Norma's desk.

Fritz's arm around her waist, Norma stood beaming. "Can we make it a double wedding?" she asked.

~ *Epilogue* ~

Smartly attired in her birthday suit, Kat leaned against the fluffy pillows on her bed, Mark sprawled beside her. She felt so damn good, she could probably light the condo's small bedroom with her high-wattage afterglow.

They'd both had a busy day at the Denham-Roth headquarters, and by six, with autumn darkness already fallen, they were eager to head home to the condo. After a quick dinner and an even quicker quickie they retrieved the briefcases for a little homework in bed. Hubby snuggled up beside her, a package of Chocolate Magic in her lap, Kat read through the September sales report as she shared bites of butterscotch fudge with Mark.

He licked a dollop off her finger, then sneaked a peek at the report's summary page. "Unbelievable. Fritz's toy line did even better in September than August."

Fritz's Critter Carvings had become the

new craze over the summer, with kids lining up at toy stores for the latest edition. "Have you seen the Christmas release? Santa's sleigh loaded with removable miniature toys."

"And Mint Meltaways in Santa's bag. Your dad brought by the prototype."

Kat scooped up a last fingerful of fudge and was about to bring it to her mouth when Mark grabbed her wrist. He'd sucked her finger clean before she could so much as protest.

She wagged her finger at him. "That was unforgivable."

Wrapping his hand around the back of her neck, he brought her close for a kiss. "I'll make it up to you."

He tasted of butterscotch as his tongue dipped into her mouth. She shifted to straddle him, maintaining the contact as she groped on his nightstand. She came up with the other package of Chocolate Magic they'd brought into the bedroom.

Scooting away from him, she ripped the plastic off the package. Mark made a grab for it, but she kept it out of his reach. She carefully tipped the chocolate marshmallow crumbles into the cream.

Mark pouted as she stirred in the crumbles. "That was a dirty trick."

"All's fair in love and chocolate," she told him as the fudge formed. "I'll give you a bite."

The wedding had been three months ago in mid-July and they'd already had their share of fireworks. But they had a mutual understanding — they'd never end the day angry with each other. Somehow, they worked things out and usually finished their arguments by making love.

She fed him a healthy gob of marshmallow fudge. "You're sure about this baby thing?" she asked. "We could wait another year."

"I'm sure. As long as you are."

"Absolutely."

The broken condom had been a false alarm. Kat had been relieved not to have to attend her wedding in the throes of morning sickness, but disappointed she wasn't pregnant after all. They'd agreed to give it the old college try for a baby. Which meant more lovemaking. Always a good thing.

Kat scooped up a blob of fudge for herself. "I got another postcard from Norma."

With Fritz so busy bringing Critter Carvings to market, he and Norma decided to delay their wedding until last month. They finally headed off to their postponed honeymoon two weeks ago.

Mark lapped another mouthful of fudge from her finger. "Fritz made an absolutely brilliant move hiring his father as VP of the toy division."

"Uncle Ned acts as if he knew all along what a genius his son is."

Mark plucked the not-quite-empty Chocolate Magic package from her hand and set it aside. "I'm more interested in what a genius you are. In particular, that clever little maneuver with your tongue."

"Which one?" she murmured. "This?" She traced the curve of his ear with the tip of her tongue. "Or this?" Shifting, she laved the quickening flesh between his legs.

He groaned, fingers threading through her hair. "That," he gasped, "will do for now."

They lingered over their climax the second time around, teasing each other to ecstasy. Later, when they lay panting in each other's arms, Kat whispered in his ear, "I love you, Mark Denham."

He nuzzled her neck. "More than chocolate?"

"Hmm," she considered. "That's a tough one."

He went up on one elbow and gave her a poke. Laughing, she snuggled close. "More than all the chocolate in the world."

~ About the Author ~

Writing has been Karen Sandler's passion since the fourth grade when she vowed she would one day "be a writer." It took another thirty years and a move from Los Angeles to Northern California before Karen could pursue her dream to write full-time. After four years of hard work, Karen finally sold her first romance novel. She sold four others within a year, but that flurry of sales was followed by a nail-biting two-year dry spell during which Karen sold nothing.

Before Karen decided that plumbing might not be such a bad profession after all, she struck gold again, selling several more books in quick succession. In addition to writing novels, Karen is a screenwriter and has several screenwriting projects in progress.

The employees of Thorndike Press hope you have enjoyed this Large Print book. All our Thorndike and Wheeler Large Print titles are designed for easy reading, and all our books are made to last. Other Thorndike Press Large Print books are available at your library, through selected bookstores, or directly from us.

For information about titles, please call:

(800) 223-1244

or visit our Web site at:

www.gale.com/thorndike
www.gale.com/wheeler

To share your comments, please write:

Publisher
Thorndike Press
295 Kennedy Memorial Drive
Waterville, ME   04901

E G Fisher Public Library

DISCARD

EGF0011973

E. G. Fisher Public Library
1289 Ingleside Ave
Athens, TN 37303
423-745-7782

DISCARD